The Sixties Man

By Ian Lennox

Published by Gordon Liberty Publishing

Printed by CVN Print
Maxwell Street, South Shields, Tyne & Wear NE33 4PU

FOREWORD

The hedonistic and exciting times of the Sixties revolutionised Britain in a way from which it has never recovered. Music, the sexual revolution, the pill, and freedom of all constraints prevailed as an explosion of awareness dominated and influenced the lives of all who lived through it. The social chains were completely broken, never to be replaced, and once the locks were off history was irrevocably changed.

The Sixties Man explores that incredible period in illuminating detail because the author Ian Lennox, a highly respected journalist and television producer, had his life completely shaped by it. Set in Newcastle and France this is the tale of a man who decides to change his life in such a dramatic way that he turns from a hedonist into a killer as he sets out to avenge a murder.

Atmospheric, this story encapsulates the authenticity of Newcastle with a remarkable insight into those vibrant and violent times, as criminals and politicians fought to take control of power in this dynamic city.

The Sixties Man is an illuminating read and a must for anyone who lived through that period and missed it or anyone who just enjoys a compulsive story with exciting pictures in the head.

Arthur McKenzie.

(Arthur McKenzie was a front-line policeman in Newcastle in the Sixties. He went on to become one of the country's most successful TV drama writers. His credits include about 30 episodes of The Bill.)

AUTHOR'S NOTE

The Sixties Man is a work of fiction. However it should be said that the character Walter Snaith was based on my impressions of the late T Dan Smith who granted me a long interview when I told him I was going to write a novel about the period.
Everything that Snaith says and does in the novel is entirely fictitious.

CHAPTER ONE

Every time he tried to tell his story of all those years ago he began with Fran who hardly figured in it really, save for one thing...if he hadn't fallen in love with her none of it would have happened. He wouldn't have gone to France where he met the film star, or to the nightclub where he met Billy, and three men wouldn't have met violent deaths.

He was called Kelvin, Kel for short. He was six feet, which was tall for those days. He had large, grey eyes with long lashes that he found embarrassing. His dark hair was brushed back from his pale, oval face and some said he looked weak and girlish; they didn't know him.

The first time he fell in love he was alarmed by the experience. He had had many women and felt at best affection for them; so to discover that there were days he could not eat because of this woman took him by surprise.

She was called Francesca but her close friends called her Fran. She had shoulder-length, dark hair, a long, slim body and outrageously simple views, which she argued with a passion.

She believed in God, England, marriage, and mortgages, but she loved to dance in the summer rain.

He'd discovered the dancing part when they were caught in the middle of Newcastle Town Moor by huge, low clouds that came from nowhere laden with thunderclaps and lightning. They were drenched in seconds and their clothes clung to them like a second skin.

They ran to a deserted park to the shelter of the bandstand but as he jumped up the steps she stayed out in the storm, then, laughing a wild laugh, bending her back into the frenzy of the rain, her body lit by lightning, she danced for him.

He stood entranced by her primeval movement, until, with one last pirouette, she ran to him. "I love you," she whispered.

The words both thrilled and disappointed him for he knew he would remember this moment for the rest of his life and yet it had so taken him by surprise that it was gone before he could grasp it.

Two months later she told him it had all been a terrible mistake and that it was over. By now he was in love, and so he felt the cold turkey of her rejection. He thought of her every time it rained.

For the fourth day in six the storm had come tumbling in from the North Sea sending the shoppers scurrying for shelter as it drummed onto the streets, filling the gutters and overwhelming the drains. And then it stopped so suddenly that people looked out into the street as though someone had been playing an elaborate joke.

"Excuse me.... EXCUSE ME" The voice was soft but insistent and had the trace of a lisp. Kel turned reluctantly from the window to be confronted by a pale, young man. He had the sort of face an artist could make mysterious by painting him as a woman. The cheekbones were high and the jaw line strong, but the eyes were soft and pastel blue, and the lips pink and pinched. His fair hair had blond streaks dyed into it and he smelt of cologne.

"I'm Gerry," he said."We met in Greys Club."

"Never seen you."

"You're with the Chronicle aren't you?"

"So?"

"So you do stories." He leaned forward. "I've got a big one."

Kel glanced uncomfortably round the room.... The snooker players were not strutting after the balls with the same bragging energy...they were listening. So was the girl by the kiosk who handed out the yellow tickets and whose eyes had followed Kel from door to window. Gerry glowed like a starlet on stage.

"We've never met." Kel let the irritation snap through his voice but Gerry was not to be denied.

"I was there in the club three weeks ago. Someone pointed you out." His eyes were large and his voice soft.

Kel felt threatened. "You said we'd met."

Gerry raised his eyebrows slightly and licked his lips. "So? Is it such a big deal?"

Kel did not reply and Gerry moved into the no man's land between them. "They said, the people who spoke of you, that you did investigative stuff...difficult stories."

Over his shoulder play had resumed. The bright lights beamed down over the green baize tables making them stand out like islands in the dark room. A slim man in a red shirt stalked the white. His Brylcreamed hair shone in the pool of light as he leaned forward. His cue flicked in and out like the tongue of a reptile on the hunt before it struck the white, which in turn sent a red rearing into the pocket. " Geddin." The Brylcream man thrust out his pelvis in obscene exaggeration before strutting round the table to stalk the white once more.

"Cretin." Gerry's voice had an edge of malice. His thin lips curled.

"You know him then?"

"Only his type."

For the first time Kel felt some sympathy. He turned away from Gerry, looked down the long, high-ceiling room and realised that it was not merely the sight of large rooms but also the sound of them that he found attractive...the way voices, sounds, dissipated into the vast space.

He turned slowly to face Gerry making no effort to disguise his disappointment that the slim man was still there. Everything about him said "I want to be a girl" and then someone had stuck a todger on him.

"Big story you said."

"It's big. Very big."

"Look if you're going to play games you can go away."

"I am what I am." His hurt, tight, little voice made absurd any attempt at dignity.

"Well try to postpone it."

"Ooooh that's really catty!" Gerry's voice rose in a squeal attracting more attention.

"There are people laughing at us."

Gerry shrugged his thin shoulders. "It's nothing new to me."

"It is to me." Kel glared at him.

Gerry smiled, then, suddenly, in a low voice full of secrets he said: "It's about contracts...building contracts...the tenders are being fiddled. There's millions involved."

He refused to give names. "Not at this stage," but he described how local hard men were using builders as a front to muscle in on huge demolition contracts.

Kel wondered what they had done to stir such a deep malice in this thin, weak, lisping man.

The players had lost interest in them as they prowled like hunters in the gloom of the room before swooping onto the tables to make a shot. But from the kiosk by the door the girl's eyes followed Kel.

Gerry finished his tale and his face lit like a child waiting for praise or at least, respect.

Kel turned to walk to the window. Below him another trolley bus splashed though the wet road as it rattled its way past Jackson the Tailors, past Woolworths and beyond the unruly queue of youngsters who were waiting outside the Odeon to buy tickets for the Rolling Stones concert.

"So...what do you reckon?" Gerry slid up beside him at the window.

Kel shrugged. "Give me a number and I'll pass it on."

"Pass it on! I'm not a bloody parcel."

The refusal cooked in Gerry for a second or so. "It's me isn't it." His natural sibilance made him hiss with displeasure.

He raised himself to the balls of his feet and rocked gently on his black, slip-on shoes. His chest heaved slightly beneath the tapered, black-check shirt and his thumbs stuck through the leather belt that pulled tightly round his trim waist.

Kel met his eyes this time. "Look I don't give a toss that you ride on the other bus. But stop honking your horn at me every few seconds." Kel looked out at the traffic again. Gerry stood his ground.

"There's letters and things."

"You can get them?"

"I think so. They're arrogant and careless."

"Give me a number. I'll get somebody."

"Why not you? Lost your bottle?"

"I'm going away." Kel smiled a thin smile without malice or affection.

Gerry left him gliding as gracefully as a cat between the tables then, as he reached the swing doors, gave an exaggerated swing to his hips, a little finale to all the eyes that were watching his performance.

Kel raised his eyebrows to the girl at the kiosk but by now he was tainted by association and she turned to her time sheets. Kel watched from the window as Gerry crossed the road and disappeared into Fenwick's. He glanced at his watch. It was time to make an appearance at the office. He walked out into the hot steamy street and turned right, towards the Haymarket and the new Civic Centre.

A television crew had arrived to film the crowd of fans outside the Odeon.

A woman police sergeant called to the queue. "Come on now, two abreast."

A shrill- voiced youth with knowledge beyond his years shouted, "Thank you mam but I don't like to share my pleasures."

The policewoman stared hopelessly into the grinning crowd seeking the culprit.

The TV reporter turned to his cameraman. "Were we rolling?"

The cameraman shook his head.

Kel grinned at the reporter. "They wouldn't have let you use it anyway."

The reporter looked at him ruefully. "True."

Kel left him and walked quickly to the top of Northumberland Street.

It took him another twenty minutes to walk around what was effectively the Northern perimeter of the inner city, down past the Empire Theatre and finally into Grainger Street where a week previously the heavyweight champion of the world, Sonny Liston, had ridden on a white horse tipping a round hat like a dandy at the adoring crowds.

Mr Liston had been a man of few words as Kel discovered during an attempted interview. He suspected him of being a simple man who, when thrown into the complex casserole of modern life, was capable of great brutality...but he had been unable to reflect this in the piece he wrote because Reynolds, the chief sub editor, had feared litigation.

Instead he had been instructed to write a story about thousands of Geordies climbing the walls on the streets of Newcastle to get a glimpse of the king of the ring.

The staff entrance to the Chronicle office faced west down a short, high-walled lane that blocked the light.

Inside the old building shuddered in gentle protest at the assault of the printing machines roaring out the second edition. The porter was struggling with the Mirror crossword. He nodded to Kel who rattled on the cage doors of the lift. Kel looked back into the gloomy foyer where a weak bulb gave off a yellow light from the high ceiling. It was as though the building knew its time was up and had given up the fight as its concrete replacement grew with increasing speed behind its back.

As the lift creaked its way to floor two he caught a faint whiff of hot oil from its ancient engine.

In the office the heavy old typewriters were clattering away for the next edition. A pall of cigarette smoke clung to the ceiling of the long room as the reporters fired off their stories. Each completed item had to be taken to the news desk for approval before being shot across the room in air pipes to the subs desk.

He stood unseen at the door and then, on impulse, turned to leave. The unmistakable figure of Edwards, the News Editor, was silhouetted in the window frame at the end of the narrow corridor that led to the lift. He was the tallest and the thinnest man in the office, possibly in Newcastle. There were jokes about him modelling for pipe cleaners until someone let it slip that three years in a Japanese Prisoner of War camp had permanently damaged his digestive system.

As they passed Edwards said: “Lunch next Thursday. The Douglas. One o’clock. OK.” He often spoke in telegram language while giving information.

They had a flat, Kel, Dave, and Paul, in a large house of black stone that jutted on the edge of a suburb called Spital Tongues which in turned looked down across a field to the Northern skyline of the city. If Kel had had a gift for cartoons, which he hadn’t, he would have drawn Dave as a bank manager on his way to a funeral...there was something long and lugubrious about him that was accentuated by his dark suits and heavy eyebrows.

Paul, he would have characterised as a ginger yapping terrier getting his arse kicked.

That evening Kel lay stretched out in the long grass enjoying the Indian summer as Paul cut through the field that lay between the flat and the city. His ginger hair glowed in the sun. His jacket was looped over his back and his shirtsleeves were rolled up displaying his freckled arms. He veered from his path as he spotted Kel.

“You missed the union meeting,” he said.

Kel looked past Paul. Across the field an ambulance was rolling silently down the road towards the hospital.” I’ve got a going-away present for you.” He outlined Gerry’s story.

Generosity always made Paul uneasy. “Hmmm.” He looked into the ground. “So what we’ve got at the moment is a tale from a raving shirt lifter who could be a malice-ridden congenital liar. And nothing in writing.”

Kel played the glory card. “But if it comes off it will take you straight to the nationals.”

CHAPTER TWO

The thing about Fran was...the thing about her was ...her naivety was fuelled with such energy and inner conviction that Kel found her overbearing, overwhelming, and intoxicating.

She was almost beautiful. She had green eyes, long hair that burned a deep brown in the light, and a squared fringe that was the fashion. Her legs were long and her skirts were short.

Fran was in her final year of an arts degree at the university. Her sketches and paintings, which she stored in the attic at her aunt's large, dusty house in Gosforth, startled him with their quality. She painted simple landscapes with such natural conviction that sometimes they had a breath of beauty. One in particular had more than that; it had power and mystery. It showed a clearing in a wood full of cold moonlight that washed away the colours. In the foreground there was a young woman and at the far end of the clearing a man. They were walking in opposite directions, neither seeing the other. There was a sense of yearning that they would meet but you knew they never would. It was as though they were already dead.

Fran found it difficult to mingle with Kel's friends and he with hers.

She told Kel that Paul would do anything to further his own narrow interests and he had better believe her if he didn't want to become a victim.

Kel told her that her friends were cocooned in mainstream professions but that was not the problem...it was their sense of superiority and arrogance that he disliked.

He was the outsider, a stunning looking man, who'd come from nowhere to capture their beautiful Francesca. They looked and waited for his downfall. They knew instinctively, long before he did, that he was never going to live the life she had been brought up to respect.

She lied to her friends and told them he was about to be made a sub editor, a position which she and they thought was prestigious.

Digby, a long, thin, young man who looked thirty-five and decorated the front of his chin with a wispy sandy beard, pursued Kel at a party. "Do you have to pass exams...you know to do your sort of thing?"

Conversation around them stopped in a ragged edge.

"Some do, some don't." Kel was indifferent.

"And you?" Digby pulled on his pipe. "Did you...you know get a degree?"

"No. I'm not very clever." Kel grinned.

"It's just...it's just Fran tells us you are about to become a sub editor. You look very young."

Later as he walked her home he asked "Why? Why did you tell them that about me?"

Fran lifted her head and her mouth tightened like a little girl who has been ticked off. "Why did you tell him you were dumb?" Her steps shortened and quickened. "You don't care what they think do you?"

"On the contrary I yearn for Digby's admiration."

She strode on quickly for a few strides and then leapt on to him pushing him back into a tall hedge. He bounced back like a boxer off the ropes but, as their bodies met, she pushed forward again until his back rested against the hedge and he sat on the low retaining wall. Her teeth bit gently into his neck.

"They don't like you."

"I know. It's fun isn't it."

On that night it didn't seem to matter, but eventually it would.

They walked on and he felt her hands wriggle beneath his jacket and then under his shirt. Her right hand caressed his back and her left stroked his chest down to the flat of his stomach.

They stood outside her aunt's house inside the front gate at the foot of the long garden. The scent of pine and roses mingled in the clear night air. A patch of bluebells gleamed coldly in the moonlight. The house stood solid, silent, and dark except where the long windows caught the streetlights.

"Do you want to come in." It was an invitation not a question.

They walked up the winding path.

He could see the moon dancing on the upstairs window where her aunt slept. The curtains were drawn. Inside the large fire in the lounge had been out for hours. She cuddled to him for warmth. "Would you like a drink?"

He shook his head.

Fran looked at him with large solemn eyes which suddenly filled with tears. She tugged gently at his arm. "Be careful the stairs creak near the top."

As they crept along the long landing to the second flight he could hear her aunt snoring gently.

They sat under the angle of the roof in Fran's room. He caressed her face.

A sepia photograph of her father hung on the wall.

She told him he had died when she was a child and he told her he had lost both his parents in a car crash when he was five. He carried two pictures in his wallet, one of their wedding and another of his father after a rugby match. She demanded to see them.

"Six years later they died," he said. "He came right through the war. Captured at Dunkirk, escaped through France, fought through D day and then there's a car on the wrong side of the road."

"It doesn't make sense," she whispered.

"Oh it does," he said. "It means live each day as hard as you can."

That night they made love for the first time and two floors down in the huge house where the moon shadows lay black and cold on the thick carpets, a grandfather clock chimed two o'clock.

He was startled to discover that Fran was a virgin and even more startled to be told that she'd been taking the pill for four weeks.

For the second time she told him she loved him and he whispered that it was too soon to know. He was right. Six weeks later she was gone.

That night he stood at the window of his darkened room staring down the slope into the grounds of the Royal Victoria Infirmary. He told himself there were people there who were being told they were dying. But the death of his love still hurt him more.

Eventually, exhausted, he lay on the bed. Somewhere a dog barked and the silver light from the moon cut through a crack in the curtain slicing into the darkness as cold as a knife.

He wanted to be happy but he didn't know how. All he knew was that to embrace her way of life, to surround himself with her friends, could only end in misery.

Great events going on around were hardly noticed, but they were to move his life on.

If...If...If the Russians had not put the first man into space....the Chronicle would not have split the page for its lead that afternoon and he would never have been asked to ring the leader of the council, Walter Snaith...and if that hadn't happened...but it had.

"I'll put you through," said the secretary in a pleasant but impersonal sing - song voice. And with that he was speaking to Snaith, the man whose attempt to lead the city out of its parochial torpor had led to him being nicknamed "Mr. Newcastle."

"Mr. Adams. How can I help?"

Kel recognized the deep voice. "Good morning Mr. Snaith. It's about the front page last week...the split front page."

"Yes I remember it."

"Well we've had a number of letters criticising the decision to give equal prominence to the two stories...big council plans for the city and the first man in space."

"And what is the criticism?"

"Basically that we are a bunch of parochial gits."

There was a brief silence and then he heard Snaith laugh down the line.

"You sound as though you agree."

"No."

"So what do you think I should say in public?"

"Something to the effect that it demonstrates the paper's commitment to the building of the new Newcastle, which if successful, will have a profound effect on the lives of everyone who lives here."

There was a silence at the other end, which seemed longer than it was.

"Put me down for that then."

Kel was about to say his goodbyes when Snaith's low, slow voice broke in again. "I should very much like to meet you Mr Adams. Perhaps my secretary can fix something in my diary."

CHAPTER THREE

Then Kel met Billy...

Paul had dressed in his new dark suit but had discarded the glasses, which he'd taken to wearing in a futile attempt at gravitas.

That week he had announced that he wanted to pursue a career in television after Kel had caught him talking to the hall mirror... "The news this morning...."

He admitted he'd been to London on a course for aspiring TV presenters.

One of the tricks of his training apparently was to grasp the vacuum cleaner and walk around backwards pretending it was a microphone and that he was speaking to camera.

He looked to Kel for approval. "Well what do you think?"

"Good idea Paul. Especially if you turn the bloody thing on."

Dave began to laugh.

Paul turned angrily on them. "Yeah laugh now but I'm the only one actually trying to do something with my life. We'll see who's laughing in ten years eh."

Dave bent double. "I can't believe you said that."

Paul was still simmering at the ridicule as they left the flat that evening and began walking down past the hospital towards the city centre.

"So are you going to join Snaith's happy few then?"

Kel shrugged. "I'm off to France."

"He's into dodgy deals you know."

"I know his reputation." Kel smiled.

"What are you grinning at?" Paul looked suspiciously at him.

Kel leapt on to the low wall that wound round the hospital grounds and stuck out his hands as though on a high wire act. "The real question is: Can he make a difference?"

They cut off through the Exhibition Park trotting under the cover of the trees as a fine rain began to fall.

"This pub sells Sunderland beer," Kel held the late edition of the Chronicle over his head as the drizzle became rain.

Paul grinned. "Maybe but the totty is incredible."

They burst through the door of the Brandling into the long room that stretched right down one side of the pub and the sound of a hundred people talking hit them like a wave.

In an instant Kel knew Paul had got one thing right. It was a room of people on the pull; all the signs were there...the exaggerated gestures, the loud laughter at everything said, men hanging on the words of the girls, men standing like roosters, the smells of perfume, after-shave, and the warm bodies newly-bathed in scented soap. Kel had seen it, smelt it all before, indeed for three years he had reigned in this world and each time he entered a room like this one he felt the same... he filled with the sudden concentrated coolness of a card player dealt four aces.

He could have lectured on the subject. The room was basically divided into two areas. To his left, along the wall by the windows, stood half a dozen tables with bench seats on either side. Here sat the couples or, on some occasions, groups of girls. But it was to the right, in the crowded standing space in the well of the floor and round the long bar, where the real action took place... the drinkers came back and forward from the bar, the bodies bumped and brushed, the drinks were spilled, the tentative jokes were passed. He thrust through the crowd at the bar to order the beers which he took to a space in a corner of the room. Dave and Paul took their glasses.

Paul moved off to chat to a girl he'd known from his university days. He gave them a conspiratorial wink which she saw.

"In your dreams," she said.

"Is that your boyfriend?" Paul asked gesturing to someone at the bar.

"Yes," she said. "But that's irrelevant to the central issue."

"Which is?"

"Which is I don't fancy you." Her eyes strayed briefly over Kel and she walked away with Paul following.

"He won't take no for answer will he." Dave shook his head in disapproval.

Kel grinned. "He tries." As he turned to watch Paul push his way through the throng Fran appeared in front of him, smiling, friendly and at ease.

"Hi," she said.

"Hi."

"I'm with some friends." She gestured behind her. They were both conscious of her get-away clause.

He looked out and across the room and caught the eye of Digby, whose raised hand dangled on a long, thin arm.

"Are you OK Kel?" Fran touched his arm to attract attention.

He smiled. "Yes of course. It's just we are in a bit of a rush." He gulped at his beer, aware that for a man in a hurry he had rather a full glass.

Her eyes softened. "I want us to be friends."

"I'm off to France next week Fran."

"Oh!" Her face fell and then she smiled. "You always wanted to go. I never knew why."

"Neither did I," he laughed. He drained his glass. "Nice to see you Fran. Good luck with your exams." He leaned forward and kissed her quickly on her head and walked towards the door. He heard her call but didn't look back. The rain had stopped and lights floated in the puddles. He hurried on towards the town fearful she might follow.

Dave caught up with him as he walked down the Great North Road past the police section house and towards the Haymarket.

"Slow down man." He was breathing heavily. His face glowed as he bent to light a Senior Service.

He offered the packet but Kel shook his head. "I've stopped."

Dave grasped his arm. "I thought you handled it very well," he said gently.

Kel shook his head. "I don't even like her any more. It's just we were once so happy. I miss being happy."

He felt a gentle pull on his arm as Dave guided him across the North Road.

Kel sighed. "Sorry to piss about like this."

"You'll be away soon."

They heard footsteps quicken behind them and Kel swung round. But there was no Fran, merely a panting Paul who cursed as he splashed through a puddle.

"Fuck me! You just left me there."

Dave ignored the remark. "Why didn't you say Fran would be there?" He saw the hesitation from Paul and pressed on. "You said you were a regular. You must have seen her."

"I ...I er forgot. I only saw her fleetingly a couple of weeks ago. Across the bar with her frightful friends." He looked away from Dave towards Kel. "I'm sorry," he said simply.

Kel shrugged. "Let's go."

"She won't be in the Coffin Box," said Paul. "Posh there is to have no spelling mistakes in your tattoos." He grinned at his joke. "She started to cry after you left." He glanced at Kel seeking a reaction. There was none.

The Coffin Box was one of a number of clubs that had been erected without frills to meet the accelerating demand in the city. It stood on two floors. The cheap carpet that covered stairs to the main bar was already stained with drink, scarred with cigarettes, and stabbed to death with stiletto heels.

There was a smaller bar on the ground floor that butted on to a dance floor and a raised area for the band. There were no musicians that night but a juke box was blasting out a selection of the top twenty and a dozen or so girls were dancing round their handbags under a kaleidoscope of coloured lights. Big bottoms and fat thighs threatened to split the home-sewn, micro skirts. The room was heavy with smoke, sweat, and cheap scent.

The girls struggled to stay in rhythm as someone selected The Animals latest hit, House of the Rising Sun.

Paul began to tell Dave that he'd written the first story about the group.

"A bloke called Jeffries came into the office and said they'd be in the charts on Monday and they were," he said.

"Really," Dave refused to encourage him. Paul had told the story many times before.

Paul moved away to the stage to look through a pile of forty-fives.

"The little shit," Dave got rid of his residual anger. "I forgot about Fran... Like hell. Just didn't care."

Kel shrugged. "It's all part of his hard-boiled reporter bit."

A tall girl with a paint-on suntan strode confidently across the floor breasting through the dancers like a ship through waves.

She smiled down at Paul who looked up from his crouched position as she spoke.

Paul's voice carried through a lull in the music. "Hell no, I'm not the DJ."

"Why the hell am I talking to you then." She turned away, her long black hair bobbing on the swing of her buttocks.

Dave who had been facing Kel turned at the sound of the raised voices. "What's happening?"

Kel grinned. "Paul has just been rejected by the stripper."

The speakers started to blast out Always Something There To Remind Me. Across the floor Kel could see a whisper of pain on Paul's face." You've not much sympathy for him have you," he said.

"Not a lot."

Kel reached out and patted Dave on the shoulder. "I'm off to the bog."

The coloured lights lit up his pale face as he skirted round the dance floor.

Dave watched Kel's tall straight figure move like a cat through the crowded room and then through the arched doorway.

A narrow landing ran across the top of the stairs leading to a large bar and twin toilets marked Blokes and Pokes.

As he reached the top of the stairs a woman staggered out of the Pokes as though she was being blown somewhere she didn't want to go.

She was wearing a black cocktail dress, which matched her dark hair. In her unsteady right hand she held a scooped glass of Babycham. As she stopped the contents spilled on to the carpet.

She looked up angrily at him. "You're not wearing a tie," she pointed to his chest.

"You're obviously a trained observer." A couple on the landing sniggered and the woman's face flushed.

"The rules are that you must wear a tie."

"Are you sure it's not a tattoo?"

"Listen Pretty Boy I'm the manager's wife." Her drink swirled dangerously near the rim.

"No one else is wearing a tie except a woman in a trouser suit."

"I'll deal with them later in the meantime," she made a theatrical gesture to one of the doormen. "Billy." She started to giggle as the dark-haired powerful man in an outsize tuxedo stepped quickly up the stairs. Kel noted his clear blue eyes...they weren't the dead eyes of your normal hard man; they were an athlete's eyes, young, and alert. Billy stood unthreatening but unafraid and just out of reach of any single movement.

His voice was high pitched for such a broad man but there was no hesitation or even tension. " Sorry, you'll have to leave sir."

Kel shrugged his shoulders and began walking down the stairs to the exit. He could see into the dance room, which by now was packed to the door. "I've a couple of friends in there..." He stopped.

"I can't let you in there sir. She's watching."

Kel turned to face him.

Billy smiled. "Please don't try to take me on."

Kel smiled back. "No way. I've seen you fight."

"Oh yeah?"

"A guy called Casey knocked you down and you reached through the ropes and had a drink of my beer."

Billy smiled at the memory. "I owe you a drink."

"I'm off to Greys."

It was warm and wet outside and as Kel stretched his step to avoid a puddle he took the ground of two men who were walking towards the club.

"Watch it!"

Kel smelt the warm beery breath as he turned.

"Sorry."

"Clumsy twat." One of the men pushed him and he stumbled backwards. His heel caught the kerb but before he fell his right palm slapped into the ground and with a quick movement of his feet to his centre of gravity he thrust himself upwards causing the beery man to miss with his kick. For a second he froze in shock and fear. Then it was all over. Billy came at them like a bull. Before he could move Kel heard the sickening thud of two heavy blows landing. His two attackers uttered no sound. They lay on the gleaming cobbles. Billy leant down to shake the beery man. "He's with me."

He looked up at Kel and saw the shock on his face. "You OK?"

Kel nodded and took a handkerchief to wipe the dirt from his hand. He sucked on a small cut.

"Frightening isn't it. Violence." Billy seemed quietly amused.

"Very." It was true. He felt the deep gloom of knowledge. He'd frozen.

On the edge of the light from the club the two men recovered their feet and slunk away down the dark lane.

Billy shouted after them "Remember what I said."

Kel felt the blood trickling down his hand again and sucked on the palm. Billy handed him a pristine, silk handkerchief from his top pocket. "Here. I want it back mind."

Kel wrapped the handkerchief tight round his hand. "You know them?"

Billy nodded. " They're tanner men." He saw the lack of comprehension on Kel's face. "They work for one of the top teams. They empty money from the one-armed bandits. Just delivery boys who think they're gangsters." He smiled his strangely boyish smile. "I know you too. I seen your picture in the Chronicle, and you're kind to the cleaning ladies."

Kel wondered where the conversation was going but Billy did not elaborate. Instead he looked at his watch. "Time for my rounds. We're going the same way." He started to walk down the lane and Kel followed as he cut across the Haymarket and passed the three-sided Eldon Square. It was a quarter to eleven and the last of the drunks were scattering across the streets raising thin voices into the night. Half a dozen men went out of their way to acknowledge Billy. To say you knew, or better still, had exchanged greetings with the tough guy of the town was a matter of primitive prestige.

However Kel soon discovered that, unlike most hard men, who acted out a humorless and monosyllabic self lampoon, Billy reveled in laughter.

Yet even when making fun of someone, more often than not, his style of speech was strangely respectful.

As they approached the Theatre Royal he said to Kel "I hope you don't mind me saying this." He stopped under the columned entrance. "But I think it was fortunate that I stepped in back there."

Kel stared at the round passive face and then burst out laughing.

Billy gestured down the street towards Greys Club, which stood in a short alley on the opposite side of the road. "Do you think you can make it from here then?"

Kel smiled. "I owe you Billy."

Billy nodded in agreement. "You do."

George the doorman, who was standing at the entrance to Greys in his long grey coat, gave Kel a mock salute as he passed into the cramped foyer. Kel walked up the narrow staircase where sometime last year a girl had groped him, on to the bar on the lower level where at least a score of girls had introduced themselves, and then up to the raised cabaret area where the pretty, black jazz singer had walked off stage at the end of her act and suggested he take her back to her hotel.

Kel bought a half of keg beer and moved back to the lower bar.

He cleared himself of his memories as he watched the pneumatic actions of the dancers, and the shadowy clinging figures at the tables round the upper room. This was where his successes had made him the envy of so many. Once he had seen his life as a circus but all the time it had been an arena.

He drank the last of his beer, placed the glass on the bar, and walked out.

George raised his eyebrows in mock surprise. "Not up to standard tonight Kel?"

"It's me not them George."

"Ah," said George. His silver hair glinted in the light as he took off his peaked cap to wipe his hot forehead with a handkerchief. He'd seen them all through the years. The usual cycle for the clubbers was about two years. But this guy had lasted longer as the local rooster.

The flat was blessedly empty and as Kel lay on his bed staring into the dark, the events of the night ran through him like a train. He wanted to be a hero and he wasn't. He just wasn't.

One of the nurses in the flat downstairs started to play some Liszt. He fell asleep amid Consolation Number Five, which was his favourite.

CHAPTER FOUR

A large, silent lift took him to the sixth floor of the Civic Centre. Snaith was standing by a long window at the far end of his office. He was taller than Kel had expected, six foot two or three. He was wearing a dark suit, a dark shirt and a green tie. His hair was groomed and expertly cut, and as they shook hands Kel detected the faint scent of aftershave.

His office was large and he had only to swivel in his chair away from his oak desk to look down across the city, his city.

"That's bollocks by the way." He pointed to a copy of the Daily Globe, which Kel assumed he had left deliberately exposed on his desk. The headline leapt at him "SNAITH MP?"

"Why the hell would I go down there? What would I do there eh? "

The secretary with the singsong voice brought in two cups of coffee on a tray.

It tasted dark, rich, and real.

Snaith took a sip before resting his cup on the porcelain saucer.

"We live in exciting times don't you think."

"I do."

"Why?" Snaith leaned forward as the question sprung like a trap.

Kel shrugged. "It's possible the world is going to change faster and more profoundly in the next fifty years than in the whole of history before it."

Snaith beamed with pleasure. "You are right of course and nowhere will change faster than here."

"I doubt it."

"Why?"

"Because we are locked into Labour dogma."

"You don't like Labour?"

"I didn't say that."

"Well what are you saying?"

"I'm saying that Labour's obsession with dividing wealth instead of creating it will make it extremely difficult."

"Nevertheless we have advantages...we're an island on an island with a fierce sense of identity."

He began to talk about his plans. There were no broad sweeping statements. His mind was adept and intricate but all the while his eyes shone with his visions as though he was conducting great music.

Kel felt mesmerised by the man. Eventually he asked, "Why did you ask me to come here?"

Snaith uncoiled his long body from behind his desk and returned to the window .He stood with his back to Kel looking down at the traffic.

"I've read some of your stuff," he turned unsmiling. "I wondered whether you were intelligent or merely sharp."

Kel's face must have betrayed his surprise for Snaith spoke on. "You are wondering why I should find time for something like that. Well I'll tell you

...You're about 25 right. The south is taking our talent...and by the south I mean everywhere from Leeds down. It's got to stop...be reversed if possible. If we don't win that battle we'll lose everything. We're in a race to take this city into the modern age, airports, the river, road and rail networks, huge shopping centres, theatres, schools, universities...these are the sort of things that will decide the conflict, but above all we need to develop and keep our outstanding people."

Kel hardly spoke as Snaith tumbled out his ideas in a slow deep voice. He wondered whether Snaith was a slightly mad, a zealot, or perhaps even a great man.

Snaith reached out and folded up the offending newspaper. "It's right about one thing however. It calls me a visionary. Do you know the prime quality of a visionary?"

Kel smiled into the silence. "Am I meant to say 'No' here so that you can answer your question?"

Snaith laughed a short jerky laugh"Yes. The difference between a visionary and a dreamer is the capacity to carry out the ideas, the will, and the arrogance to get them done." As he spoke he waved the newspaper in the space between them as though fanning flames. Finally he slapped it on to the desk, "I've told your office its bollocks by the way."

Kel smiled. "It's not my office any more." He explained his impending departure.

"I see."

Snaith rose and punctuated his thoughts with another walk to the window.

Kel heard the gentle toot of a horn from way below.

Snaith turned. "I'd rather you didn't go."

"Pardon?'

Snaith had the grace to smile at his arrogance. "We need people like you"

"But you don't know me Mr Snaith."

"I know what I need to know about you. Believe me." He smiled enigmatically.

The leader began to stride up and down the office. His body movements were slow and controlled and his voice was deep and soft... strangely contradictory to the ideas that galloped through him.

A large map of the city and the proposed development areas was pinned on the long wall to the left of his desk. Snaith's empire was coloured in red...slums down, high rise flats up...shopping centres, airport extensions, and an invading army of Irishmen armed with concrete mixers, shovels, and not a P45 between them.

Snaith leaned over the desk towards Kel. "If we don't keep our talented people up here we're buggered."

On his way out Kel was aware of a great irony. Fran had left him because she was alarmed by his lack of direction and yet here was the most powerful man in Newcastle asking him to be a part in shaping the city's future. He laughed until the fresh air hit him outside. He stood for a second facing the war memorial where he had met Fran on their first date. It was for the moment a city of ghosts and memories but soon he would escape to new sights, new sounds, and new people.

Three days before he caught the train Edwards summoned him to lunch.

Rumour had it that Edwards had discovered that the Japanese venerated the mad and so had done press ups in his POW camp every morning. Whatever, he had survived but, unlike Kel's father, there had been no escape.

As Kel looked at the long, sharp-featured face he could not pretend to comprehend Edwards's sufferings; the difference between living them and listening to them was too great.

They met for lunch at the Douglas Hotel, an appropriate venue since it overlooked the Central Station from which he was about to depart.

Edwards raised a long bony arm to summon a waitress before turning to Kel. "It's a long way to the Pyrenees," he said. "I mean by train. Why Pau?"

The waitress approached them from the service hatch, her tray held steady and shoulder high, a distant smile on her face as she navigated her route between the tables. Edwards waited for her to leave.

"I don't suppose you'll change your mind." It wasn't even a question, just something that needed to be said. "I used to think I'd never fall in love and then I did." Edwards's long fingers peeled away the upper slice of his wheat bread sandwich to reveal a crimson slab of tongue. "There are people in the office who were surprised that you fell for someone so obviously naïve. "

Kel forced himself to laugh. "She could cut to the bone when she wanted to." He stabbed his finger at Edwards in imitation of Fran. "You may think it is fashionable not to know where one is going or what one wants to do, but I happen to believe it denotes a lack of thought rather than an excess of it."

Edwards leaned back with his high-pitched "Heeh," took a sip of his lager and then shook his head. "She's wrong," he said. "One day you could do something special."

"But not by staying there." Kel gestured with his head towards the Chronicle.

Edwards smiled thinly in silent agreement. They both knew that along the narrow, creaking, winding corridors walked, in the main, ordinary men, who watched their lives edge towards the end of their mortgage, who gained comfort from repetition.

Kel had no right to say No for them of course. But he had every right to say No for himself. He feared being trapped in a similar life.

There were times when he envied Dave his suburban ambitions in the same way he envied people who believed in God.

The waitress arrived with Edwards's change, breaking his thoughts. Then as he pocketed the money his eyes fixed in a stare. "Look...while you're in France I think it'd be a good idea to write some features as a freelance." He raised a hand, as Kel was about to speak. "No strings." He looked down into his beer. "I'll miss you."

CHAPTER FIVE

The pound had just been devalued to fourteen francs and Kel had to smuggle out five-pound notes in his back pocket to avoid the currency restrictions.

He kept on feeling the bundle for reassurance as he struggled with a heavy case from Pau railway station in the river valley to the town above. Behind him to the south the Pyrenees jutted like a row of jagged teeth against the skyline.

A broad highway followed the valley round the southern end of the town. On the station side a large grandstand stood across the road from a netball court. He stared at it in wonder. A month later a girl told him he'd been standing on the finishing strait for the Pau Grand Prix.

He found a cheap room in the Rue Montpensier. It was noisy but central.

That night he walked to the southern edge of the town past the restaurants and bistros where the tables and chatter spilled out on to the streets as the French dined en famille.

As he stood under a palm tree looking over the stone balustrade across the valley to the mountains he recalled one of his father's letters to his mother. It said "If there is one place I must revisit it is Pau...if only to stand and look out once more from the Boulevard des Pyrenees."

A deep red sun stared over the purple mountains and as he stood there in his father's place he felt more distant from him than ever. He had done what he had felt bidden to do and now he was conscious of a question. So what? He turned back towards the town.

His room was furnished with a lumpy double bed, a sagging chair, and a scratched table. Under the bed stood a large chamber pot, which contained a film of disinfectant. "Luxury, fucking luxury," he murmured to himself.

He had paid two months rent in advance to the owner who ran the Bar des Sports across the street.

The wife of the manager, who worked there each afternoon and evening, could talk at three hundred words a minute in three different languages, French, Ancient French which was common in the region, and English.

Sometimes talking and serving drinks and food just wasn't enough to satisfy her energy and she sang the songs of Edith Piaf in a low, strong voice as she polished glasses and cleaned the bar. On his first evening he sipped at a demi of light beer and she leaned over the bar towards him and said in English. "Ah Englishman how come you look so sad?"

He replied in French "Be careful Madame, I am attracted to women who are slightly mad."

She laughed and two middle-aged men in the far corner turned from watching the television, which hung from a bracket on the wall.

She turned on them with friendly insults.

"Get back to your tele you boring old gits." They grinned and did as they were bid. During this exchange Kel took the opportunity to examine her more closely.

She had refused to colour her hair which was streaked with grey, and her nose was hooked. But when she turned to him, up to the brim with amusement and gentle mockery, her sparkle hid her defects.

She wagged a long forefinger at him." You are a student and poor yes?"

He thought of five answers he could have given and chose the simplest and most self contained. "I am over here to do some writing," he said.

"A writer," she said in French for the benefit of the others. "Un Ecrivain," she nodded her head approvingly. And then added in English. "Then you must be very poor. All writers are poor. All the good ones." She beamed happy at this grand statement. " I shall give you some special onion soup."

He grinned. "Yes. If poverty is the measure I'm a genius."

It was true...after his rent he estimated he could survive for up to three months at seventy francs a day.

He was told he should register in his passport at the local police station.

A smiling Gendarme took him into a back room. Two of his colleagues were cleaning handguns and the room was heavy with the smell of oil. The gendarmes insisted on lining him against a measuring chart on the wall and he stood there somewhat confused as they gathered round.

"One eighty six," one of them gave a low whistle and there was silence until a sergeant said "Yes but the General he is two metres."

"Is that all?" Kel asked.

"Yes Monsieur that will be all." The sergeant smiled. "Forgive us. Here we are soldiers. All our tall men went with Napoleon."

He clicked his heels and handed Kel the navy blue passport. "A beautiful passport if I may say so. Ours," he shrugged. "They look like notebooks."

Outside in the main square the taxi drivers smoked Galois in the sun, leaning on the bonnets of their black Citroens, which gleamed like the backs of black beetles. A warm breeze ruffled the leaves of the palm trees that stood bristling round the square.

The warmth of the autumn surprised him. Each day for a week he took bus trips to Ogeu, a village in the foothills of the mountains, and walked through the narrow rutted streets, which were fouled by cattle, and on, into the fresh air of the mountains. The landscape was decorated with beech and oak and elm. The slow chime of a church bell rose from the village below to mingle briefly but mellifluously with the calls of the cattle.

On some days he walked past the small wooden shooting lodges, across the streams, and along thin winding lanes that led off into the clouds hovering round the mountains.

In the second week he sat on a sawn-off stump of a beech tree and began to write his features. He wrote of Newcastle a small provincial city, an island on an island, that for one hundred years or more had been at the heartbeat of the world's industrial revolution. He wrote of Stevenson, of Armstrong, of the steam engine, of electricity, of the turbine, of coal, of steel, of ships and of shipbuilding and how the fruits of its wealth and invention had been hived off to London.

Newcastle was a city, which had lost control of its own destiny; it was a city whose industry was now controlled from the south, and it was a city that needed a great man. Opinions that had been gestating in his subconscious flowed with deceptive ease as he sat on the stump. Such was the feeling of elation as he wrote he found it difficult to step back and look objectively at his work.

Then one misty morning in the mountains he read the features quickly. His longhand, normally controlled and concise, had lost its shape as he chased the rush of ideas. With sudden and fearful inspiration he stuffed his work into a carrier bag and threw it in one wide, wild arc into the stream. His heart pounded as he watched the bag career through the rocks and round a bend.

That evening he sat at his rickety desk, filled his favourite fountain pen, and this time, in a neat, controlled hand, he tried once more to put into words the place that he loved.

The following morning Madame skipped across the street from the bar and handed him two letters. She watched, smiling, as he read a brief note from Edwards asking for the first of the features by return of post.

In the second Paul was threatening a visit. He was hoping to arrive the following week and would catch the Madrid express from Paris. Could Kel meet the train next Monday Tuesday and Wednesday? It arrived at 6.30 in the morning.

A PS said "Sorry about Fran. I told her you were best left alone but she insisted."

He smiled at Madame. "Friends."

She said nothing.

He returned to his room, sat once more on the bed, reopened the letter and dug out a tiny envelope .On it was his name in her small neat hand.

He read her letter in one breath. "Hi Kel, Just called to tell you I got a two one. Please write, or ring when you get back. I miss you and want us to remain friends.

Love Fran ox."

He crumpled up the note. Outside he could hear the toot, toot of the traffic and next door the butcher was opening up shop.

He wrote to her,

"Dear Fran,

We were never friends. I never liked you, but for a while I loved you. When it ended I was devastated and you were relieved. It happens. Now we've both got to get on with it in our own ways...

Good Luck."

He spent the rest of the morning writing his first feature for Edwards but his letter to Fran lay on the bed with a power of its own.

He crushed a banana in a stick of French bread and washed it down with some bitter tasting vin de table.

Then he wrenched himself back to his work. That evening he took his letters to Edwards and Fran to the bar.

"Homme de Poste," he handed the letters to Madame who glanced at the addresses.

"So the beautiful Englishman has a girl friend," she teased.

He smiled. "Not any more."

"You have left her?" Her dark eyes widened in interest.

"No."

"Ah Englishman," her hand reached out for his and her fingers softly stroked his arm as her face filled with a cocktail of Gallic emotions. "What could she be thinking of?"

He resisted the sudden impulse to tell all to a stranger in a strange place.

"I don't know. I think it was the peculiar way I made love." He winked at her darkly.

CHAPTER SIX

The following morning he timed his walk to the station, down the Rue Montpensier, past the Henri Quatre bistro in Place Clemenceau, across the Boulevard des Pyrenees, down the steps by the cinema, across the ring road and into the station concourse. It took twenty-three minutes to walk to the station's café. Johnnie Halliday was playing on the large TV jukebox. A great diesel growled into the nearside platform from Paris disgorging twenty or so Service Militaire soldiers.

The train moved away bound for Madrid and the soldiers trudged reluctantly towards the ticket collector and to the camp that awaited them. Kel stared at their young, smooth faces, tired, and sullen at the enforced return.

For the next three days he lost himself in his writing, sometimes in his room, sometimes in the foothills, and one afternoon on the Boulevard des Pyrenees until the rain came, warm and sudden.

It was still raining at six the next morning when he set out for the station. The cold from the night cut through his coat and the reflection of the street lights shivered in the empty streets. A local skier stood stiff with ritual by the Olympic flame. Four of his friends kept vigil with him, though from a respectable distance. As Kel passed one of them muttered. "Only two more hours." ...Two hours, then the flame would resume its journey to Grenoble. Kel hurried past, down into the valley. The platform was deserted save for a couple of lovers who clung in tender silhouette at the southern end of the station. The train arrived prompt at six thirty. Paul was not on it.

The following day he made the same journey ...but still no Paul. It was the same on the third day and his face felt like pulp with tiredness as he made his way back up the steps towards the town above. He turned to look across the grey valley at the same time as he heard the woman's scream. She was twenty feet below him, just past a corner of the staggered stairway. She was small and thin, fighting like an angry bird against a tall muscular man. For an instant she broke free and her nails raked across the man's face. He cursed in Spanish and struck her with the heel of his hand. She staggered, dazed, into a wall and he closed with her before she could fall. As his hands went round her throat her eyes caught Kel's. That and the sound of the slap woke him from his shock and he ran unthinking, and accelerating, down the steps. At the last moment the man became aware of him and turned away from the girl, but by then it was too late. Kel's shoulder hit him straight in the chest lifting him in the air. He took off and landed half a dozen steps away and then rolled a further dozen crashing into the brick wall where he lay shocked and winded. Kel stared down at the man waiting. The girl pulled at his arm. "Come on. Leave him." He turned with her and ran up the steps. At the top he turned again. There was no pursuit.

His mind was tumbling with disparate thoughts. The man's long blue coat and grey flannels were of the town. But the trousers and thick boots were splashed with mud.

He gestured towards the town. "The police station is near."

"No. No police," Her voice rose in alarm.

He looked down the steps and into the valley. There was no sign of the man.

He turned to face the girl who was looking at him with curiosity. "You are English yes?"

He nodded. "And you are Spanish?"

She shook her head. "No. I was born here."

"How did it happen?" He gestured to the steps.

She shrugged. "Pervert." She lit a black cheroot and leaned her head back to blow the smoke skywards. Her large, dark eyes studied him from under a black, peaked cap. Her face reminded him of Lisa Minelli in Cabaret.

"Thank you Mr English man." There was a little gap making two words of Englishman.

"Kel, my name's Kel. It's short for Kelvin" He held out his hand which she took.

"Eloise," she said. "Short for Eloise." He admired her cool.

They began to walk towards the town.

He paused by a palm tree when they reached the square. "I have a room down there." He pointed down Rue Montpensier.

She smiled "I go that way." She pointed east.

"Are you alright?

"Yes, Yes," she nodded her head quickly. "Perhaps I will see you at Henri Quatre." She smiled at his surprise. "I have seen you there. Big English man."

"Perhaps we will meet there then." He ignored her mild mockery and held out his hand in goodbye. She took it and kissed him lightly on both cheeks.

"Thank you again," she said softly.

He turned away suddenly tired, whether by his early rising or the delayed shock of his eventful morning he could not tell.

He slept across his bed.

Madame woke him with a letter. It was an apology from Paul saying he had been called away on an urgent story and wouldn't make it to Pau after all.

Kel wrote all afternoon completing the second feature, glad to lose himself in his work.

That evening he took a letter addressed to Edwards to the bar. Madame was sitting at a stool smoking a Caporal. She stood up as she saw him enter and leaned over the bar to hand him an envelope, which was addressed to "Kelvin."

"Femme de Poste. Very pretty." She wagged a finger. "No visitors after seven o'clock."

He opened the letter, which he knew could only be from Eloise. "The Bar Sud?" He asked.

Madame gave him directions and then tutted at the detail. "Here." She quickly drew a map on a menu card. "It's about two kilometres." She looked closely at him. "Is it romance then?"

"Nothing like that," He described the attack that morning.

"The man," she asked. "What was he like?"

"Tall, burly, Spanish I think."

Madame shook her head. "Stay away from this girl English. She is dangerous."

"She was attacked. I intervened...that's all."

She glanced around the room as he spoke and then leaned into him lowering her voice. "This is Basque business. Stay away from her."

He smiled. "Thanks for the warning. But I must see her. She will only seek me out. She cannot mean me harm."

CHAPTER SEVEN

The broad pavement outside the Bar Sud was cluttered with metal tables and chairs, but the cold night air had driven all the customers inside. Eloise was sitting with her back to the wall in the far corner. She waved as he looked around the room. Two men who had been sitting with her got up and left. They were small, dark, and stocky. They nodded to Kel as they passed.

Eloise blew smoke from her cigarette towards the ceiling. She was wearing a black, polo -necked sweater that clung to her slim body like a second skin. Her black hair hung in thick short clusters from under her black cap. Her pale face emphasised the darkness of her eyes. She seemed frail yet her gestures and movements were full of vitality. It was as though someone had put a racing car engine in a Mini.

She leaned forward and kissed both his cheeks and then waved her arm and ordered two whiskies. "I presume you detest our thin, weak beer," she said.

"It's different," he said diplomatically.

She sipped her whisky neat. "I wanted to thank you properly for this morning and to see that you were ok."

"I had a weeping spell this afternoon but I've recovered."

She looked at him sharply. "This is the English sense of humour, yes?"

He added some water to his whisky and took a sip. "And you?" He gestured to her neck, which was covered by her sweater.

"Ah yes," she pulled at the jumper. "It is nothing."

"He was Spanish."

She nodded. "Yes he will be back over the border by now."

"You know him?"

"His type. He is a mercenary. The Fascists send them across. There are many Basque families living here and some Spanish families in exile. We make them nervous."

"But you said you were French."

"My father fled here after the civil war. Franco stole our land. I was born here...but I am my father's child. And you. What brings you here?"

He shrugged. "Nothing so dramatic. I got bored with my job. I always wanted to live in France for a while...so here I am."

He sipped on his whisky and decided to elaborate. "Also my father ...he came here when he escaped from the Germans...to cross the mountains."

"He was lucky," she smiled again with her eyes this time. "To get away I mean. Many people helped the Germans, though none admit to it now of course."

Across the room a drunken man fell against a table scattering glasses. A waiter took him by the arm and rushed him out into the street. The drunk fell into one of the chairs by the patio where he lay, balanced, relaxed and ludicrous, before slumping to the ground. He began to snore and a group of young men by a table near the doorway showered him with cigarette stubs.

"But no..." Eloise protested. Kel turned to face them expecting trouble, but their eyes dipped before her furious stare.

She turned back to him. "In England...what do you do?"

He gave a brief account of how he had left his job and come to France to write some features for a newspaper.

"You have a lover?"

He shook his head.

"And you?"

"My husband left me." She saw the sympathy in his face. "It's OK; I did not like him in the end. He took lovers when I was pregnant. That I did not mind. But he left me when I lost the child."

"You did not mind him taking lovers?"

"Not when I was pregnant."

Her wide eyes, emphasised by her slightly narrow face, reminded him of a beautiful pixie. He wondered how many had paid the price for not seeing the whole of her; he recalled the small hand that struck out as fast as a snake at the man's eyes, the sharp nails that had raked his nose and cheekbones. She was in life to the death.

She returned his stare."You do not approve of our fight eh English man."

"I don't know anything about it."

"You do not need to know...except this: that man this morning he will never return here so you are in no danger." Her eyes flashed momentarily. "He knows that we will do to him what he would have done to me. That is the way it is here...like your Ireland eh...your Government did nothing for years while the Unionists practised religious apartheid against the Catholics." She smiled triumphantly as she saw his surprise. "I know this because I have met some of them."

"What point are you making?"

"What point am I making?" She fished for an answer. "I don't know," she said with disarming candour. "Perhaps it is that there are times when it is necessary to fight to the death to get justice. You do not understand?"

He shook his head. "I've never been in that sort of fight."

She smiled. "You have courage; you have convictions ...one day something may happen." She drew deeply on her cigarette. "I like you English man. However I will not take you as a lover. You are too tall, too conspicuous."

"Do I get a say in this?"

She grinned. "No. Women do the choosing. Men only think they do. But we will be friends...it is for the best." Outside a car tooted its horn. She looked at her watch and rose from her seat. "I must go." She leaned into him to kiss his cheek and her hand pressed into his leaving a slip of paper with a telephone number. He glanced at it and by the time he looked up she was at the inner door. Two of the young men rose and followed her. The three who remained nodded to him when he left a few minutes later.

They did become friends. As his writing took up more of his time she drifted in and out of his life like the weather. He never asked about her activities and she never spoke of them in any detail. However she did read his writing, always sitting cross-legged, gnawing on her knuckles, her large eyes hardly blinking as they sped back and forward across the lines. He told her of Newcastle. He explained to her that Snaith and his planners were trying to create a modern city, with theatres, universities, new housing, motorways, and a bigger airport, before all the talented people were compelled to move away to seek jobs.

"And you think he will?"

"I want to think he will."

"And he wants you to help him in this fight."

He smiled. "In a very small way. He asked me to stay but I was already set on coming here."

"Maybe he will win his fight. He sounds an unusual man."

That afternoon they were standing looking into the window of a superstore and Eloise turned from the display of electrical goods. "Did I tell you I am studying law," she said.

She hadn't.

"If I lived where you live I would stay and fight with him," she said.

He pulled a face. "I think I need to make a lot of money."

"Why?"

"So I can control my own life."

She smiled and shook her head.

"What?" he asked.

"Nothing," she said.

The weeks passed. He never sought her out; it was always Eloise who appeared beside him at a bar, or a shop, or in the street with a little dig to his arm. "Hey English man."

She followed his bus into the mountains on a motorbike roaring through the village of Ogeu, riding the grass verge when confronted by a herd of cattle. She swooped on him in the open land between the village and a stream, riding in circles round him whooping.

They sat on a dead tree in the low, thin winter sun that gave faint warmth when the wind was still. She'd brought sandwiches and wine. He told her that a month before he'd thrown his writing into the water and watched it float away because he had known it was the only way he would improve it to his satisfaction.

She was impressed. "Perhaps you are a great writer then. Great writers throw away their diamonds don't they?"

He watched her straight face break into laughter. He rolled over and wrestled her so that she lay on her back. She was helpless but she still laughed. "Why do you always mock me?" he asked.

"Envy," she said. And then she kissed him on both eyes. He got his own back on the way home when she allowed him to ride her bike. She clung to him for her life as he roared down country lanes taking one corner so low that their knees scraped the tufts of grass at the edge of the rutted road."

It's my passion," he explained later. "Speed is sexy eh?"

She did not reply which, for her, was unusual.

A week later and two nights before he left for England he awoke to the sound of tapping at his window.

He slept in a single room on the lumpy bed that backed on to the high windows. He pulled back one of the shutters and her face stared in white and wide eyed.

Fearing disaster he ran along the cold passage, dressed only in his football shorts, and hurried her inside.

"What's happened?"

"Nothing," she said. "I must go away for a while in the morning. I will not see you before you leave."

He pulled the blankets round himself for warmth conscious that they they were looking into the abyss between them.

Since the day in the mountain he had asked himself whether she had wanted to make love to him. Tonight he knew with sudden clarity that despite her visit to him in the early hours she did not. As a friend who was not involved in her struggle he had great value. He was her little window into another life. As a lover they would both demand more from the other...and that increased the risk of her losing him.

She was staring into the spluttering gas fire that they had lit. Her white face was strained and tired. He stroked her clustered, short hair that hid her ears that should have been pointed like a pixie's, but were instead small and round.

"We will meet again yes?" She looked up to him, suddenly vulnerable.

"Yes." He was aware the answer sounded hollow. "Some day I will come back here." He took out one of his little cards. "Are freedom fighters allowed to take holidays?"

She grasped his hand as she took the card. "You are my dearest friend. You know that."

He nodded. He felt his face soften and his eyes water.

She smiled. "Tell me, did you ever want to make love to me?"

"Yes, but you would not have welcomed it."

"Are you that bad?" She raised her eyes briefly in mockery.

"We both know that your life is here and mine is in England."

The scattered cries of a couple of drunks cut into the night. One of them banged on his window. Then they passed on into the night.

"I must go English man." She rose quickly and pushed him back on the bed as he started to rise. She leaned over him and kissed him quickly, but warmly, on the lips. "I will write to you Kelvin."

She ran to the door and, seconds later, he heard the inner and then the outer door close; there was a tap on the window and her hard heels clacked along the pavement. He knew from the sound of her running that she was fighting back tears.

His chest heaved with a sudden sadness. He fell into a half sleep where dreams are too near reality...the other women, the names he couldn't remember, the strange rooms, the secrets kept from the lovers, husbands, or just neighbours, the bursting out into strange streets, the stiffness from overcrowded single beds, the cheap mattresses, and the pleas, questions, and accusations. "Will I see you again?"... "Well we know the sort of person you are now."..."Don't tell Carol. I said I wouldn't sleep with men anymore." ... a nurse fortifying herself in a voice as cold as disinfectant: "Well I'm off to save lives ...God knows what you will do."

And above all else the great joke that he, the thriving, thrusting handsome man, was the envy of his peers. There was a pleasure in being envied. But he had not fooled himself for long. His life had been lonely and empty until he'd met Fran. And then...and then...his mind wriggled against the truth that would not be denied...her life, her horizons bored him...even when she had thrilled him there were voices whispering his doubts.

The lights were out, Fran had gone, Eloise had gone, and he was a thousand miles from home. He had seen himself with sudden clarity and he started to laugh.

CHAPTER EIGHT

Kel looked at his reflection in the long mirror behind the bar as Madame spoke.

"France has done you good Monsieur. You look more at ease."

The high lights in the room made caverns of his eyes and accentuated the high cheekbones and the strong jaw. She looked at him looking... "So vain yes."

Her dark blouse was lower cut than usual and she wobbled her eyes as she leaned forward. "No sex in France for the handsome Englishman?"

"No sex in France at all Madame. I don't know how there are forty million of you."

"Ah Monsieur this is a Catholic town. You should be here in the summer when the English and Swedish girls arrive."

He laughed. And leaned forward to kiss her cheek. "I'm off to town."

She frowned. "Be careful the Parapluis will be out tonight."

He squeezed her hand, which was hard skinned from her labours. "I'm sure they will be no worse than Newcastle on a Saturday night."

A man in a black beret paused from peeling an orange with a clasp knife.

"The Parapluis are not Service Militaire, Monsieur. They are elite soldiers, paratroopers."

He caught Kel looking at the strong clean knife and drew it slowly across his throat. " Boche," he said. His grin revealed yellow broken teeth. "He got on the escape line in the mountains. We knew he was Boche. I took his knife." He stabbed it into the bar for effect. Madame slapped his hand hard. "Will you stop doing that Jean? My beautiful counter is as pockmarked as your face."

The war hero retreated before this onslaught. Madame tutted.

Kel rose from his stool towering over the pair of them. "I must go," he announced and gave a little bow.

He walked slowly to the square. The lights from the shops held back the dusk from the streets. A couple sat in one of the window seats of the Henri Quatre. The backlight caught their bodies in silhouette as they leaned gently into each other across the table that separated them.

He ordered a demi from Alphonse, the tiny waiter. Tonight, he told himself was one of those nights where you waited to pick up your life again. He'd lived here for three months...Fran would be gone... he wanted to return to Newcastle and tonight he was filling in the time before he caught the train. The thought relaxed him and he drank the beer quickly and ordered another.

He was on his sixth beer when the paratroopers came. Five of them bustled into the room and crowded onto two benches on opposites sides of a long table with a plastic top.

A woman sitting doing a crossword at the bar glanced at them and left. The couple followed. The men shouted to Alphonse and ordered four whiskies each. Kel stared into his beer avoiding eye contact. Two of the men had sergeant's stripes and from their loud conversation and many toasts he learned that one of them was being posted to Germany the following day.

Suddenly one of the soldiers swung round as though Kel had crept up on him. His face was pink and his light, ginger hair was close-cropped. Kel met the stare from the soldier's pale blue eyes as the man challenged him. "Hey you. Why did you not leave with the others?"

"Because I'm leaving for England tomorrow and I am trying to get drunk on your French beer."

The para turned to his comrades. "He says our beer is piss."

One of the sergeants shrugged his shoulders. "Our beer is piss."

The para turned back to Kel. "Hey Englishman... our beer is piss. You must have some whisky." He gestured to the waiter. "A whisky for the Englishman."

Alphonse had been staring at this scene like a rabbit frozen in headlights.

Kel shook his head. "No thanks."

The para rose from his seat glaring. "You will not drink our whisky?"

Alphonse put his hands together and said in a small voice "Please Monsieur accept their whisky."

Kel shook his head again. "I haven't the money to buy a drink back."

There was a silence for a second.

Then one of the sergeants called out. "Please join us Englishman. We have money enough for all."

They made a space for him against the wall.

Kel took his seat and finished the rest of his beer in one gulp. The sergeant thrust a small glass of whisky into his hand.

The soldier finished off his own whisky and pushed another glass towards Kel.

Kel kept pace with him and placed the empty glass on the table. He could feel the confidence in himself rising like a song; his mind was quick, his body strong, and he was filled with a sudden joyous feeling of invincibility.

He looked across at the larger of the two sergeants. He was a man of about thirty, dark hair brushed back in a wave across the top of his head, tanned and fit and beneath the starched cuffs of his khaki shirt he saw the sharp outline of a dagger tattoo. He was the sort of man who would fight Billy the doorman without a second's hesitation. He would lose, but he would fight.

"Tomorrow I go to Berlin," he said.

Kel wondered whether there was some hidden significance in this.

"Do you want to go to Berlin?" He asked.

"Hell no." The soldier lit a cigarette.

"It could be worse couldn't it?"

The sergeant drew deeply on the Caporal.

"Better you go there than the buggers come here again eh."

The paratroopers laughed like naughty boys finding an excuse to make a great deal of noise. Alphonse glided backwards from the room.

"The sergeant pushed another glass towards him. "Good Health."

Kel sipped at the whisky. "My name is Kel," he announced.

The big para with the ginger hair leaned towards him close enough for Kel to feel his warm breath and smell the whisky. “And so Kel what do you think of the French soldiers.” It wasn’t a question, more a challenge. There was something in his tone and his pale blue eyes that seemed to give an air of menace to everything he said.

Kel sensed the others were alert to the tension and were looking for signs of nervousness. They were hard physical men who didn’t give respect without it being earned.

He stared down at the table as though giving the matter his deepest thought. “I’m very impressed. They seem more intelligent than our soldiers.”

“How so?” Again the warm breath of whisky from the big para.

“Well I’ve never met an English soldier who could speak French.”

There was a second’s silence and then the sergeant who was going to Berlin started to giggle.

Alphonse looked on from his post by the door in astonishment.

They all raised their glasses, drank the whisky in one throw down their necks, and sent the glasses crashing against the wall behind them.

The sergeant rose and steadied himself against the table.” We continue back at the camp,” he announced turning to Kel. “It is only a few kilometres. You must come.”

“Of course,” said Kel smiling as the room went into a spin. “But first I must have a piss.”

The toilets were empty, because the bar was empty and he stuck two fingers down his throat bringing up the bile from his stomach. The tap water was cold on his face and made his eyes water. He wiped himself down with paper towels.

Through the door he could hear raised voices but that did not prepare him for the scene outside.

At least a dozen gendarmes stood in a large semi circle. Some of them had sten guns angled towards the ground. Four others had Alsatian dogs snarling and leaping at leads. The young paratrooper, who had first called over to Kel, was attempting to charge at them and was struggling like a sail in the wind with his four comrades who were each holding a limb.

Kel acted instinctively, moving quickly, and quietly, sideways along the wall. The night beckoned and he ran into its welcome darkness. He ran until his lungs were burning for air and his chest was heaving. He halted and his stomach churned.

He vomited into a shop doorway, watching through tear-filled eyes as long strands of saliva strung out from his mouth to the ground. He found himself to be in a small square. A couple of large, twisted orange trees stood on either side of a small fountain, which was flanked by palm trees. He moved across to the fountain. A brass plaque said something about Verdun. He drank deeply settling his stomach and clearing his mouth of the taste of vomit.

He had run towards the east end of the town, at least a mile from his room and the air was damp and heavy, but at least the rain had stopped. He pulled up his collar round his throat and began to walk slowly back to the town. He'd fled by instinct but now, looking back more calmly on the situation, he was glad that he had. The big, ginger-haired Para would cause trouble in an empty house. He breathed in deeply and spat loose phlegm on to the cobble stone street.

He wondered what bond had held those men together beyond their respect for each other's courage. Perhaps they despised him now. They'd said he was one of them for the night and he'd fled. He shrugged. Better that than jail and a missed train. For the second time that night he thought of Billy. Billy would probably have laid out half the cops, bent their sten guns, and then started on the dogs. Billy was a world-class street fighter who, legend had it, often took on five or six men when he worked the doors.

Kel was not a world-class street fighter, and he was frightened of dogs, and very frightened of guns.

"Excuse me can you help me please?" The woman's voice was warm, steady and confident, despite a near indecipherable accent.

He turned to face her. She was standing across the street, tall and elegant in the lamplight .A black silk scarf covered most of her blond hair. She was wearing a long, leather coat and her eyes were hidden by sunglasses, which emphasised the pallor of her face. She seemed as cool as the moon and at least that far away from the world he inhabited. He wondered idly whether she was real or whether he was drunk or dreaming or both. Everything seemed to go into slow motion. He blinked and she was still there. She took a step towards him. Her light, sensible shoes clicked on the cobbles. The glasses glinted in the streetlights giving an air of mystery to her elegance and beauty.

He replied to her in French. "Of course."

She began to tell him in hesitant French that she was lost.

He smiled. "It's OK I speak English."

"Oh. You're American?"

"English. But the good news is we invented the language."

She said nothing but he sensed that from behind her sunglasses she was coolly appraising him.

"No wonder you are lost... wearing sunglasses at night."

Still she said nothing and she did nothing, which he found disarming.

He looked away from her along the road. The lights gleamed on the cobbled street and the square stood strong between the tall terraced houses with their long shuttered windows and high doors. She turned to follow his eye, and seeing merely an empty street, looked back.

He smiled. "I love those nineteenth century paintings of carriages on cobbled streets with rain on the roads and lights reaching out from shop windows. You said you were lost."

"Yes I can't find the Hotel Olympique...it's near the Place Clemenceau."

"It's about a mile. I'll show you." He saw her hesitate. "If you're wary of me I'll walk on ahead and you can follow." He strode off towards the town. She caught him in a few yards. "It's not out of your way?"

"No. Not at all." He ran ahead for a few yards and then swung round looking back along the long gleaming road. There was nothing of the twentieth century apart from the streetlights and the woman who stood poised and elegant in her expensive coat. He had always thought that the eyes were the key to beauty yet here she was, her eyes hidden by sunglasses, tall, straight, poised and beautiful...beautiful with the eyes hidden. She had the sort of shape, the sort of movement that told you she knew she was beautiful. As she walked towards him she moved across the strongest reflection of light in the wet road and to his dazzled eyes it was as if she was a wonderful vision raised from the light.

"What?" she asked. "What's the matter?"

He struggled to find a suitable evasion from his thoughts. "When I looked back then there was just you and the streetlights of this century, everything else was from another age."

She turned to look down the street then back to him. She said nothing.

He felt obliged to elaborate." I like the sight of empty streets at night. I know it's fanciful but to me it's not as though the people have gone in but more as though the streets have come out...like it's their time."

She smiled. "Perhaps I should be wary of you. You seem a very strange man." But her laugh was friendly.

"I'm sorry. I think it must be something to do with talking in English for the first time in weeks."

"Tell me about yourself," she said. "Why are you here for instance?"

Perhaps it was the drink, perhaps she merely struck a chord with his life at home, but he started to tell her about Newcastle, about Fran, about his job, about his leaving his job. He told his stories with boyish enthusiasm reliving them, as he went, not even noticing the glances she gave him as they walked slowly down the long Avenue.

"I'm sorry I've been very tedious telling you my life story like that."

"No you are not tedious." She spoke the words in a flat honest voice but he was too caught up in his own embarrassment to be listening.

"I don't know how I ever thought you were American," She glanced sideways at him but he did not catch her look. "Your accent is very English, English."

"Minor Public School," he said.

She looked at him blankly.

"Posh School," he explained.

"Ah you were lucky then."

"I hated it," he said. Then before she could pursue him he smiled.

"If you want to unload anything on to me you have just over half a mile to do it," he said.

She laughed and swung her arm round one of the thin young beech trees that lined the road. Rain fell from the shivering branches and her laughter echoed into the empty street. It was a surprisingly loud, an almost discordant laugh, which he thought, he had heard before, but of course that was impossible.

"No," she said Tell me some more. Tell me about..." She hung her long body out from the tree with just one hand taking her weight. She had the unconscious grace of a dancer. "Tell me about your first love," she said at last.

The girl came to mind in an instant.

"She was called Jane and I was very shy. I was fifteen and not able to deal with rejection. Each summer there was a gymkhana near my home and I was sitting watching it when I saw her come through the gate across the field with her two sisters. I saw her point towards me and I knew for the first time that she really liked me. They came to sit with me on a low, wooden bench and her eldest sister made room for Jane to sit next to me and as she did she smiled as though we had a secret."

He stared into a big puddle that lay in the hollow of the road. It held the reflection of the moon and he tried to think of the film but couldn't call it to mind.

"What happened?"

"We went out a couple of times. We were just kids. But as I watched her walk across that field towards me that was the most exciting rush I've ever had."

"That's a lovely story."

He looked up to see she had discarded her glasses and her eyes were soft with thought. They were also blue and bright, even in the washed-out light of the street lamps and he knew now where he had heard the laugh. He hid his astonishment and disappointment. Soon they would come to the square and then the hotel and that would be it. He wouldn't tell anybody who she was because no one would believe it.

They could see the high-sided buildings of Place Clemenceau now.

"Saved by the square... I was about to launch into another boring story and you would have remembered me as a boring git instead of..." He sought the phrase

"Instead of..." she said softly.

"Instead of a slightly loony Englishman."

"Who helped me and entertained me for which I thank him."

She had a habit of pausing before she spoke, as though giving everything she was about to say a final check. She also had a strange tone to her quiet voice, friendly, polite, but almost formal.

He bowed "Your hotel awaits madam."

She stopped, so he stopped and then she stood looking at him, placid and confident. For two or three seconds they stood silent and he sensed with amazement her increasing interest in him. Finally she broke the spell.

"And you. Have you far to go?"

"No, a couple of hundred yards." They walked on past the Henri Quatre. The windows were intact and not a bullet hole in sight; some dog dirt on the pavement was the only evidence of the drama of an hour ago. He pointed down a long road to the north.

"I've a room down there. I don't suppose you've been down the Rue Servier or Rue Montpensier."

"No."

"Of course not. They've been saying they haven't had a film star down there in ages."

"Oh." She stopped walking again and this time he noticed the faintest of smiles flirt with her still, beautiful face.

He smiled. "It was the laugh, and then when you took off your sunglasses I saw your world famous eyes."

"You didn't say."

"That's bad?"

"Oh no that's good."

Fifty yards away the hotel's neon lights glowed into the damp sky. The town was asleep. The houselights were out, the shops and the bistros had shut their shutters, the last drip of rain had run down the drains and the only sound was a splutter from a faulty streetlight.

She moved on a little in front of him and then swung round forcing him to stop again. "Very good indeed." She smiled and took off her glasses again.

"They're meant to react to light but I don't think they work properly in street lights."

He reached forward and replaced the glasses. "I was getting on fine without the famous film star."

"And then?" Her voice was low, almost inviting."

"You became hopelessly out of reach and it all became a bit like a dream."

She removed the glasses and put them in her pocket. "But I am real."

"Of course you are... or so I shall tell myself tomorrow."

"If it would help I could meet you tomorrow."

He shook his head. "I'm afraid not. I'm booked on the morning train to Paris."

"Oh," she said softly. "Walk me to the foyer." She took his arm and they strolled the last few yards across the square. She stopped just out of the light from the hotel's double doors and turned once more to face him with the confidence that he assumed came with fame.

"Have a good life Jean Smith." His voice was steady but he was suddenly filled with sadness. He watched her face closely but her expression did not change. He reached out and gently held her by both shoulders. He gave her a squeeze and then turned to walk away. He was having difficulty walking out of this dream and he managed about fifteen yards when he heard her call. "Wait."

As he turned she walked towards him.

"I don't know your name," she said.

"It's Kel. Kel Adams."

"I'm not American by the way."

"Oh."

"I'm from Canada."

She reached in her pocket and handed him a small card. "Perhaps if you're ever in London..."

"Gee thanks."

Her large blue eyes looked right into his. "Please don't write about this." She saw the resentment in his face. "I'm sorry. It's just my life's like a circus."

They stood at the parting of the ways in a strange silence.

At last he asked her... "I hope you don't find this a cheek but I've often wondered why you chose such a simple name as Jean Smith."

"Because it IS my name," she said.

"Aaah, that's a good reason."

She shivered in the cold.

"You'd best go in. You're going to catch cold. Nice to have met you."

"Nice to meet you," she said and leaned into him and kissed him on the forehead. "Please call. I mean it,"

Then this time she was gone. She turned at the entrance and waved but he had crossed the square. She watched him out of sight. He did not look back. She stood staring into the square for seconds before turning to walk into the foyer where the night porter hovered in the warm and the light.

CHAPTER NINE

The last book Kel read before catching the express train to Paris was James Baldwin's "Giovanni's Room". He, like the hero, lay across seats of the train at Pau station and pretended to be asleep in an attempt to persuade the Service Militaire soldiers to try another carriage, but in his case a big corporal barged his way into the compartment and slung a long, heavy bag on the rack above Kel's head.

That afternoon he caught a second train from the Gare du Nord to London.

There was a picture of the film star in the evening paper at Kings Cross. She was wearing her sunglasses and her right arm was round a downhill skier. The caption said something about Jean wishing him luck for the big event. Kel laughed harshly at himself. He chucked the paper into one of the wire bins and her card with it. Alone, they'd shared a brief dream but now their separate worlds were demanding that they return, hers more stridently than his evidently. Even so as the train pulled him back to Tyneside, she slipped past his defences to rear into his mind. It seemed preposterous but there had been a mutual attraction. When she touched him he sensed she wanted to feel him, to run her fingers over his skin, to arouse him.

The long, slow screech of brakes woke him as the train pulled into Newcastle Central Station. He left his case in a locker. It was closing time and gaggles of drunks swarmed the streets. He walked up the long curve of Grey Street and bore left past the YMCA and Eldon Square towards the flat in Spital Tongues that he knew he must leave. No Dave, no Paul, but the rooms were warm and filled with the heavy smell of cooked bacon. Nothing had changed. The battered, stained three-piece suite cluttered round the electric fire. A small table, surrounded by four straight-backed chairs, stood at the only window in the lounge/dining room.

The carpet smelled of brown ale and cigarettes. The kitchen sink had an avalanche of dirty dishes and grease wriggled down the side of the cooker like a runny nose. He turned off the lights, and retreated to his bedroom, which was cold and empty. Two white, polystyrene squares had fallen from the ceiling and lay on the dark carpet. He opened the window an inch to let out the stale air and looked out over the black, open land towards the lights of the city. Neither Paul nor Dave returned during the night and he lay face up on his cheap bed thinking of Eloise and Jean as a series of unrelated images drove through his head, until the pictures became dreams, and he escaped into sleep.

In the morning he walked down to the Chronicle's new office.

He took the route down the Bigg Market to the new front entrance, which did its best to disguise the fact that it was a concrete box as it faced the Victorian splendour of the Old Town Hall. A circus had put their animals on show and two giraffes stared at him from a high window in a room from which the business of the city had once been conducted.

The newsroom was open plan with the reporters and sub editors sitting at opposite ends like two opposing teams. Each reporter had a typewriter and a grey phone neatly spaced on long wooden desks that looked as though they'd been laid out for dinner.

Edwards's new office was slightly larger than the one on the old building. As he rose to greet Kel with a smile on his thin pinched face his clothes stuck to the synthetic material that coated his padded chair.

Kel's features had gone down well. They'd attracted a number of letters.

"You seem to have struck a niche," Edwards sipped on a mug of tea.

They exchanged pleasantries. He had been a legend as a reporter while working on the Daily Mail in Manchester where his reputation was such that if he scooped any other newspaper the excuse that it was Edwards on the story was accepted.

He had a gift for extracting information from unlikely, and potentially unwilling, sources. His technique was simply to talk about anything but the subject in hand until he struck a common interest with the victim. Then for ten or twenty minutes he would chat until the atmosphere became relaxed. Only then would he turn the discussion to the raison d'etre of the conversation.

"And Francesca?" he asked gently.

Kel grinned. "Norman!" He shook his head.

Edwards smiled in defeat. "Old habits, you know."

"Of course I know...you taught me."

A small clock chimed sweetly on the wall behind his desk.

"Am I allowed to comment on the mellifluous tones of French nineteenth century clocks?" He looked at Kel and answered his own question. "No...OK do you want to come back?"

"No."

"Francesca?"

"No." He owed Edwards more than that. "There's nothing between us now. She's gone."

Edwards used his phone to order two cups of tea. It was another of his tricks. Kel could not now escape with good grace until he had finished his drink.

The tea came on a Formica-topped tray carried by Miss Young, an elderly, spindly, and imperishable secretary who, it was rumoured, had once met Pitman when she was young and he was old.

Edwards sipped his tea. "Why? Why NO?" he said at last.

"I think I'm a maverick."

"Eh?"

Kel smiled. "I want to strike out on my own."

"Doing what?"

"Making money and then using it."

"How are you going to make it?"

"Dunno."

"How are you going to live?"

"In the immediate future there's some freelance work and my aunt left me a flat and a little cash. Crazy innit!"

Edwards surprised him by smiling but saying nothing.

"The alternative is that I'll get sucked back in."

Edwards stared at him and then again his thin face softened. "I had a young reporter went on holiday once. He read a book by Nietzsche on the plane. Caused all sorts of problems." Edwards took another sip "However he did not have your talent or determination."

As they said their goodbyes Kel was struck by the thought that he might be embarking on the life that Edwards had wanted to live.

He told Dave and Paul that evening that he was moving out.

"But why?" asked Paul. "We've had good times."

"Things change," said Kel. "The two of you will be off to the Nationals in a year. It's the way things go."

Dave, who was sitting by the old wooden table by the back window, gave a laugh that sounded like a cough. "And you...you're going to stay here."

"Here is home to me Dave."

Paul was preparing to go out. He'd bought a long, black, leather coat, which by some strange psychology of fashion had become the in-thing for young people to wear. Kel knew this because he'd passed the A Go-Go club on the way home and seen the long queue of teenagers in the Haymarket, their collective coats curled and gleaming like a snake's back. Paul made his goodbyes as quick as he could and the clash of the door was followed by the sound of quick steps on the hard lino that covered the stairs.

"He's off early."

"He's found a girl who fancies him. That's why he didn't go to France. What excuse did he give?"

Kel laughed. "He plays a mean hand doesn't he."

"You like him don't you." Dave's voice had a note of incredulity.

Kel shrugged. "He tries."

It was warm and they strolled to the pub that stood in the long row of terraced houses that faced out over the field.

Dave stared into his drink. Across the room through the smoky, yellow light a fat man with greased, thinning hair sang sentimental songs out of key.

"That's Newcastle," said Dave motioning towards the singer.

"That's a slight simplification, Dave," Kel said dryly.

"You know what I mean. Old fashioned, out of time, but 'Eeeh aren't we quaint and friendly.'"

Kel and Dave sat in silence for a while both aware of the gap between them.

"Tell me about France." Dave tried to resurrect the conversation. The room was crowded and noisy and he leaned towards Kel.

"I wrote some, I walked some, I met some interesting people," he glanced up at Dave watching for the effect of his next words.... "A very pretty Basque freedom fighter and then on my last night..." he described the meeting with the Paras and how it had led to him meeting a beautiful film star.

"You're pulling my todger." Dave grinned.

The singer's song ended. A few applauded, some out of appreciation, some out of relief.

Kel watched as war broke out on Dave's face. He knew Dave was saved from cynicism, the fate of so many journalists, because he wanted to believe. His irritation at Paul was not so much that he lied but that he lied so transparently that he was in permanent confrontation with Dave's first premise...that people were basically decent.

"It's true," he said. "I'm only telling you because I know you won't tell anyone else."

"Jesus Christ!" Dave whistled in appreciation. "Who was it then?"

"You won't tell anyone. I promised her I wouldn't write about it."

"No...no of course not."

He found it hard to keep a straight face as Dave leaned into him like a conspirator in a film.

"Jean Smith."

The name exposed all Dave's small-town naivete, his adoration of the famous, who despite his intelligence in other matters, he saw as being another species, a people who lived on what was an unattainable plateau for ordinary mortals. The new Royals.

"Jesus Christ!" He gulped at his drink.

Kel watched as Dave's bank manager's soul struggled between curiosity and propriety.

"Did you?" Dave believed in the legend of Kel.

"No."

Two years ago though the answer had been "Yes."...only the girl in question had been Dave's girlfriend of two months. She had come to his room when Dave had left for work and in the gloom her fingers had run like mice over his half-awake body. And then it was done...apparently in revenge for some half- hearted infidelity on Dave's part the previous week...or so she told Dave later.

Dave had felt more betrayed by Kel than the girl.

"Why Carol?" he had asked bitterly. "You can have anyone you want, why pick on Carol for your fucking collection?"

Kel had pointed out that it was in fact Carol who had picked on him.

His own life was moving on.

Edwards had asked him to write a further series on Newcastle called "A City at War"...about the Reivers when the region had been the buffer state between

England and Scotland, about King Charles staying in Newcastle after losing the Civil War, about the siege of the city by the Scots in 1644 when they'd threatened blow off the Cathedral's tower until the mayor had hastily placed Scottish hostages in it, about the Roman settlement and about the Normans who built Newcastle into one of the most important 12th century centres in the country.

He became a regular reader at the Lit and Phil near the Central Station and at the local studies department of the city library. The Lit and Phil fascinated him. Some of the great figures in the industrial revolution had met within the book-lined walls. He found a strange therapy in a place where silence was welcome and a cough was treated like cannon fire.

Within two months of his return he moved into his aunt's flat in Tynemouth but before that Fran approached him one last time at Spital. She came out of the copse of trees that stood in the fields in front of the flat. It was spring; the wind weaved her hair and the long grass whispered round her long, bare legs. He stood still and empty as she approached. She told him she was visiting her aunt and she had to see him. "I can't sleep. I worry about you."

"I told you. If you want to help just stay away."

There were tears in her eyes. "Do you hate me now Kel?"

"I hate meeting you."

She started to cry.

"Look," he said. "We fell in love at the same time. We fell out of love at different times."

Her long neck was bent as she sobbed into her hands and he knew this was her final act of exorcising her guilt.

"Oh for Christ sakes." He handed her a handkerchief.

She dabbed at her red eyes. "Take me away. We can go somewhere."

He shook his head. "No."

"You've changed," she sobbed. "You've got harder."

"Of course I've got harder. I've had to. Look. It's over. We both know it's over. There's nothing else to say."

He turned and walked towards the black stone house. He could hear her sobbing as he shut the door and stood in the gloom of the spacious hall. A single sunbeam shafted down on to the stairs from the skylight and the draught from the opening and shutting of the door sent dust particles drifting through it. He stood in the emptiness of the hall, in the emptiness of the house, listening to the silence. He stayed there for a minute before moving up the stairs to his room. And then, when he could no longer fight the compulsion, he walked to his window and looked out into the field. She had gone. He never saw her again.

CHAPTER TEN

The sunlight drew him out. Shoppers and workers sprawled in the grounds of the Civic Centre and the neighbouring St Thomas's Church eating ice creams and sandwiches. A poster outside the church announced that Che was dead. A double-deck, yellow, trolley bus glided past the Haymarket Cinema. Jean Smith's face looked down from the billposter on the sidewall. He turned away down Northumberland Street and found refuge in the snooker hall.

Gerry was at one of the far tables. He and a friend were performing, in their bright shirts, pastel jeans, wipe-on suntans, and dyed hair. There were lots of sniggering jokes about balls as they stuck out their bottoms to play their shots.

The other players laughed at their cabaret. Kel watched from the other end of the room as Gerry moved like a cat round his table.

Gerry's friend pretended to swoon. "Oooh you're not going to pot the brown."

"Later dear later," Gerry waved his cue in admonishment.

"Good God," Kel muttered to himself.

"You don't mind me mentioning this but you seem interested in those two."

Kel turned round to find Billy grinning at him.

"Interested in avoiding them."

Billy nodded. "Best way. He's twisted that one." His voice and movement gave no hint at what was about to happen.

The girl from the kiosk smiled quickly at Billy and inclined her head slightly to three men standing in a far corner, just out of the pools of light that mushroomed over the tables. Kel glanced across. The men's shapes were dark in the backlight from the large, long window that looked out into Northumberland Street.

"You're sure?" Billy's voice was low but strong and urgent.

The girl nodded and her dyed blond hair shimmered dully. It was early afternoon but she was made up to meet her public, her eyebrows plucked to a thin line, her eyelashes heavily dabbed, her cheeks touched with rouge and her lips painted red. Paul called her sort "Cavendish Girls" because, he claimed, that was the club where they spent Saturday nights chatting up footballers whom they collected like trophies.

Paul had once described their methodology at a party and was for a while quite amusing as he shrieked in a falsetto voice, "Eeeeh Aaaa've had a wunnnnerful weekend. Aaaaa've shagged the whole of the City half back line."

The sight of Billy moving at a fast walk across the floor took Kel's attention. He couldn't analyse it but he knew there was trouble. The three men came to the same conclusion as they saw Billy advance on them but by then it was already too late. He didn't say a word nor did he stop walking as he threw a punch to the first man's ribs, and then jumped forward to catch the second man with a blow to the face. The third man launched himself in a head butt only to be halted by a forearm to his throat. Then Billy's own head jerked forward and the man fell.

Billy reached forward and picked the first man up and shook him gently against the wall watching him fight for breath and told him in a voice soft with menace. "My name's Billy Latimer and she's a friend of mine. Don't ever threaten her again."

The snooker had stopped and the players stood like tombstones behind their tables. Gerry's friend gave a nervous giggle.

Billy stared into the room. No one spoke. Then he turned and walked towards the door where Kel was standing. The whole incident had taken less than ten seconds. Three men lay on the floor and Kel knew that there could have been five or six of them for all the difference it would have made. He took stock of the broad figure. He was three or four inches shorter than Kel but much stronger, and the flat pale face had wide blue eyes that always glinted with wildness. His speech, his manner, and his movement all suggested a man, who, if he did indeed fear anything, saw it as a challenge. He was known and feared throughout the city. His reputation was such that even the hard men from the outlying areas no longer came in to challenge him. What Kel had just seen was brutal, bloody, primitive, and exciting. He was completely in awe as he watched Billy plant a soft kiss on the girl's cheek. She smiled and whispered something.

Then Billy turned to Kel. "I owe you a pint."

As their feet clattered down the stairs. Kel asked. "What was all that about?"

"The owner refuses to pay so they keep coming in and frightening the girls. The girls leave and if that doesn't work they start trouble and things get damaged."

"You mean protection money."

"Aye. Except they can't protect themselves."

The bright sunlight caught their eyes as they moved out on to the street. Shoppers passed unaware of the drama that had been played out only yards away.

Billy cut across the road between the slow-moving traffic and stood with his back to Fenwick's window. Kel joined him. Within a minute the three men came from the snooker rooms. One was clutching his ribs and another dabbed a handkerchief to his nose. They looked quickly around before they moved up the road towards the Haymarket.

Billy turned to Kel. "The Turks?"

They headed off towards Grey Street. "I like working the doors here. It's a grand street at night."

He saw the surprise in Kel's face at the remark. "I've got an O-level," he announced. They crossed the road from the theatre and walked through the swing doors of the hotel. Kel felt the posh carpet give beneath his feet.

Billy ordered two pints and they sat by a window. "What did you think of that then?"

"Every time I see you you seem to be bashing someone!"

Billy sipped on his drink. "It turns most people against me when they see me work. Relatives even. It frightens them. But not you. Not this time."

Kel deflected the observation. "Why your interest in me?"

"You were respectful to my mum." He smiled into Kel's blank face and eased his large body round so that he could face the door. "Elsie the cleaner at the Chronicle."

Kel's face lifted in memory. "Aah Elsie. We're pals."

"Also I'd like to say how much I appreciate your stuff on old Newcastle." Kel wondered briefly whether the big man was taking the mickey but Billy continued. . "Actually I got eight O-levels." He lifted his glass and drank deeply.

"You're interested in history?"

"Why shouldn't I be?"

"No, no reason at all." Kel was disarmed by his directness.

"I'm from Scotswood right. There's a little one-eyed geezer with a Box Brownie called Jimmy something going round taking pictures. I asked him why and he said one day the photos would be all that's left of the streets, and the pubs, and the people. He was right. They're knocking the place down now. My old house has gone, and Sandra's, and the school we walked to every day."

It was the longest speech he'd heard Billy make.

They finished their beer.

"Do you want another?"

Billy shook his head. "No I'm in training."

"A fight?"

"Against Casey. It's in a warehouse .In the West End."

"A prize fight?"

"Bare fists."

On the night of the fight Kel rode his motorbike to Westgate Road and chained it to railings in one of the side streets. As an extra precaution he stuck a label across the speedometer, which read. "Property of Billy Latimer."

It was a two-minute walk along a derelict Victorian terrace to the builder's yard that housed a large warehouse. The roof, he noticed, was patched with rusty corrugated iron.

The fighters did not in fact have bare knuckles. They each had a strapping of bandages to protect the fists. Billy explained that without them the impact of the punches spread the knuckles damaging the small bones in the hands.

The ring consisted of one rope strung loosely round four posts to form a square. There was a ten-yard space round the ring, crammed with people, and on one side a stack of boxes formed banking for a rough grandstand. Some temporary strip lights had been mounted in the warehouse and two additional spotlights pointed on the ring.

Billy's fight was the last of five and the stone floor was already spattered with blood as he jumped over the rope. His white, hard body gleamed with sweat from his warm-up. A roar rose into the dark, high roof as Casey followed him into the ring. He was six inches taller, had slits for eyes and a skin that looked as though it had been bathed every day in vinegar. His chest was matted with ginger hair.

"God made him ugly and then asked me to hit him" was Billy's description of his opponent.

As the two men squared up a woman squealed in excitement and near her two men began shouting encouragement to Casey, and then the rest of the crowd drowned their cries.

In their previous fight Casey had boxed behind a long left lead, occasionally slipping in a hook and varying that with an overhand right. They were his three punches. All the time he moved to his right away from Billy's own right hand. But that was in a boxing ring and in the warehouse such tactics counted for little.

His first left jab drew blood from the nose but as he fired his second punch Billy ducked slightly so Casey's fist landed on the top of his forehead. Casey winced and stuck out another jab but by then Billy was at him. He pushed the heel of his left hand under Casey's chin while his right struck just under the rib cage. A flurry of blows followed from a variety of angles with incredible speed and power culminating in a chopping right that snapped Casey's head back and sent him sagging over the single rope.

There was an astonished silence as the five hundred watched the rope sag beneath Casey's dead weight until it laid him gently on to the concrete floor. A roar as primeval as the fight itself burst to the walls and the roof of the warehouse. The long, loud sound rose, and rose again to meet the echo of the sound coming back. Kel became conscious that he himself had both arms in the air and was shouting, "Yes! Yes! Yes!" as he danced in triumph. Billy gave Kel a wink then climbed over the rope.

Two of Casey's men raised the fighter from the floor. Casey leaned against them, blood dripping from his nose unseeing and unseen. Kel stood his ground as the crowd dissolved around him. He watched three men with beer bellies slap Billy's back as he moved up the steps to the office that was acting as a dressing room.

An hour earlier he had sat in there on the long, tea-stained desk, his stomach tense with nerves watching Billy as he sat on a high-backed wooden chair reading the sports pages of the Chronicle.

He knew then that Billy was a very special man. It was one thing to fight in a rush of rage but to sit reading before a fight, or to have the confidence to walk across a room and fight three tough men... that was something else.

Paul called call him a thug. But Kel didn't see Billy like that at all. To Kel he was a warrior.

The dregs of the crowd had drifted out. The window of the office had steamed up as the warehouse cooled quickly now the body heat had gone. He walked up the steps and knocked gently on the door. There was no reply and he pushed it open and walked in.

A large, red-faced man, who looked about fifty, was standing behind the cheap desk. He had a ginger wig that curled ludicrously at the neck and he appeared to be brushing non-existent dandruff from the shoulders of his light brown overcoat. The man coughed sending ash from his large cigar mushrooming out in front of him.

"Who are you?" he asked. It wasn't a 'Who-are-you' question...the way the words came out it was more a 'Who-the-fuck-are-you' question.

"I'm a friend of Billy's"

"So's every fucker in Newcastle, or claims to be."

"I'm the fucker who's giving him a lift home."

The big man coughed again. "He's in the back cleaning up. I'll send him out."

Kel didn't move." I'll send him out, I said." The man's raised voice sent the last of his cigar ash spiraling down his coat. He slapped at it, his face reddening in anger.

Kel shouted: "Billy I'm waiting outside." He turned to leave and as he closed the door he heard the big man say "Cocky fucker."

Kel moved down the steps and zipped up his leather-riding jacket. Someone had dismantled the ring and the warehouse was stripped bare save for some bricks, slates, and bags of cement in a dark recess at the far end of the building.

He walked to the centre of the warehouse. One of the spotlights was still on and he stepped on to his toes, throwing out punches, spinning, and ducking.

"Not bad. Not bad." Billy's voice echoed through the warehouse as he came down the steps followed by the big man.

Ten minutes later Billy was on the back of Kel's motorbike, one arm round his waist and the other clasping five hundred pounds in his coat pocket.

"Who's the man with the Irish wig?" Kel shouted above the noise of the engine.

"Kenny Conway. You heard of him?"

"Naaah."

"He's the Al Capone of Newcastle, fruit machines and protection. He promotes my fights. And he owns the Coffin Box. The club I kicked you out of."

Kel couldn't see the big man's face but he knew he was grinning.

CHAPTER ELEVEN

Kel's flat at Tynemouth overlooked the North Sea, which rolled in on the east wind to hiss and spit up the yellow stretch of the Long Sands. Kel stood at the front window watching the lone figure sprint from the north end of the beach... sprint ...stop... shadow box. Sprint... stop... shadow box...a flurry of fists leaping out from the weaving body.

He turned from the window and put on the kettle. Ten minutes later Billy arrived, his wet clothes clinging to his strong body, seeking his bath. They'd come to an agreement. Billy could use his flat after training and Kel could use Billy's gym, which was housed in a large, lock-up garage three miles away in Wallsend.

Billy came out towelling his hair as though he was trying to wipe off his head.

Kel pointed to the mug on the table. "I'd better give you a key. I'm off to London for a couple of days to do an interview."

He'd got the call to meet Edwards the previous afternoon. The news editor was standing behind his desk. He stubbed out a cigarette as Kel knocked and entered. "By God you're a deep one." Edwards ground the cigarette until the flimsy paper burst and the smell of smoke was replaced by that of sweating tobacco. "Jean Smith. You never said you'd met her in France."

Surely Dave hadn't gossiped. Kel kept his voice flat and casual "Yeah at Pau."

"You didn't tell anyone?"

"She asked me not to so I didn't...well just Dave and he didn't believe it anyway."

Edwards lit another cigarette.

Kel shook his head. "You do know that there's some research suggesting that those things are dangerous."

Edwards shrugged his thin shoulders. "I've survived for twenty years with the buggers." He picked up an A4 size piece of paper. Kel tried to read the letterhead upside down but Edwards held it close to his face. He'd lost his glasses again.

"This is from her London agent. You certainly made an impression on her."

"I don't think so." Kel remembered the picture of Jean and the skier. Her arm, it seemed, had been tugging his body into hers.

Edwards pushed the letter across the desk. "I got this today. Her agent says she checked up on you. She says you're the first journalist to keep his word with her."

"I don't want her spreading that sort of thing about!"

Edwards waved away Kel's attempt at levity. "She's going to make a film up here ...he says if you go down to London she'll give us an exclusive interview. But only with you."

He searched Kel's face for signs of enthusiasm and found none.

"There's big money in it for you Kel. She never does exclusives."

"How much?"

He wrote a figure on the notepaper. "The editor will go this far if we can syndicate the story."

Kel looked at the piece of paper and made some quick calculations. It was a week's work and six month's pay.

Billy's eyes widened with almost childish wonder as Kel told him about his meeting with Jean Smith.

"She's the tops with me you know." He rattled off a list of her films, describing some of his favourite scenes, and then startled Kel by adding. "What I like about her is her ability to change her style of speech...she can talk quick and brash in some roles and then slow and hesitant in others. And then there's a scene in Love Tales where she's pleading with her lover to come back and the long shot shows her raising her right foot just slightly in anxiety."

Kel started to laugh.

"What's up?" Billy seemed strangely vulnerable.

"Nowt. It's just I can't get used to you being so intelligent."

"Kel, I'd be really grateful if you could get her to sign something?"

"Sure. I'll ask." Kel grinned. He was about to say that the Billy was a bit old for autographs but held his tongue because he sensed the hard man was soft on such things.

Three weeks previously at the flat Kel had screwed shelves right across the far wall from the window and had filled them with his books. Billy was fascinated when he arrived from his training.

"Have you read all of these?" He walked right along inspecting the books.

Kel smiled. "No not all. I just like them. I like the feel of them...the atmosphere they create."

Billy continued to stare at the books. "I think they're for reading," he said. Then he turned to face Kel. "I think the best you can do is make your life a good read."

"Would you like to borrow a couple?"

Billy said he would. That afternoon he took Kel to his gym. Through the grimy windows in the door he could see the shadowy shapes of the cranes along the river.

The roof leaked leaving a dark puddle in one of the corners and the whitewashed walls were stained. Some pieces of felt were strewn about the stone floor at strategic points near the weights and benches, which were expensive and new.

Billy started his tortuous routine. He had no technique as a lifter, just awesome strength. After doing a series of sit-ups and one-arm press-ups he settled himself on a thick wooden bench under a massive bar bell that stood on a steel rest in the centre of the room.

"Stand by me head kidda. I need you to guide the bar back on to the struts."

Kel took his position and looked down at Billy whose hands were wrapped round the bar. His eyes closed as he took huge, whooshing breaths. Beneath him sweat dripped over the sides of the bench staining the floor. Then suddenly his eyes opened, his face hardened and then reddened, his arms shuddered, the muscles swelled with the effort, and the bar bent as the huge weights moved up from their supports. Higher and higher it went until Billy's arms were fully extended. Kel stared in astonishment as he watched the strain leave Billy's face to be replaced by a smile of pleasure. Kel reached out and gently guided Billy's arms until the bar stood over the supports. Billy lowered the weight, slid under the bar, and began towelling his hair and neck.

Kel sensed that he had just witnessed a great event. "How much?" he asked.

"Six hundred pounds. I nearly did it last week but today I felt good so I thought... just do it."

"Has anyone else ever done that?" he asked.

"Dunno. "

Kel was given a key and started to train, often alone, in the afternoons. He asked Billy to teach him the rudiments of fighting, how to punch, how to move, but Billy shook his head. "You'd only end up being daft in a club and trying to fight someone like me."

"No I wouldn't."

Billy punched one of the heavy bags sending it rearing on its chain. "You've got attitude. That time at the club, you weren't alarmed."

"No. I could see you were reasonable and there was nothing to fight about."

Billy gripped Kel's arm and pushed. When Kel instinctively pushed back

Billy pulled with him. Before Kel could regain his balance he jumped forward his head stopping an inch from Kel's face.

"That's what half the bouncers in town would have done, only they would have nutted you. It's called kicking off. You're a big lad see and they wouldn't be taking chances."

Kel was stung by the ease with which Billy had manipulated him. "What are you saying?"

"You're not a street fighter. You'd be thinking of starting it when I'd be finishing it."

They put him on an afternoon train and into a small hotel near Kings Cross.

He caught a taxi to the Savoy in the morning and a smooth-mannered, middle-aged man ushered him into a third-floor suite that was filled with flowers. Jean turned smiling from the window. She was wearing a loose sweater and jeans and in an instant he felt overdressed in his dark suit and tie. She raised her eyes in appreciation at his appearance. "Hmmm nice." Behind him the door clicked as the smooth man left the room. He could feel the thick softness of the carpet. He noted the cascade of bluebells from the Louis something mantelpiece. Suddenly he felt out of place, a little provincial trying to show a brave face in a sophisticated world that took class and style for granted, but was quick to disapprove of its absence.

She smiled and he noted her eyes stayed large... large and bright blue.

"You never rang."

"Is that an accusation or an observation?"

"Hmm neat. Neat phrasing." She considered the words further. "An accusation I think. Yes definitely an accusation."

This was different from their meeting in France. There she had been lost and he had known the way. She had been cool and comfortable with the situation but he had been in charge. Here she was on her home ground amid the pamper and padding that she took for granted.

"I was going to ring. Then I saw you in the paper with the downhill skier and I couldn't get my mind past the icons...world-famous film star, world-famous skier, and daft lad from a small provincial city."

Jean was staring at him with a fixed smile on her face. He had forgotten her habit of pausing before she spoke. "The skier. The picture. It was publicity stuff."

"Of course."

"He smelled of garlic."

He had no idea where the conversation was leading. He wondered whether she was playing with him.

"He was also very arrogant." Her voice, though calm, rose a little in indignation at the memory. "I'm going to win the gold, you can have me."

"I get the same sort of approaches myself." He kept his face straight as her eyes caught his. She had a large, warm mouth. A slow smile lit her face.

Jean retreated to one of the long, leather sofas and gestured that he should sit opposite her. "I thought about you a lot ...about our meeting. It was...different." She was staring at him so composed. "Probably best that we just remain friends,"

He thought of her last four reported lovers...a prince, two film stars, and a racing driver.

"Yes," he said.

The door opened and the small neat, smooth- mannered man approached from the shallow end of the posh carpet. "Just thought I'd better remind you, Miss

Smith. You have another meeting in half an hour."

Jean smiled. "Thank you," and the man hovered before leaving as quietly as he had entered.

Kel reached in his jacket for his pen and found he didn't have one. Jean saw his discomfort and laughed. She pulled a folder from an elegant drawer in an elegant desk. "It's done. It's in here. I'm coming to make a film. There's a bit about the movie and some nice things I say about Newcastle."

"Have you been to Newcastle?"

"Of course not." She read his thoughts. "Look I had the say in where it was filmed...it was Manchester, Newcastle or Sheffield. I liked the things you told me about your Newcastle... so I said that's the place."

She pressed a buzzer. The smooth, middle-aged man glided in.

"Nigel. Mr Adams needs a picture of us."

"Of course," he left the room to return with a camera.

Jean stood in the centre of the room and gestured for Kel to join her. They faced the camera and he felt her arm go round him. There was a flash, and then a second flash, and Nigel left once more. It was only after they regained their seats that Kel realised she had replicated her pose with the downhill skier.

He found his pen and notepad in his small case. She told him of her childhood in Jasper, a small tourist town in the Rockies and how for one summer week she had sat on the small green at the edge resort watching the long freight trains wind their way out to the surrounding mountains.

Jean paused, and for a moment the formalities of the interview were forgotten, as she delved into a personal moment. She smiled. "I've just realised that to me the trains were always leaving...never arriving."

She told him that at the age of ten she had visited Banff, walked up Sulphur mountain, and looked down on the valley to watch the bald eagles on their flight to Alaska... great birds sweeping their wings and gliding on the currents of air ...she had stood above them entranced by their flight, determined to make journeys of her own. She said that for much of her childhood she had felt trapped by the massive mountains. She'd also feared boredom but had always believed she could escape it through hard work.

"It would give you opportunities?"

She thought for a second staring into the room. "It would give me control...to make choices."

She watched him make notes. "Your shorthand's not very quick is it."

"Not as quick as your tongue," he said evenly.

"Neat. Neat phrasing," she smiled.

"I find it difficult to do interviews with stars." he said. "It's not as though we meet as people." He was about to add: "In the way we met in France." But she cut in.

"I hate them," her voice rose with feeling. "In the past year there's not a question I have been asked about myself that I haven't been asked fifty times before."

He looked up from his note taking and saw her face was strained.

"I know that. It was kind of you to offer me this interview."

"No it wasn't. It's just I was a little intrigued by you." She gave a harsh coughing laugh. "Don't worry I'll figure it out and then you'll find doors closed to you." She smiled to make a joke of it, to disguise some strange inner struggle, but he knew there was a truth in what she said.

He stood up. "I prefer to close them myself I think." He had asked too much of the situation. The beautiful dream of their meeting in France had gone. It was time to wake up. He knew he had a good interview but the meeting had been a disaster. He'd wanted to make her laugh, to impress her, but had been suffocated by her fame. Now he wanted to escape from her world where he didn't belong.

He forced a smile and looked at his watch. "Well it's about time for your meeting." As he spoke he knew there was no meeting. "I'd rather go before you want rid of me."

He heard her say "But wait..." Her toes were pointing inwards and her hands were clasped in front of her hips. Her mouth was slightly ajar and her eyes were suddenly filled with a little girl's fright.

But it was too late. He hated her poise, her wealth, her power and, above all, her ability to make him feel like a provincial nobody.

He forced another smile "Have a good life Jean." And then he was in a passage leading to the door of her suite. Nigel rose from behind a mahogany desk. He was about to speak but saw the anger in Kel's face and went scurrying into her room.

Kel pressed for the lift. It was floors away and going in the wrong direction. He escaped along the hallway to the stairwell.

The cold air outside burst about him as he walked towards the Strand. He decided he'd walk a mile or so to collect his thoughts and then take a taxi to his hotel.

"Mr Adams...Mr Adams." The worthy Nigel approached him at pace, slightly flushed, but still retaining his ambience of detached dignity. He slowed down for the last pace or two. A red double deck bus drowned his first words. He paused and started again. "Miss Smith says she is terribly sorry if she has upset you."

"It's only words, Nigel mate. I expect I'll recover after a warm bath and a good cry."

Nigel blinked, unused to this sort of humour.

"The fact is Miss Smith has asked me to ask you to return to the hotel to continue the interview."

He laughed. "According to your schedule she's ten minutes into an urgent meeting." He saw the transparent discomfort in Nigel's face." I worked it out."

Nigel stayed silent with stoic loyalty.

"Tell her I prefer to remember her when she was lost." He looked at his watch. "I've got to grab my stuff from the hotel. There's an early train."

"But wait...where do I send the picture?" Nigel was a man who worried about practicalities.

Kel handed him a card and thanked him for the press kit. "It's very well written," he said.

Nigel showed confusion. "But you haven't read it, surely."

"That's right but I'm learning how this place works."

Nigel had the grace to smile.

They had continued walking slowly as they talked until they reached the Strand.

Kel was suddenly aware of the theatres, the cabs, the width of the streets, and the height of the buildings...all of it was bigger, and above all else there was the bustle of the place. "I never feel comfortable here."

"I'm from Walsall myself," said Nigel.

"No," said Kel. "You're from here really. You just grew up in Walsall."

They shook hands, a brief act of mutual respect and then Nigel said. "For what it's worth her heart is in the right place." He watched as Kel made his way towards Tottenham Court Road.

He always travelled light and was packed in five minutes. He sat on the bed and started to read Nigel's press pack. He had to admit it was well written. It covered the whole range of her life and career but not in too much detail...directing questions rather than answering them. There was of course no mention of the actors, of the prince she had left, of the eagles in the valley, of the way she frowned when talking, of the cautious phrasing, or of the sudden swing of mood. However there was vivid detail of just how frighteningly famous she was ...a long list of her films. He had seen half of them, queued with girls to see them. The memories of the night in Pau drifted into his mind seemingly with a will of their own...her long, beautiful silhouette as she stood in front of the street lights, the shimmering wet road as she came towards him like something in a dream, the stab of disappointment when she'd said at the Savoy "Best we be friends,"...then his rising irritation at his own inept performance to the point that it was a relief when he walked out. Walked out from what? From whom? The cool girl lost in France or the snapping star who so obviously had a near phobia about interviews. He made himself shrug his shoulders... at least this time he was out of love before he was in it.

There was a knock at the door. "Room service." He opened the door and she was there standing like a little girl, just as Billy had described, with one foot slightly raised. She removed her sunglasses. Her eyes were full of tears. "Can I come in please?"

He stepped back into the room and she followed him, closing quickly to him, pressing her mouth on his. He felt her hips lunge into his as she kicked back to close the door. She pushed forward until he fell back on to the bed and her honey-blonde hair covered them both. "I'm sorry, I'm sorry, I'm sorry." He felt the warmth of her tears dripping on to his face, her hands tugging his shirt, her fingers trying to push through the slack of his trousers to his groin.

He grabbed her arm. "Jean the maid will be coming."

She clung to him. "I've booked for the night." She saw his face soften into a smile and kissed him again. She had sought him and he was happy.

"I've booked a room either side as well. Just in case you're an expert." She laughed deeply into his ear tickling and teasing him with her tongue. He began to stroke her neck gently allowing his nails to trail across her skin. His other hand found the line above her stocking tops and again he gently scratched her skin on her inner thigh until she shivered with sudden pleasure. He began to work his hands around her body edging to her erogenous zones, but always skirting away until she lay still shivering slightly and whispered, "Please...please."

He heard her wild calls as her body writhed out of control so that he had to use all his strength to hold her. Eventually she gave one last shudder and lay completely still. Their bodies had a sheen of sweat, the muscles ached in his arm, and outside it was dusk. His train had been and gone.

He kissed her ear until she wriggled. "Did you really book the rooms on either side?"

In the gloom he saw her mouth spreading wide into her grin. "Have you heard any knocking?"

She asked him to order a cab while she dressed, the final act of which was to tie on her headscarf and replace the barrier of the large sunglasses.

They had agreed that he was going to stay at her house and, once in the seclusion of the taxi she clung to his arm.

She whispered, "Do you remember the first few minutes that we met...before I was famous."

"Of course I do."

Her body was slightly angled towards him and he felt her stare.

"What did you feel? Tell me."

He laughed. "No."

"Tell me, tell me, tell me." Her hand round his arm was jerking into his ribs.

"OK," he pushed her hand away. "I really fancied you. And then when I saw who you were I thought it was just God having a little joke."

She listened solemnly to him and when he had finished she stayed silent for a while, and then said in an even tone. "I was never lost." She watched his face as she spoke and was gratified to see his eyes open in surprise.

In the morning he caught her ruffling the sheets in one of the spare bedrooms.

He started to laugh. "That won't fool your maid. They're trained observers." He let fly a whoosh of body spray, tossed a pair of used socks into the corner and squirted some toothpaste into the washbasin.

"There you are. No one could go to those lengths."

Jean didn't join in the humour. "It's not funny. You've no idea how many of them sell gossip. In Hollywood, newspaper people go through your trash. It's disgusting."

The maid turned out to be a young Spanish girl who gave Kel a pretty smile and followed basic instructions from Jean who shouted slowly at her with the help of a phrase book.

Jean took him for a walk on Hampstead Heath, but not before she donned her sunglasses and her scarf. They walked side by side but she did not link arms. He began to feel irritated.

"Does there not come a point when you are recognised by the sunglasses rather than hidden by them.

The effect on her was astonishing. She raised both arms as through beseeching the heavens. "My God you don't know what is involved here...what will happen to me and to you...how we will be pursued. Believe me I've had six years of this shit. They're devils."

They walked through a wide and gentle avenue of beech trees. The grass swept down in a mild curve to a lake on their left. They could hear the scattered cries of children at play. A man trotted by on a piebald mare and raised his hat.

They sat on the warm slope and he held her arm gently. Jean was shaking.

The irony that he was a journalist of sorts and her lover was not lost on him, though she did not seem to associate him with her phobia.

The warm air, the heavy scent of the grass and his late nights were too much for him and he drifted into a calm, dreamless sleep.

When he awoke she was looking at him through her sunglasses.

"Why do you stare at me?" he said.

"It's a trick I've got...a gift... I can feel people by staring at them."

"Feel what?"

"Feel their spirits, feel their hopes and fears, feel their futures sometimes."

"Really?"

"Don't mock, it's true. I knew we would meet again when we met in France."

He pretended to whip her head with a blade of grass. "Jean we met again because you contacted me."

"Don't laugh." She was distressed in an instant. "When I watched the eagles I knew I would leave Jasper. A year later my family went to Calgary for the stampede and there was a queue of us having our palms read and when she got to me she dropped my hand. She told me I had gifts and that I should always follow my instincts."

"So?"

"She also told me I would become famous." She was watching his face again. "And that I would marry an Englishman," she smiled as she saw his attention growing. "And that I would meet him in France."

"You're kidding!"

She smiled in triumph. "Yes I am actually...well some of it's true but I'm not telling you which."

He rolled over on to her and tried to kiss her but she was wriggling and giggling. Her glasses fell away and she grabbed them as though her underwear elastic had snapped.

They slapped the loose grass from their clothes and walked slowly back to her house. The large wooden gate closed on a spring behind them. The long gravel path was lined with young ash trees and at the edge of the lawn some white foxgloves were dying under a large weeping willow. A little coppice of hawthorn bushes stood like stubble before the huge facade of the house. He saw rural peace in a metropolis but Jean tutted. "He should have cleared the dead flowers away."

Kel presumed "He" meant the absent gardener.

Maria had gone and the house stood large, warm and empty with the sunlight beaming in through the high, Edwardian windows. There was a ham salad and freshly cooked bread covered with transparent paper on the long pine table in the kitchen.

She kissed him on the ear and sat beside him smiling. "We're going to a party tonight," she announced. "It's Zimani's. He's going to be directing the film in Newcastle. You've heard of Zimani?"

"Have you heard of Billy Latimer?"

She shook her head.

"Well I've heard of Billy Latimer and Zimani."

"Who is Billy Latimer?"

"Billy Latimer is the toughest street fighter in Newcastle. He is also a film fan and he told me that Zimani was an example of the efficacy of cross breeding among the refugee nations of Europe...Polish father, Hungarian mother, one set of grandparents from Estonia and another from France. Apparently he screws like a rabbit though in more imaginative positions and Billy told me that he's regarded as a genius by the critics, seemingly because of his preference for hand-held cameras to affect reality of movement."

Jean retreated from this avalanche of words. "I've upset you," she said.

"I don't like London," he said. "And I haven't got any clean shirts."

She escaped into practicalities. "Nigel," she said into the phone. "I need three shirts...No men's shirts. Neck size..." She looked across to Kel.

"Eighteen," he said.

She passed on the information to Nigel and then sat next to Kel.

"You trust Nigel."

"I do indeed."

"And you trust me?"

"Yes I do."

"Why?"

She looked at him. "Instinct." She began to pick at her salad.

He stared at her.

She had, he decided, the most beautiful face he had ever seen...large blue eyes and a straight nose, but the secret lay in the high cheek bones and strong jaw that gave her the ultimate classic look that no angle of light could distort. Indeed it was ironic that her face was best seen in strong sunlight, ironic because the sunlight could make shadows of her beautiful eyes.

CHAPTER TWELVE

Zimani's large, Victorian house stood imposingly just back from the top of Hampstead Hill behind a blockade of thick, ash hedges.

Kel was introduced to him as the man who had helped Jean when she was lost in France.

"He's a journalist so I gave him an interview. It seemed the least I could do." She was a bad liar and as Kel watched the director's large, dark eyes drift over her he knew that Zimani knew she had given him more than an interview.

Half the nations in Europe had been involved in the family history of the great man, though from his face and his gestures one would have given ultimate victory to the Italians. He looked like a cartoon version of an ice cream salesman with a few tantalising defects. His hair was blonde, an expensive dye Kel suspected, and his hands were long and sensitive. His shirt was open neck and the V of flesh under his throat hinted at a mass of black, body hair. His silk shirt gleamed darkly and the neat cream flannels, which imposed on his slight paunch, flowed down to sweep the tops of his black leather shoes. He gave the impression of a man who dressed to impress.

The hand that shook Kel's was firm. Their eyes met briefly and then he waved over to a new arrival. His eyes came back to Kel. "A writer eh...you look like an actor."

Kel told him he couldn't act and Zimani snorted in amusement. "You'll be lost in here then, the whole fucking place is one big act. Tell me about your meeting in France."

Kel briefly outlined his little adventure in Pau.

Zimani grinned and said "Neat. Neat," which seemed to be the in- phrase. On his last visit to London everyone had insisted on saying, "Yes indeed." God he hated the place.

"Enjoy!" Zimani's short arm swept out in invitation to his huge house in which the dark architecture of the mid Victorians had finally been defeated by a number of multi-windowed extensions, and even more crucially by the advent of electricity. Chandeliers hung everywhere in Damoclean triumph over Victorian gloom.

Across the room the famous mingled with the half-remembered and half-forgotten. A cameraman flashed at a couple of hopefuls who were wearing see-through tops. Their smiles went on and off like electric lights. Jean had left Kel's side at the first sight of a camera. "People to meet," she told him but they both knew the truth. He sensed her irritation at Zimani for allowing the Press to attend, but the party was a celebration of his latest film, Apache, the story of a beautiful, innocent dancer in the demi monde of Paris in the twenties. By chance he had seen the film at the Essoldo before his trip to London and had been moved by the girl's predictable decline.

Large chunks of the film had been shot in black and white, a technique which Kel had not understood.

The anthology of critiques, which were stuck among stills from the film on a large board in the hall, showed no such uncertainty, but they failed to convince him.

"You've seen it?" Zimani appeared at his side."

Kel nodded.

"What did you think?"

"Really?"

"Really...you're the public not like these ships in bottles," he gestured towards a group of animated men whom Kel assumed were the critics.

"I'm a sucker for innocence.... she was great," Kel inclined his head towards the stunning lady who was holding court across the room. "The script was succinct and well-constructed, the pictures were sympathetic but I didn't understand why parts of it were in black and white and I'm sure you're going to tell me I'm a fool."

Zimani's dark eyes had stared at him as he spoke and as Kel finished his little critique he burst into wild savage laughter that turned heads to him.

Kel looked on in astonishment. At last the director motioned to him to come closer with an exaggerated conspiratorial gesture.

"Can you keep a secret?"

"No."

"Fuck it I'll tell you anyway." He gestured to the critics again. "You know the ultimate sin of that lot...to admit they don't know."

He waved towards the board. "Have you read all that stuff about the sensitive confluence of colour and monochrome that hints at fact and fantasy...the truth is I ran out of money." He waited for Kel to laugh. "That's the truth. I ran out of dough so we had to finish it off in monochrome because I could get it cheaper." He started to giggle and Kel joined him until they encouraged each other into a state of helpless laughter. More than one young actress noted the handsome young man, who appeared to have found favour with the great man, and made plans to ambush him if possible.

As the two men recovered Kel said. "Don't tell anyone. It's funnier as a secret"

"It is, isn't it." This sent Zimani off into new spirals of laughter. When he'd recovered he tugged Kel's arm with a small man's aggression. "All that shit about lost in France...I presume...you and she..."he gave a conspiratorial wink.

"Do I look that lucky?"

Zimani studied the chiselled features and didn't answer.

He held out his hand and as Kel grasped it he noticed the wrist was covered in dark hair. "I've got to mix...but I'd like to speak later...about Newcastle. Jean wants to film there." He raised his right eyebrow to suggest to Kel that he knew the real reason why.

Kel saw Jean being talked at by a man with a Beethoven haircut and jam jar glasses who appeared to be giving her the benefit of his opinion about her career.

Kel strolled through the long, elegant lounge, which was lined, on both sides with black leather sofas and armchairs. He walked through an alcove past the indoor pool where a couple of girls giggled and attempted to splash him. Two bikini tops floated at the far end of the pool. A long bar had been erected in a smaller lounge beyond the pool. Half a dozen young girls in black skirts and white blouses were serving drinks while staring at famous faces.

Kel waited until there was a lull before ordering an orange from a bright-faced girl with smiling eyes.

She stared at him as she handed him his drink. "Excuse me," she said. "Are you an actor?"

Kel smiled. "No, just an ordinary guy."

The girl blushed slightly as her colleagues giggled.

Kel approached Jean side-on through the crowded room so she didn't see him until he was standing next to her.

"How you doing pet, flower, love, and hinny?"

"Hinny? What's a hinny?"

"Dunno beyond a Geordie term of endearment."

"Wasn't it used in factories?"

"No that was a spinning Jenny."

She was coolly appraising him again. "I'm going to have to leave you again," she said gravely. "Otherwise I'm going to grab you."

"Right well I'll see you in ten minutes in the small lounge in just your vest."

"I don't have a vest."

"Then make it five minutes."

She left him and he stood sipping his orange in the centre of the large room. Critics and writers swirled about and he found himself being confronted by Beethoven who was telling him in an accusatory tone. "I don't appear to know you."

Kel introduced himself and told Beethoven that he had come to London to interview Jean.

Beethoven allowed himself a weak smile. "Aaaah a provincial."

"Yes, but I've got an O-level." He turned his back on the critic and walked through to the big lounge to be confronted by Monica Southern who was leaning against the large Adams fireplace. Jean had told him she was famous for being famous. No one could remember how it happened but she had now become a permanent fixture in the gossip columns, yet she had never made a film, appeared in a TV series, or acted in a play. She was said to enjoy a colourful love life, in addition she was adept at one-line witticisms and on the strength of that had become a sought-after guest at celebrity parties. It was estimated that more column inches had been written about her than many of the major stars. Such was her status that she had only to stand in a room and people would come to her. She watched casual and confident as Kel approached. "I say," she caught his arm as he moved past. "I say. Weren't you one of my lovers?"

"I don't remember." Kel smiled and moved on towards one of the hard- backed leather couches.

"Weren't you one of my lovers?" A pretty, dark-haired girl flopped down next to him.

"Ah you heard."

"Yes I've been following you."

"Why?"

"Outsiders are interesting."

"Is it that obvious?" He looked at her with interest. Her face had a puppy-like quality, her eyes were round, her nose small and snub, her lips had an exaggerated bow that one minute seemed voluptuous but the at next gave her a huffy or sullen air. It was as though two sculptors had had a hell of an argument on whether to make her pretty or plain.

"Well," she said. "You're not performing and Jean keeps glancing at you so I expect you're her latest lover."

He laughed: "Daft Geordie on weekend trip would be more accurate. And you? Are you a star or a starlet?"

She shook her head so violently that her long hair hid her face. She emerged to say. "No thank you. I'm Little Zimm...daughter of the great man." She gestured to Zimani who was talking to two women in mini skirts who seemed to find his words very amusing.

"Little Zimm...is that really your name?"

"No it's what I'm called."

"You live here in this splendid house."

"God no! I only come into London for a fuck." Her eyes challenged him.

"Ah," he said keeping his voice calm with some difficulty. "I suppose there's more choice here...three million male adults ...there must be a couple worth the bother."

But she wasn't going to let him off the hook that easily. "What about you?"

"I came to London to do an interview with Jean."

Little Zimm laughed. "You might have thought that but you came to London to be shagged by Jean. She always plays her cards close to her considerable chest."

"Well she hasn't played with me close to her considerable chest."

Little Zimm began to giggle. "You really are a dreadful liar. People who look like you are never just friends."

"I'm just friends with you aren't I?"

Zimani approached them through the crowded floor dabbing his neck with his handkerchief. His dark shirt was stained with perspiration.

Before he could speak Little Zimm opened fire. "Daddy this man won't let me screw him."

Zimani grinned. "He probably knows where you've been." He turned to Kel. "Her favourite game is to try to shock me."

"It's my favourite way of getting attention." She took hold of Kel's hand and pressed it to her bosom staring at her father. Kel withdrew his hand.

Zimani appeared not to notice. "You know you're my favourite daughter."

"Only because you don't know who the others are."

They were shooting words at each other. Kel got the impression that this was not an uncommon scene and that they both took perverse pleasure in it.

Zimani brought the exchange to an end by leaning aggressively over Kel. "In half an hour we're off gambling."

"He's inviting you." Little Zimm locked arms with him staring at her father. "You must have done something to impress him. There's no charity here." She reached out a hand to press her father's breastbone.

"Right," said Kel. "I must go to the bathroom."

"You play roulette?" Zimani pushed his face forward like a deaf man seeking an answer.

"It's just simple sums really."

"You good at sums Kel?" Again the head was pushed towards him.

"Naaah. I never earn enough to have to be."

"Use my toilet upstairs," said Little Zimm. "It's the third bedroom on the right."

Zimani grinned. "It's OK. I'll stop her following you."

Kel told himself later that Little Zimm had known a copulating threesome occupied her bedroom but by the time he caught up with the plot he was past the bed and in the washroom. He locked the door behind him and looked through the latticed window down the long lawn as he relieved himself. The two girls from the swimming pool were embracing on a garden swing.

When he returned to the bedroom one of the blondes was waiting for him leaning against the bedroom door. She was naked and he noticed her pubic hair had been shaved. He assumed she modelled swimsuits.

She smiled "Hi Big Boy. How are you?"

"I've got syphilis how about you?" Then he was on the landing and heading for the stairs. Zimani was shouting, "The fucking taxis have arrived."

"There is in fact a fleet of fucking taxis." Jean was at his side as he stepped into the hall. "Enough to take fifty fucking guests off to the fucking casino."

"Exfuckingtrordinary." Kel pulled a face and she laughed.

They clambered into one of the taxis. "I've got no money," Kel whispered to Jean. Her hand, which had been resting lightly and out of sight on his thigh, disappeared into a handbag to emerge with a huge wad of notes. "I've got some," she said and peeled off a month's salary. "Here," she said carelessly. The whole thing was so casual he felt he would be shown up if he argued. He took the bundle reluctantly.

The taxis pulled up in a convoy.

"Oh Christ," Jean scrambled out of the taxi, briefly mooning the other occupants as she bent low for a racing start past the flashing cameras of three pressmen. Then she was in the club.

Kel walked in with Little Zimm and the cameras flashed again.

"You didn't tell me you were in the news," he said.

"I'm the daughter of 'the legendary film director Zimani,'" she said putting the words in to quotation marks. "That's the way they always describe me," she said cheerfully. "Only the adjectives change." She reeled off a list. "Wayward, wanton, wild child, high-spirited, even vivacious by one particularly kind writer."

Jean was waiting under a massive chandelier in the main hall.

Little Zimm pressed Kel's arm to her breasts. "Where did you find this one then?"

Jean smiled but didn't answer. Her story was being received with transparent disbelief and so her new tactic was to let the facts filter through like a process of osmosis to her select friends. But Little Zim was ahead of the game. "He doesn't sing, he doesn't act and he's got no royal blood, so what's he good at eh? You looked shagged out by the way..." Jean shook her head at this outrageous torrent. Kel pretended to survey the huge room.

Seven roulette tables formed the main column down the centre of the long room. Smaller blackjack tables backed on to both the main walls and a large bar served customers at the far end of the room.

Pretty girls in skimpy costumes offered free glasses of champagne from silver trays.

Little Zimm looked across to her father who was already at one of the tables and said cheerfully: "Dad usually loses a fortune. He can't add up."

On cue Zimani proceeded to spray counters all over the table. In half an hour he'd lost nearly three hundred pounds. Ten minutes later he won it back and then hit a losing streak again. Win or lose he had the same intense look.

"He's mad," Kel whispered to Little Zimm.

"It's a drug."

His eyes took in the draped curtains, the chandeliers, the ornate furniture, all imitations of an eighteenth century drawing room.

"Drugs are cheaper than this," he said.

"That depends," said Little Zimm. "Are you going to play?"

He shrugged. "Sure. Jean gave me a wad of cash." He took out the notes and bought some chips.

Little Zimm and Jean followed him to the nearest table. The players made room in deference to the star. Kel watched for three or four minutes before placing a five-pound chip on black. The wheel span and the little ball danced until it rested in a red socket. Jean nipped his bottom gently. "I could have told you red," she whispered. "It'll be red again. I feel it."

"Faites vos jeux." Kel leaned forward and put two five-pound chips on the black." Again the ball came up red.

"I told you I told you," said Jean. She sounded irritated. He grinned and placed fifteen pounds on the black and won.

"What are you doing?" whispered Little Zimm.

"It's a betting system," he said. "I wait for two consecutive colours then bet against them. If one of the next four of my colour comes up I win five pounds. Then the staking plan gets tough. The next bet I lose ten pounds if I win and the next bet I lose twenty pounds if I win. It works on odd and even numbers too."

"It sounds dangerous if you get a losing streak."

"Yeah. You have to tailor your winning ambitions to your stake." He flicked at his chips. I have enough here to cover eight consecutive losing bets. If that happens I lose the lot."

Little Zimm put her hand on his chips. "Do you think you could teach dad how to play?"

Kel shook his head.

"Why not?"

"I want to win. He wants to gamble."

Kel turned back to the tables and started to play again. Jean came back with some more chips. "Here stake me in." Within minutes a crowd had gathered to watch the man who was playing for the great star. At the end of an hour he had won £50 for each of them. He pulled in his chips. As Jean went off to collect her coat one of the men in evening dress approached him. He smiled and held out his hand. "Justin Jacobs, I'm the manager here. I was impressed by your methodology."

He waved his hand and a blonde waitress approached with champagne. Justin took two glasses and offered one to Kel.

"Do you play much?"

Kel wondered where the conversation was heading. The clink, clink of the little balls the slap of the cards, the pretty women, and the sharp edge of winning and losing... sometimes he found it alluring, exciting, and at other times superficial.

"Not much," he said. "It's easier here. In Newcastle some of the clubs have two zeros."

"They could get done for that. There again they might not." Justin said. "We can't afford the scandal of being prosecuted so we play safe... without noughts."

"I've never played before on a table without a zero."

"We still have the advantage. We never run out of money and we don't chase bad odds."

Kel had assumed that the manager was chatting away in the hope of meeting Jean when she returned. But he looked at his watch. "Nice meeting you."

Likewise," said Kel. "I'll come for advice if ever I open a club." They both laughed and then Justin reached into his pocket for a business card, "You could do worse. There's big money to be made. Especially in the provinces."

Jean appeared at the far end of the room with her coat. "Must go," said Kel and the two shook hands.

"Who was that smart looking chap?" she touched his arm lightly as they crossed the reception area.

"The manager. He wanted to know how a girl like you got off with a guy like me. I said you were just born lucky."

He gave her all the chips. "We won fifty quid each," he smiled.

"Great," she clapped her hands like a little girl. But he sensed she was acting.

In the cab on the way back to Hampstead he glanced at her shyly. "That's more than a week's wages to me."

Her eyes softened and she reached for his hand. "Did you think I was after your money?"

The cab dropped them two hundred yards from her home. She tipped the driver and thanked him by name. They took a route along a bridle path to the back of her house. Without warning she pushed him roughly into the tall hedge that marked the end of her garden.

He twisted her round as she came at him, scooped up her mini skirt and pushed her into the hedge. The moon caught the whiteness of her legs; she'd removed her tights and knickers in the cloakroom. Her eyes and her lips glistened with desire and she was moaning, "Come on be a bastard. He pulled her dress right up at the back, pushed her roughly into the hedge, and thrust at her. Twigs snapped under the weight of their bodies. They scratched his hands which held her naked back and hips and he heard her gasp in pain as the hedge scraped into her. They rocked in and out of the hedge in waves of pleasure. He became aware that both of them were moaning and then she shuddered, her legs gave in, and her arms clung to his neck seeking support.

Two dogs began to bark in the neighbouring garden. They scurried up the path giggling and reached the sanctuary of the house before they could be discovered. Later she laid face down and naked on the bed and he rubbed a lotion into the scratches on her buttocks and thighs. She lay face down and silent as he tended to her and then, without warning, her left hand reached out and felt the hardness in his groin. "Dirty bastard," she laughed. "I'll never trust a doctor again." Later they drifted in and out of sleep. It was warm and the curtain billowed in the breeze through the open window, as though a matador was playing with the moon.

In the morning she made him scrambled eggs to the music of Puccini but told him he must help with the washing up. She was wearing a kaftan of such flimsy material that it seemed to drift around her when she made a sudden movement.

She sat on a high chair and the kaftan billowed away from her lower body. She was naked underneath.

"Tell me about Kenya," he said.

"The country?"

"No. You said you were doing some work there next week."

"Ah. I'm doing a short for Zimani."

"A short?"

"It's what I call them. They ask a star to play a cameo role in the film...you know a one-scene part...I get paid a lot for a week's work...they get my name and everyone's happy providing the film's OK. Zimani you can trust but some have found themselves in the middle of really bad films and that's dangerous."

"Dangerous?"

"It's dangerous to be associated with failures." She was becoming agitated again as though the conversation was raising hidden fears. "It's a business and I'm a product with a brand name. To the companies films are not art they are the business of art. It's only to people like Zimani that films are art and they only listen to him while he makes them money." She drank the last of her coffee. "They're like all big businesses. To protect their product they'll lie, and lie, and lie." In a couple of sentences she had lost her serenity and was stiff with outrage.

Kel made an attempt to change the subject but his words were lost on her.

"I can name you half a dozen top stars who've been persuaded to marry to contain rumours about their homosexuality."

"Why?" he asked. "Why do they allow it to happen?"

"Why?" She was astonished that he could ask such a question. "Why? Because they can crush you."

As she spoke he watched the sudden passion light her face, her beautiful body become urgent and animated under the drifting kaftan.

"You're mesmeric," he said.

The tension and the energy fell from her in a second as she returned his smile.

"Tell me something about yourself," she said.

"There's not a lot to tell," he said.

"There's always a lot to tell."

He told her about the death of his parents, about his mother's sister who had brought him up out of a sense of duty. She hadn't liked children, hadn't liked men, and had sent him off to a minor public school where he'd survived bullying, beatings, and bad food.

"Sounds horrible," she smiled in sympathy.

"It was worse than that. I was also the poorest boy in the school. No money."

"That's bad."

"It gave me an edge. But not a purpose."

He reached into the sink and started to wash the breakfast plates.

"Go on," she said. She picked up a towel. The gentle sounds of Turandot drifted through from the lounge.

He told her about his meeting with Snaith and his ambitions to become a person of influence in Newcastle.

He helped her to dry the last of the cutlery and they walked into the lounge. She lay face down on the long deep sofa and swept her hair to one side. "Stroke my neck," she said. He knelt by her side and moved his nails gently up her back.

"Tell me about Fran."

The question startled him. "Why?"

"Because she's part of your life."

He told her of the events that led up to Fran, of his shyness as a teenager, of his natural feelings of being an outsider and of the party. It had been one of those parties where the parents of the host reluctantly disappear for a few hours, hoping all the beds in the house will remain undisturbed.

"What happened next?" She turned her head to smile at him.

He told her that one of his friends had called him a fool in a friendly voice and told him that he was the only person who didn't realise that every woman in the room wanted him. Even the mother. He'd looked up and caught the stare of the older woman.

Jean smiled. "So then you stopped being a fool."

"Yes."

"On a grand scale."

"Yes. Two, sometimes three a week...three in a night once."

"That would be crowded."

"In different flats."

"The marathon man."

"I didn't know their names... many of them."

"Few people would have the memory."

He hesitated before her gentle teasing.

"And then I met Fran."

"And Mr Lost became Mr Love."

His nails were leaving little red tracer marks down the pure skin of her back.

"You're really rather good at that," she murmured.

He told her about Fran...about her blend of gentleness and simple certainties, about her immaturity, about her natural talent for painting, and about her naivety which he had mistaken for innocence.

Jean turned her head. "I've never understood the difference?"

Kel paused from stroking her back. "She told me she loved me and I believed her because I thought she was innocent. I wouldn't have believed her if I'd thought she was naïve."

Jean turned to her side. "When you look sad," she said softly. "You have the eyes of a woman." She pulled him to her and kissed his ear. "Is it Fran?" she whispered softly.

He shook his head. "No Jean it's you." He smiled at her. "Soon I'll be off to my small provincial city and you'll be off whizzing round the world like new royalty."

"Come with me," she said softly pulling him into her body. "Come with me."

"No," he said. "I can't."

CHAPTER THIRTEEN

Years ago, salmon had swum up the Tyne in such abundance that the apprentices on the river were promised in their indentures that they would be given a limited supply. Now only the most determined fish ventured up the river fighting for oxygen under the film of oil and industrial waste that stained the waters.

He was travelling to the coast, on a trundling train, in a litter-strewn carriage, on a hard, lumpy seat, heading for his flat through a scattered skyline of cranes and ships down on the dirty river.

She was thirty thousand feet up above an ocean being pampered by sycophants to make less tedious her flight to another continent. Her rivers were pristine and stocked with leaping salmon running a gauntlet of hungry bears...well something like that.

He felt like a man who'd just jumped from a plane and not checked whether his parachute worked. The trouble was she just pulled him in until he melted into her. She even laughed at his jokes.

Yet...yet in twenty minutes he would walk into a cold flat with a view of a cold sea, a light bulb would have gone, the gas meter would need feeding and there'd be a week of dust on the dining table.

And she...she'd be cosseted in some five-star apartment with a bunch of penguin-suited men waddling to her every whim and telling their friends and families: "You'll never guess who I met today."

Their lives, their worlds were incompatible. Eventually it would become an issue and the clock was running. Meanwhile he prayed for the strength to enjoy the moment.

In the hour before they parted she had become tense. He assumed it was because they were leaving each other for their own disparate worlds. Without warning she kissed him. She was trembling with nerves. "I know you won't write about us," she tried to make a statement out of a question. She saw the pain in his face and pulled herself into him. "I'm sorry," she said. "I'm sorry." The serene maiden became an anxious little girl. He couldn't fight it.

That evening, in his flat facing the sea that lay out in the darkness he wrote about her, about the girl who had watched the trains leaving, always leaving, about the child who had seen the eagles and had wanted to fly with them, about her determination, about her desire for control, about her ambition to achieve all that she could.

He described the great star who feared publicity and who went to great lengths to protect her privacy, but who, nevertheless, had been generous enough to allow him rare insights into her life because he had helped her in France.

He stopped. That wasn't the way it was. She'd fancied him from the very beginning. He'd been picked up coolly, almost arrogantly, summoned to her court, and he wondered where and when she would put him down.

He fell into a shallow sleep at his desk, woke shivering with cold, and stumbled his way through to the bedroom where, in the morning, he was greeted by the sun glancing across his bed through a gap in the curtains.

It seemed only seconds later that he heard the key in the door and then the sound of Billy indulging in his favourite fantasy that he was in fact an undiscovered opera singer. He heard the water rushing into the bath. Ten minutes later Billy appeared at his bedroom door. "How was she?"

Kel's face squinted in the sunlight. "Beautiful and friendly."

Billy's face squinted at this ambiguity. "How friendly?"

"Friendly as in why don't you come to Kenya with me."

Billy's edged his head to one side. "So what are you doing here?"

Kel yawned in bravado. "I don't see myself as MD of Jean Smith Ltd, a high-pay, high-risk job, in which I'd be counting the money and the days until I got the sack."

Kel pointed through to the desk in the front room. "She gave me a present."

Billy picked up the case of LPs. "Puccini." He began to sing again in a made-up language that sounded like Italian but wasn't.

Kel leapt out of bed and pulled on a pair of jeans. He took one of the LPs and placed it on his player, relieved that Billy at least had the taste to listen.

"Oh yes and she gave me this for you." He handed Billy a photograph on which she had written her signature and a short message.

Kel walked over to his typewriter and shuffled the foolscap pages from the previous night's labour into a neat pile.

"That about her?"

"Wanna look?" He offered the sheaves to Billy who took them and without a word, began reading.

A few minutes later he looked hard at Kel but said nothing.

"What?"

"I wish I could write." Billy replaced the paper with surprising delicacy.

Kel laughed at himself. "It's not real writing." He shrugged. "What the hell, it's a good read."

The phone rang, and when he answered, a soft voice said "Zimani here."

Kel laughed. "Zimani? Hi Paul"

The voice continued in a soft tone. "Jean gave me your number. I hope you don't mind."

"No...no," he felt his voice falter in confusion.

Billy listened in astonishment until Kel put down the phone.

"It was Zimani?"

Kel nodded.

"Christ," Billy digested this piece of information.

"He wants me to work for him...on his film."

"A star part?"

Kel laughed. "No he wants me to do some research... its called initial locations research. He wanted to film in Sheffield but Jean insisted on Newcastle so they're miles behind."

It was simple work for anyone who knew the area...all he needed was a list of scenes with simple instructions and against each he would be expected to provide photographs of three possible locations, the names and telephone numbers of any relevant owners, and any other useful information...it was two months work and Zimani was offering five thousand plus expenses.

"My God! That's ten hard fights." Billy shook his head. "Well, ten fights."

A week later a package plopped through his letterbox with a list of some twenty scenes typed on two A4 size pieces of paper. He shook the package and a smaller envelope fluttered to the floor. Inside this was a note from Zimani and a cheque for a thousand pounds. The note said. "Part-payment in advance. Work fast."

He was overcome by excitement but amid it all he was asking himself. "Why me? Why so much money?"

He looked at the list...bridges, beaches, a castle, a country mansion, two night clubs, and three pubs, a scenic street in the city, a terraced street running down to the river, a quayside location near the bridges...it was all so simple. It was all so strange.

That afternoon he visited Edwards in his office.

The news editor told him his story about Jean and the eagles was not due to go out in the Chronicle until the following week but it had already attracted interest round the world.

"There are so many doors opening for you, you could get blown over in the draught." His face broke into a rare grin.

Kel smiled. "Thanks but I don't see myself as a reporter to the stars. I'm moving into films." He outlined the job he'd been given by Zimani. "The thing is," he said. "I need a good locations photographer."

"What sort of camera?"

"I'll let the cameraman decide that. It may vary from job to job"

Edwards nodded his approval. "It's not the usual Pressman stuff. There's a bloke called Stead, lives at Tynemouth near you. He's a gifted amateur. His grandfather was one of the original postcard men...you know the touring chemist's shop."

Stead turned out to be a small man in his fifties. He wore large tinted glasses and, as far Kel could tell, appeared disinterested until he was offered two hundred pounds for the job. He looked at the preliminary locations list and chuckled. "This'll not take long."

Kel voiced his surprise. "There are about two hundred photos."

Stead opened a large cupboard from which shoals of pictures spilled out.

"Shite, shite," he crawled on the carpet retrieving the pictures. "These what you're looking for?"

He spread out a pile of photographs taken along the quayside, looking down from the High Level Bridge, mean lanes gleaming in the gas lights, a long row of terraced houses with a huge ship stuck in the yard at the bottom, Bamburgh Castle booming out of the dunes, the jutting portico of the Central station, the castle keep overlooking the river.

Kel looked at him in amazement. Stead smiled. "Me hobby son."

Instead of two months on locations they spent three days taking interiors of pubs and clubs with Billy standing by to protect the cameraman. His reputation was enough in all the premises except for the Vic and Comet, which was the drinking den of the Irish labourers who teemed into the city for the building work. Here Billy achieved hero status in ten minutes by felling two large labourers who had insisted on baring their bottoms in front of Stead's camera.

"Jesus sir," said the bigger of the two. "That's a fine fist you have. Might I buy you a drink?"

Kel spent three more days compiling a list of phone numbers for permissions and then rang Zimani's office. The great man was still in Africa but Andrew, his personal assistant, assured him that he was desperate to get the locations as soon as possible. "Well I've been working night and day," said Kel. "I've got sixty locations with names addresses and telephone numbers and two hundred and fifty photographs."

Andrew whistled. "Good God. Zim will be delighted."

He sent the parcel off by registered post that afternoon. Two days later he received a cheque for four thousand five hundred pounds, the remainder of his fee plus expenses. The following day Zimani wrote him a letter of thanks and enclosed a cheque for a further five hundred pounds as a bonus.

With his money from Jean's interview Kel calculated he had earned seven thousand pounds in one month.

That afternoon the Chronicle printed the first of the articles he'd written about his meeting with Jean. The lead in story on the front page had a blow-up of the photograph taken at the Savoy under the headline Our Star Man meets the Star Lady. Underneath there was a précis of their meeting in France and a lead-in to the full story on Page Three.

He was looking at the coast edition and wondering whether they would meet again and persuading himself that it was probably better that they didn't. Then the phone rang and his heart betrayed his mind because it gave a little leap at the thought that it might be her.

It wasn't. Through the wonder of telephone communication his dream of the beautiful Jean was transformed into the reality of the abrasive Paul.

"Hi Handsome. Shag her then?"

"Hi Paul. Still wanking?"

Paul hurried on. "Look mate I've lost Gerry."

"That's careless."

"I mean he's disappeared. I was wondering whether you'd heard anything."

Kel said he hadn't.

"I've been seeing him once a week and he hasn't turned up for the last two meetings." Paul began to itemise Gerry's inadequacies. Kel looked down at the picture of himself and Jean and realised he had been right. It was exactly the same pose as she had made with the skier.

"So what do you think?" Paul was saying.

"Try the snooker hall in Northumberland Street."

"It's closed."

"Closed. What happened?"

"Who cares?"

"I do."

Paul was puzzled. "What's all this got to do with Gerry?"

"Nothing."

"I don't understand."

"It's quite simple. The conversation moved on from something that interested you to something that interested me."

There was a pause. "Have I upset you?"

"No."

Again there was another silence on the line until Kel said. "Look I'll ask around about Gerry."

He found Billy at the gym sending the heavy bag rearing into the air with mighty blows. Billy nodded and continued punching as Kel stripped to his boxer shorts.

Billy looked up at the clear- eyed handsome man. The training had added more muscle to the long clean limbs and he noted Kel's easy balance as he started his warm up routine.

Billy grinned suddenly. "What's it like? What's it like to have women chucking themselves at you?"

Kel didn't pause from his warm up. "The first two weeks are the worst," he said. "Why are you taking the piss?" But Billy just laughed and started punching again.

They trained for an hour until their sweat spat onto the dusty stone floor. Billy had begun to take Kel's training seriously. He was a natural athlete. He was also focused and had a gift of rhythm and movement.

Billy knew that his own skills were limited to street fighting. He was always going to be too short and too heavy for the ring where strength was less important. But this kid was long, lean and fast, and he danced like Cassius Clay. He didn't punch his full weight, but he had fast hands. No sooner had the thought been born than he killed it off. He was too decent to make a fighter. Kel began to towel himself oblivious to Billy's thoughts.

"Did you know," Kel said. "That each roulette wheel plays about 35 times every hour."

Billy looked at him with mild curiosity. "No. Oddly enough that had escaped my attention."

Kel grinned. "I'm thinking of opening a casino... a nightclub. I was kind of hoping you'd join me."

Billy said nothing. They pulled on their clothes quickly before the heat could escape from their bodies and stood facing each other in the yellow light from the single bulb. The gym still smelled faintly of oil from its previous life as a garage. Billy had refused to clean the place thoroughly. He said a fighter's place was amid muck and grime.

"Listen man," Kel pursued his point. "Say there's an average of £10 goes on each spin... that's £700 each hour with two tables and even without the noughts the clubs work on a profit of ten per cent. That's seventy pounds an hour or one thousand pounds every 14 hours 30 minutes.... that works out at about four grand on a seven day week."

"I suppose it does if you can find ten people to stand around each table for 14 hours."

"Be serious man."

"What's brought this on."?

"A sudden rush of money and a chance meeting in London. I've got about seven grand. What about you?"

"Kel man you know nowt about the business."

"But I know people who do."

Billy stared at him "You're dangerous you know that. You're about as vicious as a butterfly...and you haven't a clue what's going on."

Kel felt stung. "Like protection rackets...like corruption."

Billy opened the door to the street. "Ooooh big deal." As he bent to lock the door, Kel walked away. He wanted respect and he wasn't getting it.

"Like your friend Gerry." Billy called after him. Kel stopped dead and turned round. "What about Gerry?"

Billy walked to him and said in a low voice. "He's been in a furnace for the past two weeks." He allowed the incredulity to set in on Kel's face. "They had the decency to shoot him first."

The shock hit Kel like a cold wind. "Dead," he said. It sounded so stupid but it was all he could think.

"It was over some tanners."

"Sixpences."

"About two tons of them. Gerry's job was to collect the tanners from the fruit machines. He found out that they had a design fault. When they filled up they spilled out into the main frames of the bandits...so every few weeks Gerry would switch the machines round to empty the frames. It took two men to carry the body away and four to take the tanners."

He swung round and grasped Kel by both shoulders. "Listen. I'm going to tell you what's really been happening."

In simple sentences he told Kel that the corruption that Gerry had been talking about was wide of the mark. Gerry merely knew the rumours.

Billy ended with a knock out. "He was stringing you and your little ginger friend along."

"But why?"

"Because it made him feel important."

They were walking up the slope away from the river. Behind them the shipyard cranes pointed into the sky. The afternoon buzzer signalled the end of the shift at Swan Hunters and hundreds of men rushed out into the street, racing to get home, to get to the pubs, to simply get away.

"There'll be more killing before it's done," Billy gestured towards the city. " There's too much money coming in too quick...fruit machines, pubs, clubs, building contracts and protection...it's all easier than robbing banks."

They were jostled in the crowd of hurrying men now.

"Give over," Billy shouted. "If you buggers were as keen to get to work as you are to leave, the country'd be ok."

No one stayed to argue.

Kel and Billy took the bus to the coast and walked down to the beach past Tynemouth open-air pool. A couple of teenagers jumped off the twenty-foot board hunching their bodies at the last moment so that they bombed into the water. A line of body builders lay gleaming with sun oil on the slope beside the pool. It was one of those warm days in May that gave hopes of a hot summer. They weaved their way through children on the beach. The calm sea hissed along the sand.

"Put your chips on the star," Billy advised. "You've got your chance to live a great life. Come back in twenty years if you really want to do something for Newcastle. It'll all be settled by then. This is not the wonderful place you think it is. If you get in the way you'll end up dead. And you'll not even know why."

Kel was looking at the sea as Billy spoke. A gentle wave lapped at a newly built sand castle and then seconds later a larger wave swept it away.

"I'm telling you this because we're mates," said Billy.

"I won't let go." Kel turned to face him.

"Why not?"

"Because everything else feels empty."

"Even Jean?"

"She's from a different world."

Kel turned and walked up the sands. "See you Billy."

"See you Kel." Billy watched the tall figure walk away. He never looked back.

There was no mail in the porch when Kel arrived home and then he saw that a card had been wafted down into a dark recess in the hall by a gust from the open door. There was a picture of a lion and on the back of the card Jean had printed in capital letters. "In the wild. No phones, no postman. Have hired a man to run for six days to deliver this to nearest town. Missing you. Love J."

His Jean, his sudden money, his plans for a casino, he'd been riding a great wave sweeping in on the tide only to dash against the sea wall of Billy and now everything was swirling in confusion.

"Shit," he remembered Paul and the promise he had made.

He phoned the flat in Spital. Dave answered and told him that Paul was out.

"Is it anything important?"

"Tell him to forget about Gerry. I can't say more on the phone. I'll explain on Monday. Tell him it's very, very important that he does what I say."

The evening loomed long and empty. He could smell the dust in the flat. Some fish and chips left overs from last night lay in their wrapping paper on the table. He chucked them in the waste bin but decided to leave the hoovering until the morning. As a compromise he left the large front window open on the sash before he left the flat.

He walked along the promenade to the river and sat under Lord Collingwood's statue looking out over the flat sea. The mud banks shimmered as they emerged in the ebb tide and with them the brica brac of the river, dead branches, rusty petrol cans, and an abandoned bath all coated in slime and promising the stench of putrefaction.

Billy had hurt him. He had taken it for granted that Billy would back his plans with enthusiasm. Hell. He was on edge with Jean. He knew it was madness yet she pulled him in.

The parrot was still in residence at the Gibralter Rock. "Buy us a drink. Buy us a drink."

The landlord beamed. Kel ordered a pint.

"Mine's a half. Mine's a half," said the parrot.

"Clever aint she!" The landlord started to polish some glasses.

"Not really. It's his round."

He got a laugh from some of the customers sitting at the tables.

Kel unwrapped his pullover from his waist and pulled it over the cage.

"Time please. Time please," shouted the parrot.

"You see he canna even tell the time."

He retrieved his pullover and pulled it over his head.

"It's a she actually," said the landlord, slightly miffed.

A couple rose to leave. The man was wearing a suit that didn't quite fit. There was something odd about him. It was as though he had been told to dress up in a suit because it was smart, but his appearance lacked any inner conviction. The man made an excuse to the girl and disappeared into the gents. The girl smiled, looked out the window to the sea, and then suddenly turned to Kel. "I haven't seen you at the club for a while."

The memory of her came in a rush. She was the stripper who'd humiliated Paul.

She moved closer to him and spoke softly. "You should say hello sometime." She smiled as though in casual conversation. "Loved the parrot bit." She strolled towards the door her bottom straining at the confines of her tight yellow mini skirt. Her long, black hair shimmered as it bounced at each swing of her buttocks. The big man came out of the toilet and they left arm in arm.

Kel finished his drink and walked slowly home. The emptiness of the flat hung round him like a bad smell. He put on one of Jean's Puccini records and waited for sleep to take him into the new day.

Paul rang the following morning. "What's it all about?"

"Not on the phone Paul."

"Why not?"

"It's bad news."

There was a pause. "When can we meet?"

"I've got an appointment with Snaith this afternoon. I could come in early."

They met at The Brunch, a coffee shop in the Bigg Market. The site on which it had been built was medieval which meant it was long and thin. The tables stretched back thirty yards from the door and Kel insisted on taking a seat right at the back.

He told him of Gerry's fate and could see Paul putting on his tough-guy face.

He started to ask questions and Kel stared in disbelief as he detected a faint American accent in Paul's voice. Without thinking he grabbed Paul by the lapels and pulled him roughly towards him. "Listen to what I'm saying you crazy bastard. They'll know what you are doing long before you get enough to print anything and you'll be dead. It's not a game."

"Oh yeah. What's your source? It's your mate the thug isn't it," Paul said triumphantly.

Kel leaned his face close in to Paul. "He's trying to save your life you stupid shit. If you threaten them they'll kill you." He tried a new tack. "Look being brave is not enough. They'll get to you."

He could sense that the bravado was fading in Paul. Left on his own he would see sense. "Have you got any proof about anything?"

Paul shook his head. "Just rumours."

Kel leaned over the table once more " That's all Gerry knew ...rumours. It was all an ego trip."

Paul looked doubtful. "Do you believe that?"

"Yeah. I don't think he had access to any documents."

"Well why was he killed?"

"He was fiddling fruit machines and he was talking."

The tension fell from them both, and the sounds of the place returned to them, the clatter of cups, the chatter of the customers, and the calls of the waitresses to the chef through the hatch.

Paul fingered his scone but didn't eat it. "Sounds as though you're in pretty heavy. What do you see in this guy and what does he see in you?"

Kel didn't answer but he saw Billy's mum in his mind's eye.

Her large bottom was bent over a pail that smelt of disinfectant.

"Christ Elsie," he'd said. "It's like the eclipse."

She laughed like a witch and retorted. "I'll give you clips in a minute you cheeky young bugger."

And that was it that was how it had all happened with Billy. His mum had mentioned Kel kindly.

"Well?" Paul was waiting for an answer. Kel decided to change the subject. "I'm going to try to start a new night club," he said.

He repeated the same sentence an hour later in the long high office at the Civic Centre.

Snaith looked at him over the steepled tips of his fingers from behind his large desk. "And you want me to help you in this venture. Why?"

"Because in the past two months I've made seven thousand pounds and I want to invest it in a business up here rather than outside the region."

"If you're making that much money why not continue with what you are doing?"

Kel shook his head. "That would take me away from here."

"So why go into clubs?" His calm eyes took in the energy of the young man opposite him.

"There are two niche markets in this city that have enormous potential...casinos and the football club."

"The football club?" Snaith sounded incredulous.

"Oh yes, especially the football club. It's light years behind what it should be but the potential is enormous. But that's years down the road, and in any case the club's shares are tied in. No it's the casinos where the money is to be made here and now."

"But there's talk of closing the casinos down."

"That'll never happen. Too many people saw what happened during prohibition in America. If you make something illegal when there's mass demand all you do is create a criminal class. The choice is not whether we will have them or not. The choice is whether they'll be run by gangsters or businessmen and under proper controls."

"And you know all about them of course."

Kel ignored Snaith's gentle of sarcasm.

"I know people in London who do. Believe me the casinos up here are light years behind."

He told Snaith about the premises he had planned...the former snooker hall near the police station. Snaith said nothing and stared over his hands down at his beautiful desk. Kel felt a sudden warmth for the man despite his big car with personalised number plates, his silk ties, his close fitting soft collars, the soothing smell of expensive after-shave, the delight he showed in his intellect, and all the stories about his dubious dealings. Despite all that he was possibly a great man, never small-minded, never petty, a man like himself who felt for this small, provincial city.

"So what do you want from me specifically?" Snaith said at last.

"Your backing basically. There'll be a change-of- use application, planning permission...that sort of thing. I need someone like you."

He stopped and Snaith looked up. What Snaith saw was not a man hesitating but a man who knew he had one more thing to say but who had decided not to say it. Kel became aware of the intrusive chimes of the Civic Centre's carillon. The bloody thing ended its exhortation for Geordie Hinny to keep his feet still and Snaith spoke into the ensuing silence.

"Provided it doesn't hinder any overall plans, and I can't see that it will, then yes. I will help you."

He watched a boyish delight break out on Kel's face.

"You did the right thing by the way... not to offer me money."

And that was that.

Kel walked across to Snaith's window and looked down on the black stained stone of St Thomas's Church. A century ago the road round the church had been dressed in cobbles. He somehow doubted the Civic Centre would live that long...concrete crumbled...concrete against stone...compared to the church this building was just bluffing.

From the height of the office the buses glided silently in and out of the station. He followed a red single-decker, as it turned left past the Haymarket Cinema, which was adorned with a huge poster of Jean. He missed her, her stares, the slow spread of her smile, the firmness of her body, and the cute way she paused before launching out on a sentence.

She wasn't 23 she'd told him. That was the PR spin. She was 28, two years his senior and she saw the relief on his face but didn't ask why.

He thought of the minions from the PR department writing her life for public consumption...how would they see his intrusion? The enchanting, essentially romantic story of a sophisticated beauty and a small-town man... or a dangerous vignette of the Princess and the Pauper, which, horror of horrors, could end in messy publicity.

What had she said...They lied and lied until, at best, the truth was merely a convenient coincidence...the sexy swinging sixties...the birthplace of the corporate lie more like.

That night he addressed a letter to Jean's empty house in Hampstead.

He wrote:" I love you." He wasn't sure it was true but he wanted it to be.

CHAPTER FOURTEEN

"She doesn't like you," said the landlord.

The parrot sat on the top rung in its cage and tilted its head looking at him with its right eye.

"I prefer cats anyway," said Kel.

"She doesn't like you," said the landlord with finality.

Kel dabbled with the idea of telling him that he doubted that parrots had the capacity to like or dislike much beyond irritation of things that obstructed their eating and breeding.

Instead he announced it was time he went home.

It was dark outside and the half moon danced on a rippling sea. The west wind was warm as he walked to his flat along the promenade that followed the line of the beach. Below him a man walked his dog on the sands. In the distance the light from the window of his flat beckoned him like a beacon. For a second he stopped in a no man's land between the light and the sea feeling desperate and lonely.

He walked on and then suddenly Jean was there in a rush of feet, calling his name, her arms round him and his arms round her.

"I tried to ring you from the airport," she said.

"How long have you been waiting?"

"I got a taxi and when I got to the house I knew you were near. I could feel it."

He put the key in the door, kissed her, and she pulled him to her. "Oh Kel I've missed you." She followed him up the stairs with both hands on his buttocks. "Don't turn on the light," she whispered.

Ironically as they made love on the carpet in the dark, she became clearer to him because she seemed to lose the distance that her fame gave her. As he lay looking at the long shape of her, half hidden in the gloom, he became aware of burns on his wrists where he had supported her body above the carpet. She complained of a similar pain at the base of her spine and rolled over to allow him to inspect it. She shrieked when he dabbed it with Dettol.

She refused to dress but wore one of his shirts loose.

She examined the room as he made a cup of tea, commenting on the huge bookshelf that ran along one entire wall, the high ceiling and the large marble fireplace, which now housed a gas fire.

"Gee this is amazing. Heavyweight novels, history, sociology, and Jeffrey Farnoll for God's sakes."

"You've read Jeffey Farnoll?"

She smiled. "My dad has all his books. Like you. Why do so many men like him...He's basically a women's romantic writer isn't he?"

Kel shrugged. "His books are dreams."

He looked at her and saw she didn't understand. "Also he describes great days in people's lives. I believe in great days...days that will come to mind like a beautiful dream when I'm old."

Her ice blue eyes were suddenly soft. "And I ...what do I believe in?"

He was mesmerised by her. She had the face of a great star that could fill a screen without the distraction of a blemish and communicate with the tiniest movement of the lips or of the eyes. "I don't know," he said. He was meant to smile but he felt his own eyes fill with tears.

"What's the matter?" Her voice was as soft as a mother's.

"Nothing," he said.

She reached out and stroked his lips. "I think I believe in you."

"I think you believe in yourself."

Her eyes softened again and her lips spread in the slow smile he'd come to love.

"You're frightened aren't you."

He nodded.

She pulled his head to her and kissed his ear.

He woke in an empty bed to the gentle sounds of Turandot. She was sitting on the settee by the window sipping a cup of coffee and looking out at the rolling waves and the skeletal outline of the Priory ruins.

She didn't turn round but said. "Jesus, this is amazing. It's like having a masterpiece in your window."

She turned to him. “Hold me. I’m not Royalty” She gripped his arm with surprising strength and pulled him to her. “Hold me.” He held her until her body was warm against him.

“Can I stay? Can I stay here?” she whispered.

Her clothes had been sent on to the Gosforth Park Hotel. Her chauffeur had driven up overnight but she didn’t want him to know where she was.

She emerged into the day as she had come in the night. Her large sunglasses didn’t look out of place. A woollen scarf held her hair and her loose dark coat hid her long body.

They took a bus to Bamburgh and when she saw the huge castle she gave a whoop and demanded to walk across the cricket pitch that lay under its towering walls. They moved north along the beach past the golf club and on to the long golden sands.

“So this is your smoky slag heap North East,” she said.

“It’s one of the locations in the film. I thought you might like to see it.”

She looked back at the castle that stood with the strength of stone above the dunes. “ Wow! It’s amazing. How old is it?”

“About eighty.”

“You’re kidding. It’s zillions.”

He grinned. “No most of it was built by a Victorian industrialist. Mind you it’s been a castle site for centuries.”

She looked out to the ghostly shape of the Farne Islands that stood as a purple smudge on the skyline in the azure light. “This is a place of magic.”

He helped her over some rocks that jutted out into the beach.

“This is on a good day. On a bad day you can’t get moved for film crews ...Vikings crashing on to the shore for rape and pillage, medieval knights charging towards the castle...even Polanski on Holy Island making Cul de Sac and now there’s rumours that droves of melancholic Swedes are about to plod along the sands looking for a place to soliloquise.”

He turned and kissed her mouth. “But today I’m very glad to say you are the only film star in miles.”

She smiled softly at him and pushed her hand through his hair. “You really are proud of this place.”

“Especially when the cliché cretins from London write about thc filthy North.”

She shook her head. “You shouldn’t waste so much energy on bitterness.”

She took his hand and thrust it under her jumper. For a second he felt the warm softness of her breast and then she shrieked “Too cold.” and pulled away. He offered his other hand which he’d held in his pocket but she shouted “Too late!” She snatched his scarf and ran laughing into the wind.

He gave chase shouting, “Stop alleged thief.”

Suddenly she turned into him "Cautious bastard!" Then she collapsed laughing into his arms.

They followed the dunes round into Budle Bay and then turned south back to Bamburgh.

They had an hour to wait for the bus so they sat in the Lord Crewe Arms drinking whisky. He told her the sun had caught her face and she said she would have to buy some sun block because she was to play a pale-faced city girl.

The film, she said was the most important of her career. It was a sort of Romeo and Juliet set amongst gangsters. In the middle of a power battle she falls for the son of her father's rivals with the inevitable tragic results.

"It doesn't sound inspiring," said Kel.

"It will be with Zimani," she said with almost childlike sincerity. "You've got to understand he will weave the plot into the contrasting landscape here."

"Does he direct you line by line then?"

"Oh no. He knows I never intellectualise a part. I read...I read again and again until eventually I feel her." Jean's face lit up with enthusiasm.

"Zimani understands how I work. His strength is also that he understands it filmically and intellectually. He's slightly dyslexic and he seems to have a natural understanding of visual things and also of structure and scale. He will demand changes sometimes major changes but I trust him on the film set at least," she laughed. "He's a dirty little bastard off it."

Kel was absorbed. For a second he could see Fran in her. She had painted by feeling and Jean acted seemingly by a similar method.

The bus, which arrived early, was almost empty. The conductor stared briefly at Jean. Kel could read the "No it can't be" in his face before he retreated to his place by the driver.

Back at the flat she looked out to the sea and declared, "This has been a great day."

"Thank you," he said. "Thank you for today."

She closed in on him. "I haven't finished yet," she whispered.

It was dusk when they dressed.

"Show me your night club premises," she said, so they caught a train into town and walked from Manors Station up Northumberland Street. He pointed to the three-storey building..."There it is," he said.

"I hope you'll be wearing a penguin suit," she squeezed his hand. "It's my fantasy."

They strolled up to the Haymarket cinema and he told her she could treat him to her film.

"I hate watching my films," she protested. But in the dark of the cinema she clutched his hand and whispered, "I kept fluffing my lines in this scene. It was the day after you left Pau."

As they left the cinema he raised his voice in supposed conversation.

"I think she rather spoiled it," he said.

"Rubbish. She was just great."

As they crossed the foyer a woman approached them. "Excuse me." She smiled and spoke with exaggerated politeness "Aren't you the man who writes those history articles in the Chronicle."

"Yeah that's right."

"I just wanted to say how much I enjoy them." She smiled, nodded, and with that she was gone. Jean pinched his arm "If you ever ever tell a soul about this I'll kill you slowly."

"Tell as in 'Who's that lass out with Kel Adams the famous Chronicle writer.'"

"Exactly right."

That night was the first time he lost his inhibitions. He forgot she was famous, he forgot why she wore her large sunglasses and loose fitting coat. He forgot everything except that she was great fun to be with.

She had, he discovered, an extraordinary confidence in her insight into people.

He took her to Wallsend and as they walked down the High Street towards Billy's gym, amid the clanking of the shipyards and the swing of the giant cranes, he told her: "This is the other end of Zimani's rainbow...the rough, tough cliché of Tyneside, flat caps, back-to-back houses, men who belch at the dinner table, get legless on a Saturday night, and get a leg over on Sunday morning."

He stopped outside the garage. "You are about to enter a fighting man's gym. It's dark, dirty and ...words fail me."

"I'm not made of glass," she said evenly.

The light from the open door burst breifly into the gym. Then the door closed and the glow from the single yellow bulb prevailed.

Billy was half way through his press-ups routine dressed in T-shirt and black shorts. He stared into the gloom and said to Kel "Is that who I think it is?"

Kel nodded.

Jean took off her sunglasses and scooped her hair from her scarf.

She walked towards Billy smiling.

"Hi me Jean. You Billy." She gave him a hug and kissed him on the cheek.

Kel had expected Billy to be in awe of her but if he was he hid it well.

"So it's true," he said. "Your aren't one of his fantasies."

"My God Kel," she stepped back. "He's built like a lumberjack."

"I was going to do that but all my family are boxers...except my mother she's a cocker spaniel," he said solemnly.

Jean looked straight-faced for seconds and then bent with laughter.

"You are seriously mad. You know that."

Billy grinned and punched the big bag lightly.

"Do you two, you know, box each other?"

Kel pulled a face. "He won't teach me."

"Go on," she smiled at Billy.

Kel had never seen her brimming with so much fun. She'd taken to Billy in the same way Billy had to her.

Kel walked up to the bag and threw a flurry of punches at it.

Billy shook his head and spoke to Jean. "Did that look impressive?"

She nodded. "Yeah I guess so."

"Nah. They were just arm punches." He moved to the bag and at the last moment dipped his hips slightly left while bending his shoulders slightly right as he let loose a right uppercut. The bag reared. Jean was impressed.

He gestured for Kel to approach. "Hips left, shoulder right, and as you begin to come up from the dip throw your right. Just your right."

Kel did as he was told and this time saw the bag rear."

Billy shook his head. "That was fine as far as you went but you launched yourself off balance so you would not be able to throw a second punch never mind a third.

He went to the bag again and launched a four-punch combination with power and speed. "It's not about effort and strength it's about timing," he said.

Jean was impressed. "I made a film last year and we had some of the top boxers coaching a couple of the guys. But they weren't as clear as you," she said.

Kel stood back watching the two of them. He had never seen her so relaxed with anyone. She made a strange sight there, her long hair dancing on her shoulders, her classically structured face half in shadow from the one weak yellow light, all set against the stained damp walls. For the first time he dared to think that there was a chance for them.

The three of them locked the garage and caught a taxi back to Kel's flat where Billy cooked what he assured them was his speciality, Spaghetti Bolognese. Kel hastily started to play La Boheme from Jean's collection before Billy could start on his own repertoire.

They chatted about films over the meal. Billy asked her how she changed her laugh and her style of speech from film to film. She told him the trick was to change the speed at which she spoke. The rest followed on from there with help from diction experts. She rolled the pasta round her fork with expert ease and then slowed the rolling motion down so that she appeared to fumble the food. "Pace is the main thing," she said

The food eaten, the dishes washed and dried, Billy announced that he had to go. They walked with him to the door. "Look after my Kel," she said.

As they walked back up the stairs she smiled and clung to his arm.

"Happy?" he asked.

"I'm so happy I'm trying to live in slow motion."

He told her he had a secret love and took her to the small garage at the back of the house.

"There she is," he said proudly pointing to the Harley Davison that gleamed darkly against the far wall. He took her north into Northumberland, into the Cheviots where the roads ran like thread through the winding valleys and into the round hills. They walked half way up the hill at Greaves Ash where two thousand years ago the hill fort commanded the valley.

"This is a strange place, a mystical place," she said.

"In the Iron Age about twenty thousand people lived in these mountains. They were obviously breast men," he said gesturing to the round summits of the hills. "Seriously, they would be seen as important for fertility."

As he spoke dark clouds came rushing up the valley and they ran to the shelter of a copse of trees. The storm broke above and around them bursting through the sheltering leaves. She clung to his wet body pulling his hand to her breasts. "Come on," she murmured. She pulled him down on top of her, slithering on the wet ground as the rain lashed around them. Her white thighs gleamed in the heavy light as she yanked her skirt over her waist. While they made love the storm passed as suddenly as it had come.

When they ran to the bike, their feet slapping through puddles, she gave a wild laugh and shouted. "Come on the wind will dry us off." So he rode fast as he dared until the road became a path and the path faded into nothingness and they were alone in the hills where the burial mounds looked down as they had done for a thousand years.

Down the valley the weak sun highlighted the ridges and furrows left by long-dead farmers.

"I don't know which I like about you the most...when you are sensitive almost feminine or when I see you challenged and I know you're going to fight your corner." She smiled softly and stroked his hair back from his forehead. "You like people to underestimate you don't you."

He didn't answer.

They shared a bath back at the flat hunched knee to knee and hunting for the soap in the most intimate places.

That evening Billy called with a girl he'd met at a party.

"Rachel this is Jean and Kel. Kel and I are going into business together if he'll still have me."

Rachel was staring at Jean. "You look like that film star," she said.

"Yes," Jean smiled. "People often tell me."

Rachel started in amazement as the three of them burst into laughter. "Oh my God," she said. "Oh my God."

They sat round the dining table and played vingt et un or blackjack as Billy called it.

Billy showed a remarkable talent for the game. He told them he'd learned to memorise the cards by associating them with pictures near to his heart.

"You know...like the ace is Al Capone, the jack is my favourite cosh." There was a horrified silence among the other three until he gave a slow wink.

As the night went on Kel could sense Jean's unease at Rachel's presence. She said nothing until he went through to the little kitchen to make some tea. She followed him and whispered. "She's OK isn't she?"

It was a question seeking reassurance rather than information. Her eyes followed him anxiously, her body dipped in doubt.

"Billy trusts her," he said. "And you trust Billy."

He watched her fall into an uneasy calm.

"Do you think I should, you know, pretend to leave before they do?"

He sighed. It was as though somebody had filled him with happy liquid, and then pulled the plug on his big toe.

"Billy already knows about us," he said quietly.

When they returned to the room with the cups she was smiling. She was a very good actress.

The following day he took her to another of the locations, the flat muddy estuary at Alnmouth that stood in gentle pastel colours in the Northern light. They walked inland beneath the rail viaduct and along the slow moving River Aln.

When they reached the little stone village of Lesbury he called at the paper shop to buy a sandwich. She followed him in and there on the counter was a pile of Chronicles with the picture of them both taken in London.

Above it a headline declared "Friend of Film Star to open city casino."

She stood stiff. It was though she had found a body. He bought a copy and they read the story as they walked from the village.

The licence application was little more than a vehicle to cast innuendo about Kel and Jean. It reiterated the story of them meeting in France and how she had offered to give him an exclusive interview about her coming film which was to be shot in the North East. It mentioned that "Handsome Kel" had a reputation in the office as a lady-killer and concluded that no doubt the two would meet again when filming started in August.

She muttered "Oh Christ, Oh Christ" at every paragraph and then began to weep.

"What's the matter?"

She tore the paper in her rage. "What's the matter! This is what's the matter!" She held up the strips of paper in a rage. "Newspapers have destroyed two affairs of mine already. You have no idea have you."

"Obviously not." He said icily. "To me it's just a nothing story."

She wasn't listening. "Back home it's an industry. They ruin your lives and they snigger while they're doing it."

They'd reached the end of the village and she threw the torn paper over the bridge. His alarm was being replaced by anger. "For Christ sakes get a grip on yourself." He took hold of her arm but she shook him off.

"Our little world's about to change big time." she said.

"Jean we've done nothing wrong...this is just gossip."

She laughed mockingly at him. Her normally beautiful, cool face was as wild as a witch's. "Welcome to the circus. Wait until there are twenty cameramen outside your flat...wait until you can't stand at your window without being blinded by flashlights. Wait until every time I yawn I'm tired of you and every time you yawn you're tired of me, wait until we hold hands and therefore we must be in love...every little detail oversimplified, distorted. Wait until we're the main characters in a story to entertain simple people. That's what it's like in the US of A and it's coming here as sure as the plague."

"We've done nothing wrong."

"I have. The studio have been writing stories romancing me to Summerbee Clifford to disguise the fact he's a homosexual...it's called protecting their product."

"Well tell them to fuck off."

"And have them wreck my career."

There was no arguing with her. They'd crossed the bridge now. He looked at her. His beautiful Jean had gone and in her place was a little girl in a panic.

She ran back over the bridge to a phone box. He knew his dream was over; that she was summoning her chauffeur to take her away. He sat numb on the stonewall and watched her shouting into the phone.

When she came out he asked her where and she said: "Alnmouth. On the bridge."

They walked on. A rook croaked into the silence.

They turned back towards the viaduct and the coast.

"I'll get the bus," he said.

"We can drop you off."

He laughed harshly. "Tynemouth will be ringed with spies by now."

She began to sob quietly. "That's not fair."

"I'll get the bus."

He helped her climb the fence that ran under the viaduct. She stumbled into him and clung briefly to him but his arm held her away from his body.

She began to weep again. "I still feel deeply for you."

"One stupid story does this. We haven't got a chance."

"Not at the moment. Not when I'll be working fourteen hours a day on this film."

"A film," he could not keep the bitterness out of his voice.

She gripped his arm with a passion. "Not a film. This film. Zimani can make it into one of the classics. It's what I've worked for for ten years. At the end of it I'll have the power." Her voice, which had been harsh with tension, lifted with sudden hope. "All I'm asking for is three months grace. Surely you can give me that."

The bridge lay in the distance and beyond that the tall pastel-coloured houses that looked down on the inner estuary. Two hours ago they'd stood there happy and holding hands. Two hours it might as well have been two years. He could see her limousine crawling across the bridge.

She saw the car approaching too and pushed him for an answer. "Well?"

He looked at her and she saw the sadness in his eyes. "You're kidding yourself Jean. You've made a pact with monsters. There'll always be an excuse. Three months. Look what's happened in two hours."

"Go to hell then," she turned angrily and summoned the car. He sat on the wall staring at the ground. He heard the door slam and the car drive off past him. It was some minutes before he realised he was on the wrong side of the road for the bus.

CHAPTER FIFTEEN

That weekend she wrote him a letter. It said: "Supposing you were the film star and I was the 'ordinary' person... would you give everything up?" Kel did not reply.

He trained hard every day now, usually alone, in front of the heavy bag ,loosing off venomous blows until his knuckles stung.

Billy had taught him how to move his upper body to left and right to gain leverage for combinations. He lost himself in the physicality of it, and through exhaustion escaped, for a while each day, from his misery.

Out of the gym he tried to lose himself in his work.

The fittings started to arrive at the club.

Five weeks before they were due to open three large men joined them from Liverpool. They said little but were reserved and polite. Billy called them John George, Paul, and Ringo. He said John George had lasted seven minutes against him in a fistfight. Kel assumed this made him very good indeed. Paul was actually called Mark and Ringo's real name was Lawrence but the joke had gone too far, so Paul and Ringo they were. Billy described them as "Security."

Kel asked "Why Scousers?"

Billy grinned. "They'll not be spying for Conway will they."

The following day Justin Jacobs came on the afternoon train. Kel had persuaded him to resign from his London club with the lure of a percentage of the take and the prospect of returning to his native Tyneside.

Kel took him above the club to the casino. Four roulette tables were banked down the centre of the long room and two blackjack tables stood at either end.

Kel was worried. He'd heard that customers could now demand to take over the bank at every third play.

Justin shrugged. "They've got to prove they can cover the losses of the bank."

Kel had taken to Justin from their first meeting. He was, Kel had discovered later, the rebel son of an Orthodox Jewish family from Gateshead. His tall frame was slightly stooped but he always looked eye to eye and he had a soft confident voice. He told Kel he favoured wheels without any zeros but in a recent court case the defendants had fought off a prosecution so Kel had insisted on one zero.

Justin outlined his own priorities. "The important thing is that we set ourselves as a class apart from our competitors. Not very difficult." His white, almost saturnine, face melted into a rare smile. "Remember most of the players up here are hopeless compared to the punters in London. They play bad odds. The second thing to remember is that we don't lend anyone money they can't afford - they'll only disappear to other clubs. The third thing is Never Bankrupt the Customer. We Want Them To Come Back." His wagging finger made capitals out of the last few words.

Kel's talks with Justin had exposed his ignorance of the gaming business so he decided to take an educational tour of all the nightclubs on Tyneside.

By the end of the second week his eyes felt as though someone had put sandpaper in the lids as he watched the ball bounce, bobble, and then finally rest in a socket.

The girl leaned over raking in the winnings, her low-cut dress fighting a heroic rearguard action against the forces of gravity. It was his fourth club of the night.

Across the table a fat, bald man wiped a stained handkerchief on his neck. His eyes watered in the smoky light. Perhaps, thought Kel, he was crying. He had every right; he'd just doubled up five times and lost on every play.

The fat man dabbed his neck once more and then made his final gamble.

"I'll take the bank," he said with false calm. There was an air of finality about the flatness of his voice. Kel knew, as did others, that he was broke.

About a dozen players put their counters on to the table. A big man, who Kel had last seen with the stripper at the coast, suddenly thrust his way forward and put a five-pound chip on number twenty. The girl turned to the fat man.

"You must prove you can cover the bets." She smiled.

The fat man looked at the counters and then gave a deep sigh. "Sorry," he said and walked away.

The big man picked up his chip. "Don't feel lucky now."

Kel looked around the table. Half the punters were drunk and some of the others couldn't count past their fingers. In the far corner an elderly lady marked down every number after each roll and hastily referred to a graph. She was one of the better players...at least she was losing slowly.

He turned towards the exit and found himself face to face with Kenny Conway.

"You're Billy's mate aren't you?" It sounded more like an accusation than a question. His ginger wig looked as if it had been steam cleaned and its lip turned up at the back to rest over his collar. His small piggy eyes attempted a smile.

"Yeah."

"Out spying tonight?" He leaned towards Kel aggressively. But then, Kel told himself, he was the sort of man who would boil an egg aggressively.

"We open in a couple of weeks."

"We?"

"Billy's come in with me."

"I'd heard." Conway smiled a false smile. The big man came up to him and without looking at Kel said. "I'm off downstairs to the club."

Conway gestured after him. "Big George there reckons he's the man now."

"Really," said Kel.

"He says he could take Billy. What do you think of that?" Conway leaned into him again.

Kel considered the question for a second. "I think Billy would just go out and do it."

Conway was called to one of the tables. Kel took the opportunity to leave. There were no taxis at the rank so he decided on a last pint at the Tatler Club. Upstairs the resident band played "There's Always Something There to Remind Me." He stopped at the bar to listen. As they finished to a smattering of applause the stripper from the Coffin Box appeared from a dark corner across the room. She was half drunk, on a night off, and she said "Evening Boys" in a husky voice to the band as she took the microphone. Everyone knew her and waited for her to dance and relieve the tedium. But she didn't dance. She started to sing in a strained voice that couldn't hold the notes. Kel noticed Big George and two of his friends applauding feverishly from the back of the room, but she knew she had lost the rest of the audience. She walked back to the three men and sat down. Kel turned away and strolled over to the bar. He was trying to think of work but Jean would not be denied. She ambushed him from newspapers and advertising hoardings. It would get worse when the filming started.

"Hello again." He turned to discover that the stripper had followed him to the bar.

He smiled, but over her shoulder he could see the three men staring across the dance floor.

"I meant what I said about saying hello."

"I'm sorry pet but I'm attached to someone at the moment."

He saw her eyes harden and searched for the words that would soften his rebuttal but it was too late.

"Is he bothering you Doreen." It wasn't a question.

Kel started to protest but he might as well have tried to stop an avalanche as the three came at him kicking and punching.

He backed off behind a table upsetting the glasses. Panic, then pure fear, reared in him as he fell against a chair. He heard a woman scream and then they were at him as he tried to regain his balance. He went down and tried to roll away but they followed him with short balanced steps kicking him until he was still and then kicking him some more until Doreen screamed, "You'll kill him."

"Shut it you cow!" The three men straightened their ties and left unhurriedly.

Doreen knelt by Kel's unconscious body. She sobbed as she cradled his head. "For God's sake call an ambulance."

Kel awoke to waves of pain in hospital with a constable at his bedside. He said he didn't know his attackers or why they had attacked him.

The constable looked hard at him but said nothing.

Four days later Billy asked the same question at the flat as Kel peered at him from his good right eye.

"Names?" he said.

Kel eased himself painfully on to the couch.

"The main man was called George. He was with Doreen the stripper"

Billy nodded. "I know him. And I'll know the other two. They used to go round the town picking fights. You should have kicked off as soon as he started talking."

"It happened so quickly."

"No it didn't happen quickly. They used her as an excuse. You just didn't realise it."

Kel made to rise from the sofa and sank back groaning.

"Anything broken?"

"Cracked ribs."

"The bastards." Suddenly Billy's face was dark and evil. He looked like a man who was about to launch himself into a fight. His voice deepened and he spoke in a low voice. "Stay away from the Coffin Box for a couple of weeks."

He was still dizzy with painkillers when Jean rang him that evening.

"You've made the papers down here," she said. "Friend of film star beaten up in night club brawl." She sounded bitter and waited for his reaction.

He held back for a second stunned by her selfishness, then the anger that had been in him for days found a focal point. "If it's any consolation I have one eye still closed, three cracked ribs, bruises all over my body and the pain killers I'm on are so strong that I can't think straight."

When his tirade ended there was silence between them. He put down the phone. It rang again thirty seconds later. He knew she was fighting back tears when at last she spoke. "That's not fair."

"Not fair! I was unconscious for an hour, I had three days in hospital and all you've rung about is to complain about the fucking publicity. You're sick."

"I miss you," she wailed. "That's the real reason I rang."

His stereo was playing her record of Madame Butterfly. He knew she could hear it and that in her mind she was back in the flat looking out to sea." I'd still like to see you when we start filming," she said.

He was trying not to weaken. He knew she was pulling him in again but he kept his voice steady. "Billy's found out who beat me up. It's going to get heavy."

Two days later Kel made his way painfully down the stairs to answer the door of his flat. A tall man, who'd gone prematurely bald, showed him his warrant card, and introduced himself in a quiet flat voice as Inspector Johnson. He had a strange air of placid menace and his eyes were of such a light blue that they seemed to fuse into the white surrounds.

The detective noted Kel's uncomfortable progress up the stairs.

"Still hurting?"

"Only when I laugh or roll over in bed."

Johnson followed Kel through to the kitchen where he was brewing some tea. He took in the bachelor untidiness of the flat with little interest until he saw the cuttings of Kel's article on Jean Smith pinned to the cork reminder board.

"Wow you're the bloke who wrote the stuff about Jean Smith right."

The detective studied him with new interest. "The papers say she's got a temper."

"Yes. I can confirm that."

Johnson sipped his mug of tea. He took in the rows of books and the plaintiff sounds of La Boheme. "I suppose you meet a lot of famous people," he said.

"A few. I interviewed the Beatles once."

"Never!"

"Yeah they were trapped in a hotel trying to write a song. People envied them because girls were chasing them. They would have given anything just to go out."

Kel moved through to the front room and Johnson followed him.

The sweet sound of the tenor filled the room.

"Puccini?" The detective sat on the long sofa.

"It starts to scratch in a minute." Kel got up and pulled the player's arm to the rest. Again he winced as his body stooped.

"They knew what they were doing these men." The detective stared at him. Kel got the impression that here was a man who had to pretend normal human concerns.

"Have you started to remember anything?" Johnson's soft voice broke into his thoughts.

Kel shook his head. "It happened so fast, for no reason."

"Strange that."

" Strange?"

The inspector's smile was almost conspiratorial as though they were both sharing a secret joke. "It's just that there are three blokes in the General. They said something happened very fast to them."

Kel was wary. Billy, it seemed, had landed. "Really."

The inspector allowed his eyes to stray across the long line of books. The pale eyes turned back to stare at Kel and it was as though he was speaking his thoughts to himself. "A well-read man. Three thugs beat him up and then three men are in hospital. Three vicious men in hospital. They won't press charges and anyway your friend Billy will have an alibi and no injuries."

The detective smiled his humourless smile. "Who would believe that one man could take on three like these?" He paused for effect before answering the question. "Me...I would. In fact if it had been five of them I would still believe Billy capable."

"What is your point?"

The detective leaned his face in closer to Kel. "My point? My point is that he's not a normal man you see. These other three they're nasty bastards but they're not in the same league. You meet a Billy once in a lifetime. The trouble is that one day something will go wrong and then it'll be too late."

Kel stared into the shining face. "You seem to know a lot about Billy."

"I used to play football with him. I was thirty he was seventeen. Half the matches ended in fights, so in the end I just walked away. He's a dangerous enemy and a dangerous friend. Walk away while you can."

"He's a good friend to me," said Kel.

"If one of those men had talked you could have been on a conspiracy charge and that means jail."

"He's an evil bastard that Johnson," Billy said. "There was once me and a mate were locked up and four or five coppers went into my mate's cell. I could hear it all, the screams, the thuds, the fists, the boots, and I couldn't do anything about it. They never came into my cell. But Johnson looked through the hatch grinning.

They were standing at the bar of their club as Billy told the story. Above them glittered the newly-fitted chandelier. Kel had looked questioningly at Billy when it arrived. "Chandeliers don't fall off lorries," Billy said. The springy wooden floor had come from an old dance hall and the bar had been constructed from some leftover teak at the shipyard by a couple of joiners who owed Billy favours. Upstairs the four roulette tables stood side by side along the middle of the floor like ships waiting for their launch.

Kel trained every day now as a release from the pressures... an hour at fitness, followed by an hour at fighting technique. At first Billy had been good-humoured but sarcastic. Now as he watched the speed and balance of his friend he applauded in appreciation. Kel found there were times that he hit such a rhythm in training that his mind went to another place.

He stopped and wiped the sweat away from his face and neck. "Well?"

Billy nodded. "Aye."

"Aye what."

"Maybe you could fight pro."

Kel was full of himself. " Maybe...maybe."

Billy grinned. "Maybe kidda... maybe you'd curl up if you got hit... maybe you wouldn't want it enough when you met someone as good...maybe you're too much the nice guy... maybe it's just a game to you. There are lots of maybes." He pushed his arms impatiently through the sleeves of his jacket. "We're going visiting tonight," he said. "The Coffin Box."

"Will we be welcome?"

"Billy grinned. "That's why we're going...to find out."

Everywhere Billy went in the town he was recognised. On every street there was always someone who wanted to greet him...to baste his own self-esteem...to tell his friends he'd been chatting with Billy Latimer... "Oh yes I've known Billy for years." On Tyneside there were hundreds of men who "knew Billy." Most had never even seen him.

As they walked away from the casino up Northumberland Street Billy told him of one night he'd been working the doors at a club when he'd been confronted by an aggressive man who'd said he'd lost his membership card. The man had threatened to summon the assistance of his friend Billy Latimer if he wasn't allowed in.

"So what did you do?" asked Kel.

"I let him in," said Billy. "I said I didn't want to tangle with Billy Latimer." He grinned. "It helps the legend."

As they passed the Haymarket cinema Kel glanced at the Billboard. Jean was gone.

Billy caught the look. "Missing her?"

Kel didn't reply.

They turned up past the Co-op and into the Coffin Box club. The two doormen nodded at Billy.

They walked straight up the stairs to the landing where they had first met and turned into a large square room that had a bar jutting out of two walls from the far corner. Conway was sitting facing two men who had their backs to the door. Billy walked straight to the bar and ordered two lagers.

"New muscle?" Kel had not seen either man before.

Billy shook his head. "They're blowers...safe blowers. The bloke on the left is supposed to be the best in the country."

Kel looked around the room. The pubs were still open and the room was empty apart from Conway's company and a couple holding hands at a table. There was a smell of fried food. The record player behind the bar was playing a Joan Baez LP.

She was dealing with Go Away From My Window when they took a seat at the bar and had moved on to I Still Miss Someone by the time the drinks arrived. He hoped that Jean was still getting reminders of him as he was of her but somehow he doubted it.

He broke free of the thought to ask, "What happens now then?"

"We wait." Billy took a sip of his drink. "Conway'll come to us."

Joan Baez was starting Birmingham Sunday when the two safe blowers rose from their seats, shook hands with Conway, and left.

Conway made to follow them out but stopped as though he had just seen Billy.

He motioned to the barman. "Same again." He gestured to Kel and Billy, and then sat down heavily and precariously on one of the high stools at the bar.

The barman pushed the drinks across the bar. Conway paid with a pound note. "Keep the change," he said grandly.

He sipped at a whisky. "You're looking well Billy. Very well."

"Yeah. I haven't had much action recently."

Conway raised his eyebrows. "That's not what I heard. I heard you had to give a spanking to some people who were out of order."

Kel watched both men as the conversation progressed with the rigidity of a formal dance.

"They were doing disrespectful things."

Conway glanced fleetingly at Kel. "I heard they were out of order." His eyes glared in sudden anger. "There's enough trouble kicking off without people fighting over nothing."

The barman who had been hovering just out of earshot moved over to them "Anything else Mr Conway?"

"No," Conway got up and shook Billy's hand then, as an afterthought, held out his hand to Kel. His grasp was surprisingly limp.

They left together but Conway suddenly halted at the door.

"Shit," he said. "I've got to ring the wife." He moved quickly back into the club.

Billy and Kel stepped out into the cool night air. The pubs had just closed and the streets were noisy and busy. "Come on," Billy took his arm and hurried him down Northumberland Street towards the Casino Club.

Kel had noted in the past that Billy was uneasy in the raucous environment of the city. His instinct was to face trouble and make sure he kicked off. But that assumed a specific opponent or opponents. In a violent, but diffuse, atmosphere he was left waiting for something to happen and that put him on edge.

Kel waited until they reached the club before asking him "What was all that about with Conway?"

Billy grinned. "He wouldn't leave with us because he thought we might be about to hurt him."

"You're kidding"

"That's the way his mind works. He's on edge. There's been a fall out at the club. One of his men got stabbed last week. Then there's us."

"Us?"

"He's frightened we're going to take his trade away."

They were standing in the empty casino. Billy flicked on the strip lighting and looked round the room where the four roulette tables stood in line in the middle of the room. He turned to Kel with his frank open face. "You're in this to the finish now aren't you."

"Are you?"

Billy nodded. "But I haven't got a film star wanting me. And I'm used to rough stuff."

Kel met his eyes and held them "I'm here to the finish," he said.

"Before you promise there's something I want to tell you. Your beating up. Conway organised it."

"How come?"

"He wanted to scare you, and he wanted to see if I had lost my edge."

His eyes held Kel's again. "What I'm saying is that it may get wild. Do you think you can handle it?"

"Do you think I can handle it?"

Billy studied Kel's face. "Yes I do."

"I'm in till the finish then," said Kel.

Billy spat on his hand and held it out. Kel took it. "What a disgusting habit." They both laughed.

The following night as Kel walked past the Chronicle buildings on his way to Greys Club the billboards told him that the film stars were arriving in the city.

Dave was upstairs in the club, sitting at a table beneath the raised cabaret area. A neat dark suit, a cream shirt, a maroon tie...the same old Dave. They saw each other maybe once a month now...a big enough gap for Kel to notice the sameness.

He waved to Kel. "Good to see you." The smile was genuine as always. They shook hands and Kel sat opposite him. "Where's Paul?"

"Manchester. An interview with the Globe."

He looked around the room. He was too late for the cabaret, the lights had dimmed and shadowy figures sat around the edge of the dance floor.

"Nothing's changed I see."

"Not now you're back. Are you in circulation?"

Kel shook his head. "Grand tour. The Casino Club opens next week."

"And the famous one?"

"Gone to her firmament in the sky."

Dave looked closely for wounds. "I'm sorry," he said. He could say the obvious with enough sincerity to escape sounding banal.

They were joined by a pretty girl who stared frankly at Kel. Her short dark hair bobbed as she sat next to Dave and linked arms. "Jenny...this is Kel," he said.

He knew by the way that Dave introduced her and by the way she held his arm that Dave had found his next stepping-stone. He had chosen her, or she had chosen him, for the house, the family, the mortgage, and the career, the full package.

Confirmation came when after five minutes of pleasant chat Jenny rose and announced that she was going to get her coat because she and Dave were going to have to leave.

Dave watched her depart. "I'm sure she will tell me how devastatingly attractive you are but..."

Kel knew he was referring to the ghost of a girlfriend past. "It all seems like a silly game now," he said.

The band began to play and couples shuffled round the floor in the smoky light. Dave watched him watching the girls. "Picked anyone yet?"

"I came here to see you and Paul. I wanted to talk."

"Did you get close to her?"

"Too close. Closer than I thought." He smiled. "Though this time I crashed eyes wide open."

He reached across and took a sip of Dave's beer. Dave took back his glass. "You must have known the dangers."

"Yes. She's suffering from an incurable illness. It's called being famous. I hated that."

Jenny returned with her coat. It was short but slightly longer than her dress and he noticed she had long shapely legs. Dave had always been a leg man.

She noticed the slight slump in Kel's posture. "Is there anything the matter?"

He forced a smile. "No."

She offered her hand to him. "Nice to have met you." Then they left.

Kel sipped at Dave's beer and then followed them out. He watched them as they walked up the graceful curve of Grey Street. The sight of their bodies leaning into each other emphasised his own loneliness. He sighed and then cut away through High Bridge towards Northumberland Street.

The lights from Grey Street cast thirty yards into the lane and then fell short of the light from Northumberland Street. Just inside the linking darkness a man crouched in the doorway of the sex shop groaning and clutching his arm. Kel was about to walk by when he saw at the very edge of the light a patch of blood staining the paving stone.

"You OK?"

The man groaned and stepped back into the doorway.

Kel heard a rush of feet just before they came out of the gloom. There were two of them and he had no time for thought just instinct. He moved into them quickly staying bent and then rearing up so that his head hit the underside of the first man's jaw. He heard and felt the man's teeth break before he went down without a sound. A knife spun away landing point-down between the cobblestones. Kel's impetus had taken him to the left and as he regained his balance the second man came at him fast. He got in two glancing blows before Kel pushed him away with the heels of his hands. The two squared up to each other and then Kel began to dance on his toes. He had his back to the streetlight and he saw his attacker was one of the men from the Tatler.

"Fuck you." The man came at him fists upraised and lunging with his head. Kel danced back half a step and hooked to the head with his left fist. He felt the shock of the blow reverberate to his shoulder. He was filled a wild primitive exhilaration but there was no one left to fight. He stepped forward and kicked the second man in the ribs, then heard the breath whistle through his teeth. "Hurt donnit." For a second he stood in triumph over them and then he ran down the lane.

CHAPTER SIXTEEN

The Club Casino opened a week before the film crew arrived.

Paul was sent over to interview Kel, notebook out and pencil poised in deliberate self-parody.

Kel showed him round the club with its small bar, discreet dance floor and thick carpets. Paul whistled in appreciation.

"You've not seen anything yet," Kel took him upstairs to the casino. There, under the splendid light of Billy's chandeliers, the roulette tables stood solid and silent.

Kel and Billy had gone five thousand into debt fitting the room out with a thick, dark-brown carpet that gave the eyes rest from the brilliant chandeliers.

"I'm impressed," Paul stood taking in the room. "How did you raise the cash?"

"Train robbery," said Kel. "No. We raised some ourselves and borrowed the rest on a business plan. The banks agree with us that there's a niche for an upmarket club."

It was half of the truth. The other half was that Snaith had opened doors and put a smile on the money men's faces. He also seemed to have a conveyor belt of painters, decorators, and jobbing builders at his disposal.

Paul asked the usual questions and got the usual answers. They had an air of two bored people playing tennis. Then Paul asked the question that Kel had known was coming.

"About Jean Smith. Everyone knows that you are friends...you open...she arrives on a film shoot...will she be coming to the casino."

"Film stars work fourteen hours a day so I doubt it."

"Will you be seeing her?"

He leaned into Paul taking his space and spoke quietly. "Hey look, we're mates right. You know she hates this stuff so back off."

Paul held up his hands. "Sure, sure. It's just I thought the publicity would help the club."

He had to admit Paul had a point. Five hundred members had signed up by the time they opened and that doubled in the first week.

Paul and Dave visited him on the first night. "I'm starving." Paul headed for the cold buffet and returned with a plate of sandwiches and a coffee.

"The guy says it's free," he looked suspicious.

"Tonight and every night." said Kel. "We want people in here early not coming late after a meal." There were about a hundred players around the tables and another thirty playing cards.

"Made much?" Dave gestured towards the tables.

Kel felt a stab of panic. He had not kept track. He caught they eye of Justin who relieved his fears with a quick thumbs up

"How much?" As he mouthed the words to Justin Kel felt slightly embarrassed by his lack of class.

Justin raised one finger and wobbled his head left and then right.

"We're winning! About a hundred I think," he told Dave.

Dave laughed. "I think he means a thousand."

"Good Lord!" said Kel.

By the end of the night the profit had dropped to five hundred. A group of businessmen came in late and had a run of luck. A large florid-faced man with a Manchester accent, who'd told the checkout girl to take particular good care of his coat because it was a Crombie, had won consistently for twenty minutes. He smiled into the room wanting to be, if not liked, at least envied.

"If you've got a bob or two you speculate to accumulate. That's what I say."

"What a twat!" Dave looked across at the businessman.

"Nice guys don't count," said Paul who was sipping from a flask of whisky he'd smuggled into the club.

"I can't believe you said that," said Dave.

Kel turned to Paul. "I forgot to ask. How did the Globe thing go?"

"I start in Manchester in two weeks."

"Great." Kel looked at Dave.

"I'm still here a while."

"He wants to marry Jenny."

Dave caught the look on Kel's face.

"What's wrong with that?"

"Nothing." Kel draped his arm across Dave's shoulders. "It's just for a couple of years time seemed to stop didn't it.... I mean for the three of us...I mean we made a valiant attempt to shag half of Tyneside...we thought it was a way of life for a while."

Dave smiled. "No Kel, you used to shag them. I used to drive them home"

Paul took another swig from his flask. Kel decided against telling him that the drinks as well as the food were free.

Kel went home slightly richer and drunk on nostalgia.

There had been a time in his life when he'd spoken with Paul and Dave every day, when they had surrounded each other with their lives, and now they would soon be scattered. His relationship with Paul had always been uneasy but they had shared space and some adventures. Perhaps Dave had been right. They had been living and he had been playing.

Perhaps Dave had been right about Paul as well. "He's a little shit," he said succinctly. But at least Paul, and Dave too, had always had an overall plan whereas he had had nothing but his weapons: his looks, his capacity for study, and his love of Tyneside. But, without an overall objective, all his little triumphs had had a hollow ring, all his women mere tricks to win applause, and all the while life had been moving on. He hadn't been living he'd been performing.

The morning lights of the shipyard gleamed to his right as the taxi moved quickly along the coast road. He sighed. He had an urge to share his thoughts with Jean. But she was not here.

It was four o'clock when the taxi dropped him off at his flat. He fell asleep on the couch clinging to a cushion as though it was a comfort toy. He woke to the sound of the doorbell ringing. It was six o'clock. He stumbled downstairs.

The shadowy shape of a woman stood before him in the weak light and his heart bounded; then he realised it wasn't Jean.

"Little Zimm!"

"Guilty," she grinned. Her hair was bunched into pigtails and as she advanced into the hall he saw she had had freckles painted on to her face.

"I was passing so I thought I would call." She gave a giggle. "You may have noticed that I have been drinking." She breathed heavily at him. "I also appear to have lost some clothes." She opened her long, white mackintosh. She appeared to have lost all her clothes.

She walked past him and skipped up the stairs.

All he could think to say was "Do you know what time it is?"

"Time for a cup of tea?" she said brightly.

"Where have you been?" He asked.

"Oh don't ask," she said. "My bum's marked." By way of proof she flicked her coat at the back. Her buttocks were striped with four welts. She had penetrated his cool with ease, as always.

"Who the hell did that?"

She was encouraged by the anger in his voice. "Don't know his name. He seemed a nice chap at the time. In fact he was quite a good sport. He allowed me to whack him back." She lay face down on the couch. "Got any cream?"

Kel shook his head. "Sorry."

"Ice then?"

He went to the fridge and returned with a tray of cubes.

She was still lying face down though now she had raised her coat at the back. "Would you?" she asked brightly.

He shook his head. "I think you'd better."

She reached for the tray. "You're so straight really aren't you."

He did not reply and she pouted. "Is it me?"

He saw an opening to attack her. "Partially," he said. "You're like a little girl at a party who's not getting any attention so she takes her knickers down."

She took his best shot with ease. "Well I've certainly taken them down in my time."

"You'll pack this in one day...if you stay alive."

"It's Jean isn't it." She pursued his weakness. "That's the real reason. Not partially...totally. She gave me your address. She doesn't mind if we screw." She saw she had wounded him and moved in for the kill. "She doesn't give a damn any more."

He tried to hide his emptiness. "But I do," he said and retreated to his bedroom to emerge with a pillow and blanket.

She saw the hurt, which she had caused. "I'm sorry," she said. "I didn't really mean it."

He looked at her. "That's your trouble isn't it? You can hurt every one but your dad."

He went back into his bedroom and returned with an old pair of football shorts. "Try to keep them up for more than ten minutes."

Kel shut his bedroom door and turned the lock

He woke at noon and she was gone. A little note lay propped against the sugar bowl on the table in the front room. The loopy feminine hand surprised him. "I really am sorry. Jean does care for you." It was unsigned.

Billy told him he was going out on patrol. Each night he took John George, Paul, or Ringo on a tour of the clubs.

"I think I'll call you Cinderella," Kel told him. "You're always back in before midnight."

"I'm just spreading the word," said Billy. "I want people in the town to know who's with me." Billy grinned. "Your turn tonight."

They started at Billy Botto's, moved up to the Cavendish, and then Greys, the Sixty Nine Club, the Bird Cage, the Coffin Box, the Club Agogo and finally they walked into the Tatler Club.

He heard Little Zimm's voice before he saw her. She had a wild challenging laugh and she came out of the shadows from one of the tables back from the dance floor. "Hi Kel." Little Zimm flung her arms around him. "Who's your friend?" She stepped back to take in Billy. "Wow he's massive. He's scared them shitless back there." She gestured to her table. Kel made out George and his two friends and he stiffened in alarm. Billy walked straight to the table and stood before them. Kel found himself at his side. The men stood up and as they faced Billy the room went quiet. Then George nodded. "Billy."

"George." And that was it. Short on words and long on meaning, as Billy said later. It seemed entirely natural that Little Zimm should leave with them.

"What was all that about?" she said cheerfully.

Kel explained the recent events and realised immediately that he'd made a mistake.

"Wow Gangster Kel!" She began to laugh.

He found himself shaking her by the lapels of her long leather coat. "Listen you crazy little fucker. Stay away from them."

He loosened his grip. "Bad I like," she said and then reeled away as he slapped her face. He moved towards her threateningly and then felt Billy's grip on his arm.

Little Zimm licked the cut in her lip tasting the blood. She stared at Kel. "Christ," she said. "I bet you're a good fuck."

"I assume Jean told you," he said and turned on his heel.

He walked quickly to the Casino Club. Justin was chatting to the coat girl in the foyer.

"Anything the matter?"

Justin grinned. "Relax. The big mouth from Manchester dropped two hundred."

Kel felt like a small boy facing a sophisticate. "I'm not used to this yet."

Justin shrugged. "Trust me. The stake limits against our guaranteed capital are conservative by London standards where there are some expert players. Here..." He shook his head eloquently.

Billy joined them. "I put her in a taxi," he said. "I think you made an impression."

Kel still felt the need to lash out at her. "She's out of control. It's like she wants to pilot the plane just so that she can close her eyes."

Justin glanced from Kel to Billy and then back again. "Who's this?"

"Little Zimm."

"Aaah," he said with some eloquence.

"I'll put it about she's a friend," said Billy.

Little Zimm was back the following night in the Zimani entourage that came to the club. There was no Jean. Zimani made straight for Kel in his usual aggressive fashion. "Thanks for last night," he said. "Little Zimm said she was in a fix and you got her home."

"It was Billy." Kel introduced his friend and Zimani introduced Larry James a tall, elegant, dark-haired man who was playing opposite Jean. The star held out his hand but Kel saw his attention was on Billy. He apologised for his rudeness and then turned to the big man. "I think we've met," he said.

Billy shook his head. "I always remember film stars."

"Yes. Yes." Larry James insisted. "Two years ago in New York in a warehouse...you tonked a huge Negro in under a minute. Am I right or am I right."

"You're wrong. It was a minute and seven seconds."

Larry raised his arms theatrically. "Zimm this man is amaaaazing." He waved the stills man over to him and put his arm round Billy's shoulder. "Do you mind?" The camera flashed before Billy could reply.

Billy gestured to Little Zimm.The camera flashed again. Zimani joined the group with Kel and another picture was taken. Kel asked for a copy so that they could put a frame in the foyer.

Zimani advanced on the tables and began spreading his chips round the table. After a couple of plays he came over to Kel to complain. "Hey what's this about five pound limits on single numbers?"

"What part of that do you not understand?"

Zimani's face twitched in irritation. "What I mean is why?"

"Because any higher stakes would make the risk of breaking us unacceptable."

Zimani spread out his arms in protest so that his cream sweater tightened round his slight paunch. "For Christ sakes that's what it's all about aint it? It's a gambling joint." He slowed his speech to underline the last two words.

Kel shook his head. "It is for you. For me it's business."

Zimani shook his head as he took Kel's measure.

"You're a cool young bastard aint yuh." He moved away and then turned back... "By the way thanks for those locations."

At ten past twelve each morning, Kel and Billy took coffee in the little office at the back of the club bar.

Billy looked up from his Journal as Kel sat opposite him across the wooden desk.

He smiled but said nothing.

"Tell me about New York?"

Billy's face lit with humour. "Impressed eh."

Kel nodded. "Tell me about New York."

Billy shrugged. "There were some Yanks saw me belt a gypsy in Holborn. They thought they would get some good odds fighting this big guy in New York so they paid me two grand to go out and fight him."

Kel opened a bottle of lager. He offered Billy a glass. Billy shook his head.

It was a warm night and they shared a taxi home beneath brooding clouds.

Billy left him quickly and disappeared inside his small terraced house. Ever since Paul had called Billy a thug Kel had tried to come to terms with his own fascination with the big man. He'd concluded that the answer was probably simple. Of all the men he'd known, Billy was the best equipped to survive and prosper in any time down the ages.

As Kel tipped the taxi driver he shivered as suddenly he felt Jean's presence. He shrugged off the feeling as fanciful nonsense. He'd read of her arrival in the North East...the rest was subconscious wish-fulfilment.

He was right and he was wrong.

When he reached the flat it stood cold and empty. But five hours later when the doorbell rang she was standing before him.

She was holding the same huge sunglasses and over her shoulder he could see the limousine waiting at the far end of the street.

He was standing in his football shorts and a half open shirt. His heart leapt at the sight of her but there were bitter things he wanted to say. He said nothing.

"Can we talk?" she smiled her slow smile. He moved aside and she walked up the stairs ahead of him. He saw that she was clutching his letter written a lifetime ago. "I love you..." Her knuckles were white. He got the impression that she had read it often.

She looked out of the window to the sea and then she turned to him.

"Little Zimm called last week," he said. "She said you gave her my address."

Jean nodded. Even with her face in shadow he could see the strain.

"Why?"

"She asked me for it."

"You know she's out of control running round with gangsters."

"So are you."

"You knew she would want to sleep with me."

"From what you say lots of people do."

"So she sleeps with me and you say I'll never see the two-timing bastard again."

"I don't make sex the Plimsoll Line on a relationship. I've always wanted to see you again." Her voice was level but her hands were held tight.

"So what's changed Jean?"

"The truth is," she said. "The truth is that the filming is going very well."

She took a deep breath. "The truth is I'm thinking of cutting down on work after this."

She searched his face for a reaction and was gratified to note his astonishment. "What do you think?" Her voice was level and cool. He suddenly saw her great qualities, and was speechless. She had an ability to step away from herself and make big decisions, while he struggled with love and loyalties and sometimes between them. Her temper and her phobia about publicity were startling, and potentially disastrous, but there were times when she seemed to have the ability to make them peripheral elements of her character. She seemed slightly amused as she looked at him. "What do you think?" she asked again.

He tried to collect his thoughts. "Is all this for me...for us?"

She smiled at the thought he'd prompted. "When I was struggling I thought fame would be one of the rewards for what I did. It's not. It's the price. I've thought of you a lot."

He reached out and held her hands. "I don't know what to say."

"That's good." she smiled. "Zimani says it'll take six months to set up a business package and then we can tell the studios to stuff themselves. Can you put up with my obsessions until then?"

"I'll try."

She moved into him and wrapped her arms around his waist. Her head fitted just under his chin and he felt her warmth and smelt the sweetness in her hair.

"There's just one thing I want in return." She was warm and sweet but her voice was steady and determined. "It's your club: it's too dangerous."

He tried to bluff her. "There's no danger, who's being telling you that?"

"Little Zimm. I know all about the gangsters."

He sighed. "I gave my word to Billy...that I'd see it through."

"I'll see Billy," she said.

"It's not that simple. He's burnt his boats coming in with me."

"I'll see Billy," she said. "I'll bring in an army if need be."

He said nothing. There was nothing he could say because she was giving up so much.

She stroked his neck. "We'll make it work. We must make it work," she murmured. "Zimani will deliver on time. He always does. Then it's up to us."

They moved to the couch and lay still together. She had her back to the window and as he looked at her shadowy shape it was as though she was in a dream. He fell into a gentle sleep and when he awoke she was hovering over him smiling.

She kissed his ear with warm, soft, lips. "I've got to go to work."

He closed his eyes. Once again she had hauled him in and he was glad.

She brought a blanket to him and tucked him in. "We'll make it work," she whispered. "Oh Kel, I've missed you so."

She put a disc from La Boheme on the turntable and waited until it started to play softly. "It's freezing and the people of Paris are starving in their garrets. There's no penicillin and no anaesthetic...think how lucky we are." Her breath was warm in his ear.

"Will you ring?" he asked.

She leaned over and kissed him warmly on the lips. "You know I will," she said.

But she never did.

CHAPTER SEVENTEEN

Two days after Jean left Kel's flat Paul started his career on national newspapers with a story about the new man in the life of film star Jean Smith.

A picture of Jean was brandished on the front page under a headline declaring "SECRET LOVE". Beside that there was a snap of Kel and Paul taken at a nightclub. They'd taken a little licence with the photograph accentuating Kel's high cheekbones and painting shadows at the edge of his eyes. He was made to look the sort of guy any film star would be lusting after.

He felt sick as he turned to the inside page to read the full story of their meeting in France and their clandestine liaisons in London and on Tyneside. There was an insert from the Globe's Film Critic claiming that the original plan had been to shoot her latest film in Sheffield but the star had insisted on the location being moved to Newcastle. A spokeswoman for the studios was given a salutary couple of paragraphs at the end...just time to say that Miss Smith and Mr Adams had met in France and on a couple of subsequent occasions but they were just friends and she had no intention of seeing him in the near future because of the pressure of work on her film.

Kel knew that the last sentence was really a message to him. Her hotel refused to put him through to her room and when he travelled to one of the locations in the West End security guards barred him.

He turned his bike back towards the city, to his old flat at Spital Tongues.

Dave answered the door, black stubble pricking out from his pale skin. He saw the emptiness in Kel's face and invited him inside.

"I told you he was a little shit."

Kel slumped on the sofa but didn't speak.

"He always was a little shit and he always will be."

Kel stared into the floor. "Does he know what he's done to me?"

"Good God he won't be thinking about that, he'll be basking in the herograms."

Kel got to his feet and walked over to the back window where he looked out on the drab slate roofs. "She won't see me, talk to me."

"So what are you going to do?" There was gentleness in Dave's voice that reminded Kel of why he had always liked him.

"I think I'll go down to Manchester and show Paul that I'm not a nice guy."

Paul was easy to trace. The Gothic monstrosity of Manchester's town hall stood dark against the night sky as Kel sat at the base of a statue and stared down Albert Square to the large double doors that were the entrance to the Press Club.

A dozen times he stood up as the doors opened to spill light down the steps as members entered or left... then he saw him, or rather the outline of him...the slightly stooped walk and the light burning in the ginger hair.

"PAUL!"

Paul glared into the gloom recognising the voice but not the possibility that its owner could be in Albert Square at four in the morning. "Kel?"

"You bastard." Kel moved in quickly and, without another word, was on him with quick blows to the ribs and a short punch to the jaw. Paul fell to the pavement and rolled into the gutter. A taxi came roaring round the corner. The wheels hit a small puddle spattering Paul with dirty water. Paul looked up gasping for air and trying to make sense of what was happening. Kel leaned over and pulled Paul back on to the pavement. He punched him in the mouth bursting his lip. There was no astonishment in Paul's face now, just terror. Kel stood over him, his primeval rage dissipated by the sheer incompetence of his opponent.

"You bastard! Never come back to Newcastle. You hear me!"

Paul started to sob. "Kel, I'm sorry man."

Kel leaned into his face and spat. He caught the early train back to Newcastle and was in his flat by ten o'clock.

There was a brief angry note from Jean lying on the doormat. It said what he knew it would say.... that her studio had complained to her; that it must have been his loose tongue that had tipped Paul off." Then she started on a tirade.

He scribbled a reply and posted it on the way to the gym.

He left the light off and strode into the cold, deep, dark cavern where he punched the heavy bag in a fury until the skin came from his knuckles and his triceps and biceps were numb. He clung exhausted to the bag sobbing for breath, sobbing for her.

"Conway wants a meet," Billy's voice came out of the gloom and then he switched on the light. Kel's face and body gleamed with sheen of sweat. He stepped back from the bag. He wanted to be so exhausted that he could think of nothing and he still had a fair way to go. Billy's arrival had forced him to abandon the journey.

"I'm sick of that twat and his Irish wig."

Billy laughed. "Where have you been?"

Kel told him of his trip to Manchester and his confrontation with Paul.

"She really got to you, didn't she."

Kel's face was red with effort and anger. He walked over to the damp wall and picked his jacket from a bench. "She sent me this." He handed Billy the letter. "She thinks I betrayed her to Paul. She thinks I'm a dreamer dressed up as something else, incapable of making the really hard decisions. She thinks she should have realised all this in France. She thinks I was running away then and that I'll run away now. "

"That's all a bit sudden isn't it?"

He looked at Billy and sighed. "Perhaps she's right. I'm not a big enough person for her." He shrugged. "I wrote back saying I'd had enough of her over-reactions and then I wished her a happy life. I felt better for about ten seconds after I posted it. Then I came here." He held up his skinned knuckles.

"I'm fighting a week Saturday." Billy threw a right at the punch bag. "Some gyppo from Leeds." He punched the bag again and looked across at Kel noting his sculptured shape as he leaned hands on thighs recovering his energy.

"What do you make of Conway?"

Kel looked up surprised at the question. "I dunno. He's tough, evil, and thick. Why?"

"Best you know what you're facing. He grew up in a different world to you. When you were trying to get on the school team he was trying to get on the tough team. He was a good thief. He was handy with his fists and his nut and he never grassed. He did his bird and he didn't bottle...he got into armed robberies and was accepted by the hard men because he was a hard man."

"What's your point?"

"My point is: Don't underestimate him."

Kel was stung. "I know him."

Billy's voice rose. "No you don't. He might not know the capital of Scotland but that's not thick that's ignorant. If your friend Paul had done to Conway what he did to you he'd be dead. He'd have to be or people like George would think he was getting soft."

Kel saw the logic in this "OK. So what should I be doing?"

"Don't let him see all of you. Don't let him know you can fight."

Kel put his arm round Billy and patted him on the back. "Why are you bringing this up?"

"Because I think he'll be asking for protection money and he aint getting any."

Four days later Billy called at Kel's flat in his red Jaguar. He'd bought the second hand car a month ago but still polished it every day.

It gleamed pristinely as Billy drove along Scotswood Road and through the decaying west end of the city. The new, high-rise blocks of flats were sticking into the sky but around them the end was nigh for the rows of terraced houses that had been built during the Victorian expansion of the city.

Billy's street had already been reduced to rubble and Kel sensed the anger in him as a huge ball swung from a chain smashing through the bricks and mortar, splintering the wood, shattering windows and raising dust from the rubble at each blow.

They headed deep into the council estate where Conway had been raised and where he still lived. Conway had prospered. The family had taken over two semi-detached houses and knocked them into one. Conway greeted them with false warmth and ushered them into the front room of the right hand house where he poured out glasses of cold lemon. He sat in a high throne-like chair with his back to the window so his face was dark, almost in silhouette. He introduced Ben and Ronnie as two of his associates. Kel recognised Ronnie. He'd seen him in the ring, a halfway heavyweight who'd rapidly descended from being a fighter to being an opponent. Finally he had settled for the easier way, threatening men who couldn't fight instead of going on the back foot to men who could.

Ben looked to be a man with a similar history as they stood like bookends at either side of Conway.

The doorbell rang and Ronnie opened the door to a small bespectacled man who dabbed his collar with a handkerchief that reeked of after-shave. His anxious eyes flitted left and right over the room as he attempted to ease his tight fitting collar.

"I'm sorry I'm late. I'm sorry I'm late," he panted like something out of Alice in Wonderland.

"This is Sorry Sol, my bookman," Kenny waved an arm introducing him to the rest of the room.

"Accountant, actually Kenneth." Sol gave a nervous laugh.

"Accountants are just fucking book keepers on twice the rate." Conway seemed to think this was some sort of profundity.

Conway turned his attention from Sorry Sol to Billy and Kel raising his glass to them. "Respects," he said.

Kel suppressed a desire to laugh.

Ben and Ronnie were staring at him. He nodded and they nodded back. Anybody who was the close friend of Billy had their respect.

Conway leant forward towards Billy. "Ok for next week?"

"I'm fit."

Conway's eyes half closed. "They say he's quite useful this Bannion kid."

Billy didn't answer and Conway was drawn in. "You look confident."

"I'd fight him for a sandwich," said Billy. Then staring at Conway he added. "If someone called me useful I'd hit him." With extraordinary speed for a man of his size he moved forward and grasped one of the rear legs of Sol's table chair. With a forward motion he tilted the chair in towards himself and lifted it with one hand to chest height. Sol squealed in alarm before Billy laid him gently to rest. "Sorry Sol," he said. "I get these urges."

Sorry Sol adjusted his spectacles that had fallen off one ear but said nothing. Conway was not amused. "Bannion'll not be sitting on a fucking chair next week."

"He'll not be standing on his feet for long either." Billy kept his voice monotone.

The door opened and Mrs Conway came in with a tray of tea mugs and a pile of Penguin biscuits on a plate.

"Forgive fingers," she said. "The maid's day off." She turned to her husband..."And I don't want any more language like that in the house Kenneth." She wagged a finger at the crime boss who apologised.

She was pretty, like a cheap doll, with her hair dyed rusty red and the lashes on her large eyes painted heavily. Her large breasts fought to escape from her low-cut dress as she bent to distribute the mugs. She smiled at the room in general and Kel in particular.

Kel had a vision of her as a Beauty Queen in the Fifties, telling the world that she wanted to have children and to travel.

She broke into the thought. "You're Kel Adams aren't you? The papers say you've been..." Mrs Conway searched for the appropriate word.

"Shagging" suggested Conway.

"Oh Kenneth don't be so coarse," she giggled and handed out the last of the mugs...."That's been going out with Jean Smith. She's my favourite," she said to justify her curiosity.

"She used to be mine." Kel took a sip of his tea.

"They've gone their separate ways," Billy smiled at Mrs Conway.

"Oh Kel I'm so sorry," Mrs Conway's impressive chest heaved in false sympathy. This was True Romance writ large.

Conway yawned intrusively. Ben and Ronnie stared their hard man stares at Kel. Kel said nothing and didn't meet their eyes. Let them think he was a flash pretty boy. One day it might make them careless.

Billy decided the throw a bit of petrol on the fire. "It was down to one of Kel's friends who wrote about them...that's what caused the difficulties." Mrs Conway reacted like a sentimental lady who's just found a Mills and Boon book she hasn't read. "Oh how terrible. What happened?"

"We went down to Manchester to speak to the man," said Billy before Kel could answer.

"Oh," said Mrs Conway. "I wouldn't speak to anybody who had just done that sort of thing."

Billy smiled at Mrs Conway again. "We had harsh words."

Sorry Sol's nervous fingers scrambled at the catch on his briefcase. He rustled through some papers coughing gently.

Conway turned to Billy and Kel and asked about the club.

Kel decided it was time he said something.

"It's a bit early to say. But I think we're going to be OK."

He returned Conway's stare. He could hear him wheezing slightly. Fifteen years ago he'd been the toughest Teddy Boy in town but now a heart condition had him fighting for breath if he took the dog for a walk.

Sorry Sol knew his cue. He wafted his papers. "Our club is down about five per cent on last year. And other activities are even worse."

Conway translated. "He means that other bastards are saying why should we pay for protection when the Casino Club doesn't."

"There's a simple answer to that," said Billy. "We're able to protect ourselves. How long do you think I'd last if I paid for protection?"

He stared straight at Conway amid the tense silence in the room. The world seemed to stop and Kel had visions of large men wrecking the room as they fought fiercely.

Sorry Sol's eyes widened in alarm behind his dark glasses. His matchstick limbs would be in peril from any violence.

Conway's expression didn't change except for a slight twitch at the side on his right eye. And then he roared with laughter. "Bugger me. I'm not suggesting that. What I want is for you to continue to fight for me ... and to stay out of the trouble on the street. If you get offers."

"No problem," Billy stood up and offered his hand, which Conway took.

Business was concluded. Billy and Kel got up to leave. Mrs Conway waved to them from the doorstep. A sudden shower drummed on to Billy's red Jaguar and they sprinted to the car. The shower had turned into a storm by the time they headed east along the riverbank.

Kel turned to him. "What the hell was all that about?"

"He was trying it on...protection."

"Maybe he got what he really wanted. Your neutrality."

"Maybe."

The wiper on the driver's side was frayed leaving the nearside view obscured. As he slowed down at the approach to a roundabout Billy leaned forward to widen his angle of vision. As he did the driver's nearside window shattered and a blast of glass peppered their faces. Kel froze in shock. He heard the brakes screech. The wet air hit him. There was blood in his eyes. He screamed, "I've been shot. I've been shot."

There was another bang and a bullet gouged its way along the roof of the car until it fell exhausted into Kel's lap burning his thigh. He jumped in pain slamming his head against the roof. He pushed open the door and fell into the gutter as a third shot rang out. The car was empty. Across the road behind them the gunman fired another shot. Kel hugged into the nearside wheel. The shock was beginning to dissipate. The blood from his face dripped into the gutter staining the rainwater. He stared as it ran into the drain. His face was stinging. There was no deep or numbing pain. He wiped the blood that had been running into his eyes and a couple of fragments of glass fell onto the road. Some of the bricks from the demolished houses had spilled out onto the pavement. He looked across the road. He could see the gunman now quite clearly, advancing from behind the parked cars, moving towards him with his rifle held hip high. Then he brought the rifle to his shoulder and turned in a 180-degree arc. Kel leaned back and grabbed some of the rubble. The first half brick he sent in an arc so that it bounced to the gunman's right. As it landed he rose and flung a second brick at the man's chest. The gunman twisted towards him and fired but the brick caught him just beneath the throat. He staggered and screamed as Billy came at him from behind one of the cars across the street. He tried to face this new attack but even as he moved his face opened in fear because he knew he was too late and the faster it got the slower it seemed. Billy's impetus lifted the gunman from his feet and he was thrown into the gutter. He was half conscious and in pain but he still managed to bring the rifle up into firing position. Billy stepped in without hesitation and kicked the gunman's left hand that grasped the stock of the weapon. The man screamed and his hand went limp from the wrist. The gun clattered far back in the rubble. The man screamed again as Billy kicked him in the ribs and the air left his body in a whoooosh and came back stretching the broken ribs in pure pain.

Kel was on his feet now limping towards the two men but Billy didn't even glance at him. Instead he stared deep into the man on the ground.

"Who." He said. It wasn't a question it was a demand. The gunman stared up at him helpless.

"You've got five seconds," said Billy. "Then I'm going to break both your legs and both your arms and bury you in the rubble over there." The rain dripped down his dark locks and on to the man's chest.

He wasn't a big man and he hadn't a fraction of Billy's physical strength but he had his own currency; he was prepared to shoot people.

The man met Billy's stare. "I'm dead anyway," he said. From the far gutter a dark Cortina moved out at a sharp angle and accelerated across the road. Kel shouted a warning but was too late as the car rode over the gunman's chest. There was the sharp cracking sound of bones snapping and then the car reared from the body into Billy who lifted his arms as though to push back the speeding vehicle, and then even he succumbed as the Cortina rose over him like a great black beast. Billy was swept to the ground his head smashing into the edge of the kerb. The Cortina continued upwards and then, its wheels still spinning, hit the ground and rammed into the Jaguar. Kel saw Big George's head smack into the steering wheel, saw the blood spurt from his nose. Then the tyres screamed as Big George put the car into reverse. Metal pulled at metal and the Cortina tore free. Kel picked up a brick and threw it at the windscreen. It struck at an angle and bounced across the road where it dented the wing of a parked car. Kel threw another brick as George reversed at speed down the road into a junction where he spun the car round to race down towards the city.

Kel turned to Billy who was lying in the roadside, the great body limp, the head resting sideways on to the kerb, and the blue eyes open in a dead man's stare. Kel started to sob. The eyes were the most terrible of all, still and staring from a man who had always been so full of life.

Kel ran one hundred yards back along the road to a telephone box. The broken windows presaged his worst fears. He picked up the receiver. It had been torn from its cord. As he ran back to Billy he could see a policeman struggling up the hill on a bicycle. He was about to ride past when he saw the smashed Jaguar. He dismounted and then spotted the two bodies,

"There's been a shooting." Kel shouted at him.

He looked at Kel with disbelief and then Kel pointed to the rifle jutting out of the rubble. The constable asked a couple of basic questions before leaving to find a phone in one of the flats. He summoned help and gave a description of the car.

Five minutes later he took out his notebook and asked. "The driver. Did you get a look at him?" The policeman was large, fair-haired, inexperienced, and trying his best to contain his mounting panic.

Far away down the long straight road a tank rolled out of Vickers works and rumbled slowly towards them. Kel stepped out into the gutter and laid his jacket gently over Billy's eyes.

"Did you see him?"

"Aye I saw him."

"What did he look like?" The policeman licked his pencil like a man waiting for the off.

Kel wiped the rain and blood from his eyes. "He was dark haired and in his thirties. It was just too quick you know."

"Is that all?"

"Yes." He said the word quickly to get past it because once said there was no turning back. It was a defining moment... the exact moment he moved from one side of the law to the other.

"Your friend...was he THE Billy Latimer."

"Yes."

"The hard man."

Kel looked down to the roadside and started to sob. There was no blood, there was nothing.

"Hard man. Hard man." Kel shook his head. "He should have realised. The only way they could get to him was with guns."

CHAPTER EIGHTEEN

They took Kel up the road to the Casualty department of Newcastle General. A short, stocky nurse, who smelt of disinfectant, bathed and bandaged a scrape on his knee, put a plaster over a small cut in his forehead, stuck a needle into his backside, and declared him fit to leave.

A small group of doctors, nurses, and auxiliary staff watched as he was treated. Two policemen waited in the corridor.

He stumbled towards a table where a man was lying holding a bandage to his head. A nurse called out in alarm and a detective took hold of his arm.

"Nowt to do with you Mr Adams."

They took him across the road to the police station. A posse of Press people had gathered and he had to walk through a wall of flashing cameras. He asked for a cup of tea with two sugars. It came in a large blue mug.

He'd forgotten about the seen-everything eyes of the inspector who'd played football with Billy. He'd got it wrong. They weren't the eyes of a tired man, but of one who was deeply sinister.

They sat opposite each other across a table.

The inspector told him he'd visited the Casino Club and chatted to Billy. He'd been pleased to see Billy building something.

He offered Kel a Senior Service.

Kel shook his head. "I don't."

Johnson smiled. "Been trying to give up for months. Can't. Too much stress. Tell me about this afternoon."

Kel described the attack and then the visit to Conway's house.

"Why...why were you there?"

He spun him a story that fitted in with the truth...one that he knew Johnson would know all about.

"Billy was a fist fighter," he said. "Conway promoted some of the fights. Billy was on next week. Conway liked to take a look at him before a fight. I think Conway liked having someone like Billy call at his house. Billy was the toughest man in town and Billy was his man as Conway saw it."

"You and Billy. How did you meet?"

"He was rather polite when kicking me out of a nightclub."

"Hardly the seeds of friendship."

"He was interested in history and the stuff I was writing at the time. And I knew his Mum. She was a cleaning lady at the Chronicle. She and I were pals."

"Do you think the shooting could have something to do with your club?"

"I suppose it's possible."

"Any threats...demands?" The soft voice was deceptive. Kel knew Johnson was searching his face for an answer beyond the spoken reply.

"No one threatened Billy."

"So they got a gun." Johnson's face shone in a wintry smile before blowing a smoke ring spinning out over Kel's head. It took Kel back with Pavlovian certainty to the Coffin Box where he'd seen Conway sitting in a darkened corner away from the bar talking to a man who'd stayed in the shadows. But out of the gloom he'd blown a perfect smoke ring that drifted spinning out on to the dance floor. He remembered too the low, flat voice of the man in the shadows.

He glanced in alarm at Johnson. There was no mutual recognition of the moment.

Down the corridor a drunk started to sing in his cell. His voice echoed off the tiled walls, encouraging the prisoner's fantasy that he could chant with the best of them.

Johnson drew on his cigarette. "Who knew you were going to see Conway?"

Kel shrugged." It was no big secret...no big news either...a few people at the club and some of Billy's friends."

Johnson was joined by a sergeant, a large, fat, red-faced man whose shoes creaked as he walked across the hard floor.

They took him through the killing again...every detail from the moment he had left his flat... who had said what to whom...the windscreen wiper that had saved their lives...the second third fourth and fifth shots...who had been where...who had shouted what...who had done what...the bricks... the distances thrown...who had said what to the gunman...the threat of broken bones from Billy.

The sergeant eased himself over the table. His dark bloodshot eyes stared at Kel. "What did you think when your friend made a threat like that?"

"What do you mean?"

"Were you shocked?"

"I'd just been shot at half a dozen times. I was already shocked. I wanted to jump on his legs myself. I wanted him to be terrified like me."

The sergeant ignored Kel's outrage. "You said 'I'd been shot at' not we."

"OK. We'd been shot at then. I presume he was shooting at both of us...anyone he could see. It just feels like every shot is at you. I was behind the car. Billy had got across the road somehow."

"So he was firing at you."

"In my direction. I don't think he could have seen Billy get away from the car."

"Why do you think that?"

"Because he started to walk towards the car pointing his gun

"Tell me about the other man...the driver."

Kel hesitated. He was on the last bridge leading to an unknown road. "I never saw him clearly. It all happened so fast. He came from nowhere and then I flung myself clear. He hit Billy's car and then reversed away."

Johnson spoke for the first time since the sergeant had entered the room.

"When he reversed there must have been some point when he faced you." "I'm afraid I was cowering behind Billy's car most of the time." He shed himself of his embarrassment. "What about the gunman? Won't his identity lead to the other man?"

Johnson shook his head. "The gunman's a well-known shooter from Leeds. The driver will probably be local."

The sergeant came at him again. "These are strange men for a person like you to be involved with?"

Kel stared back at him. "Not really officer. As Inspector Johnson said in your absence, Billy was in the process of bettering himself...whatever that means. He was one of the finest men I've ever met."

The sergeant leaned into him again, close enough to betray a mild case of halitosis, and for Kel to see the lattice of broken blood vessels across the bridge of his nose. It was a boozer's face and a bully's face, a face that had lived and prospered in a thief's world, a face that snarled threats at snouts. The sergeant and the inspector, fresh cops back from the war...they were that age... out of the war into the force, hated paperwork, dealt with crime in their own way (a punch-up in a back lane as like as not)...they knew who to hit and who to do deals with. They never went home empty-handed whether it be sucking on a bottle of brown ale or dipping greasy hands into a packet of fish and chips. But they were wary of men in suits, wary of people like Kel, who had a business, who knew Snaith, and went out with film stars... wary of him because he didn't fit any of the stereotypes of their simple, brutal cynical world...but most of all they were wary of him because he just might nail Big George and through him, Conway for murder.

Kel knew that he wouldn't survive very long if they believed that. Something would be arranged... a false charge to discredit him, or something more violent and permanent. He wondered which of them would speak to Conway first.

Johnson glanced at the sergeant and they came to an unspoken agreement that they could go no further for the present. They gave him a lift. Kel asked for the car to be stopped near Collingwood's Monument. He sat on a bench looking at the statue as the evening sun rested gently on the curl of the river.

Lord Collingwood's silhouette stood dark against the sky and the cannons, which had been among the first to fire at the Battle of Trafalgar, pointed out over the river, heavy and black in the low light. The great man had sat shaving with a cut-throat razor as the French and Spanish guns blasted at his ship. He envied Collingwood his coolness.

In the distance he could hear the sounds of revelry from the Gibralter Rock. It was there that he had first encountered Big George.

The Press besieged his flat when he returned. They hadn't turned out for Jean Smith but they came in their droves for Billy Latimer. He muscled his way through them to his door ignoring their questions.

In his room he sat on the sofa staring at the window until the light dropped from the sky and the darkness enveloped him.

He woke with the cold and pulled a blanket from a drawer. On it he smelled the faint remnants of Jean's perfume. By the morning the fragrance had gone.

The Press were still there though, or a new shift of them. There are some stories so big that you can't stop telling them even if there's nothing new to say. They'd had time to get out the files and Jean was splashed across the front pages.

In the Globe Paul had written a full page of his life and times and their nights on the town.

He sat in the flat waiting for the call from Conway that he knew must come. But Jean rang first. He felt a shock at the sound of her voice. "Oh Kel I'm so sorry."

He felt the tears welling for the first time. The man who had been so full of life was dead. He found himself describing the events. He ended suddenly and there was silence. He thought for a moment that they'd been cut off and that he'd been talking to a dead line but then she spoke.

"Is there anything I can do?"

"Nothing Jean."

"Come to London."

"There are fifty reporters outside my house. And there's the club to run."

"There's something else, isn't there."

"I can't say on the phone."

Her voice rose in alarm. "Meet me."

"Come to the funeral."

There was silence and then she said. "You know I can't."

"I don't know you can't. He would have gone to yours."

"Not if he would have had to face the consequences I would face."

"He would have gone to yours no matter what."

He heard and felt her sharp intake of breath. "Perhaps he would."

There was a silence again and then she said.

"I'll come up...but not the funeral Kel. I'll come up on Wednesday...the film stars beach. Two o'clock." He said nothing and he heard her start to weep.

"Two o'clock," he said and put down the receiver.

From the other room he could hear Puccini's Un Bel Di from Madame Butterfly...One fine day we'll see a thread of smoke on the horizon on the distant sea.

He looked out of the window. There were no ships. But he fancied he could hear Billy singing in nonsense Italian.

The phone rang again. "Conway here Kel."

He hugged the phone to his ear and said nothing for seconds as the adrenaline of hatred coursed through him.

"Hello, Mr Conway," he said at last.

"Just rang about Billy you know...to say he was respected by everyone."

"Yeah, I know."

"You OK?"

"I think I'm still in shock." He kept his voice flat and dull.

"I heard it was a crew from Leeds."

"The police think so."

"I know so. They're trying to move in."

"But why Billy?"

"Billy was the toughest man in town and he fought for me. It's a warning."

"I'll see you at the funeral." Kel put down the phone.

Billy's mum stood at the door of the crematorium, small, white-haired, and frail. He wondered how someone so tiny could be the mother of someone so strong. But they had the same wide blue eyes. She still had her smoker's cough. In fact this was the first time he'd seen her without a cigarette. His first sight of her had been on the early shift along the narrow, cold corridors of the old Chronicle offices, sloshing and slopping, kicking her bucket forward, and all the while retaining an inch of ash with the dexterity of a dedicated smoker.

It was seven in the morning the beginning of his shift and the end of hers. He winked at her and she winked back and as he passed he blew at her ash so that it trickled down her flowered pinafore. He walked past without a word and she gave a laugh like a pirate. He turned back and she was grinning at him. "I've just cleaned that bit." She pointed at the ash stain.

He took her mop and wiped the floor.

"Ye divvent dunch it like that." She retrieved the mop and twisted it into the colander head of the bucket to squeeze it dry."

He gave her a hug and walked away.

The pinny had gone, replaced by her best coat, which smelt of lavender. He held her to him longer this time squeezing her hard as though he was hugging Billy.

"He loved you," she whispered. For a second they noticed the tears in each other's eyes and then he walked out into the light and the huge crowd that had gathered outside the crematorium. He stood there looking at the faces of strangers. Most of them were young men standing and shuffling, smoking in awkward groups, like customers waiting for the pubs to open.

"Not one in ten fucking knew him." Conway was at his side. "The wannabe hard men. The pubs will be full of them tonight...Billy and I said this...Billy and I did that." He fluted up his voice to make the words sound ridiculous. "They'd have shit themselves if he'd looked at them." He spat on the gravel. "Seen the filth...they're snapping away over there. Disgusting. No respect." He gestured angrily towards a policeman crouched behind the hedge. "Fuck off."

His thick neck reddened, He was a man who looked as though he was wearing a suit for a joke. The finest Italian cotton, the silk black tie and the black polished patent leather shoes were no match for the round, barrel chest, the short, thick legs that defied the efforts of any master tailor... and the angry tufts of red hair growing like weeds from under his ill-fitting wig merely exaggerated the joke.

Kel stood watching the young men leave. Conway had got them about right, half-scared to go on, half-scared to back down, they had seen Billy as the man who stood beyond the fear they had to conquer.

Conway came back to him. "We should talk," he said. "They'll not stop at Billy. On your own they'll pick you off. Wanna lift?"

"I've got my bike." He gestured to the shining black Harley Davidson that leaned into a tree.

"We'll meet next week," Conway gave him a curt nod and strode off without waiting for a reply.

Kel took his leathers from a case on the bike and rode past the reporters.

He took the road for the coast and headed north to Bamburgh. He was early. He planned it that way. He sat in the Lord Crewe drinking orange in the same seat he and Jean had once drank whisky, then he walked across the empty cricket pitch, glancing at the huge castle before turning north along the coast. When he reached the golf course he walked down the incline and on to the long flat empty beach. The sand was dry and warm as he stretched and lay in a hazy reality between sleep and rest.

He must have heard her approach because it was in his mind that someone was coming to him. Then he heard her voice.

"I loved him too you know."

He looked up. Her honey blond hair was in a bun. She was wearing a loose, red-checked shirt and tight, blue jeans. She was carrying slip-on shoes... a picture of chic beachwear a la catwalk.

"His mother was a cleaner at the Chronicle you know...a lovely lady. I often wondered why he took to me. He told me I was kind to his mum...a laugh and a joke with her." He shook his head. "And that led to all this."

He felt her hand warm on his shoulder. "Come away with me...away from all this."

"I can't. They killed him Jean."

"So leave it to the Police."

He laughed. "The man in charge is in Conway's pocket."

"So walk away." He would not look at her. He was staring out to sea. "Walk away from this small provincial city and live a great life."

"I can't."

"Why not?" Her voice snapped with irritation.

"There are things to do."

"What things?" Her voice rose in alarm.

"Things he would have done for me."

She knew what he meant and her voice rose in alarm. "For God's sake you are not him...you never were him or even like him."

"Maybe not but he uplifted me every time I met him and he never walked away."

She ignored the barb so great was her alarm.

"Listen Kel. You are not a gangster. You are not a killer. Do you think Billy wanted you to become that?"

He was still staring to the sea though now his eyes were filled with tears. She reached out and pushed her fingers into his hair. "He looked for you to lead him out, not for him to lead you in. Don't you understand he looked up to you more than you did to him."

He could hear her crying softly. She knew she hadn't moved him.

"I cannot put it down," he said. "There are bonds up here between men that you can't understand."

She held his eyes for a second and then said softly. "And what of us?"

He laughed harshly. "Jean you've walked out on me twice because of something in a newspaper."

"I can deal with that now. I promise you."

He smiled but his eyes looked beyond her and she knew that for the first time she could not reel him back in.

"You don't believe me do you."

He smiled again. "He thought the world of you and he was my greatest friend. He was my comrade and my brother. And you couldn't go to his funeral because of the publicity and you are asking me to believe everything's changed."

His eyes held hers. He'd humiliated her with the truth and they both knew it. "You won't want anything to do with me in a few weeks." He turned to stare out to the sea.

She pressed him to say what he meant but he wouldn't and then he heard her sob "Damn you" as she walked away.

That was the last he could remember clearly until the cool wind hit him on his speeding bike.

That evening he sat in his flat writing a letter. Dear Eloise..." He posted it on the way to the club where he summoned Justin and the three men from Liverpool. They sat by the dimly lit bar on the long stools. "Are you in?" Kel cast anxious eyes over them. They all nodded and Justin said: "I know some people in London."

Kel shook his head. "No. Too risky. All I want from you is that you keep the club going."

"And what of you?"

Kel smiled. "It's necessary they think that I am frightened and weak."

He poured out five whiskies and handed out the glasses. "To Billy," he said. They clinked their glasses and drank. He pulled out four envelopes and handed one to each of the men. "You've each got ten per cent of this," He waved his arm in the general direction of the club. "And believe me you'll earn it."

That night he stood on Tynemouth beach alone and lonely in the long, clear moonlight, throwing flat stones into the calm sea. He looked back towards the Priory along the stretch where Billy had trained. It was flat and smooth. His footsteps had gone forever.

CHAPTER NINETEEN

There was a scene that Kel remembered. He and Billy had been sitting out on the low wall that sloped down from the cliffs by the open-air swimming pool at Tynemouth

Billy had gone into business and Kel had beaten up Paul.

Kel had laughed at a thought that came like an arrow from nowhere. "Perhaps we've met going in opposite directions."

Billy smiled. "You don't want to go where I've been."

But he was going where Billy had been. His Harley glided past the swimming pool then followed the road inland towards North Shields. He left his bike on high land above the fish quay. The steps to the quay were as steep as he'd remembered. A lifetime ago he'd run down and up them on a daily journey to gather the white fish landings which someone, somewhere, sometime, had deemed a matter of local interest for the paper.

The smells of the quay were the same...fish, dirty water, diesel, and seagull shit...a heady cocktail hanging in the damp air. The boats were in and a scattering of fishermen lounged around the vessels, waiting for the pubs to open. Red, raw hands and clean nails... hard men, wild, in drink... superstitious men too.... they hacked splinters off a wooden statue believing it would keep them safe...afloat on a splinter in the North Sea. Some chance! The same men had held a whip-round to buy a dolphin snared in their nets, and then they'd set it free.

The trawler he was looking for bobbed at the far end of the quay. He climbed carefully down the metal steps and jumped on to the wooden deck. The noise brought out the man he had arranged to meet. They stared at each other for a second and then Kel said, "I'm Billy's mate."

The skipper stood for another second taking him in. He didn't look like any of Billy's mates but this was the man that Billy had talked about often...from the posh end of Tynemouth...the man who'd loaned books to Billy. He noted the soft hands and the smooth open face, almost girl-like, and then the easy balance on the shifting boat. He remembered Billy talking about the boxer in the gym, his natural movement and fast hands. The man with the film star looks who was shagging the film star. He spat and sent a glob of white hockle out into the filthy water. A seagull swooped, seeking food and then soared away.

"I seen you in the papers," the skipper said at last. He belched and farted at the same time and his pock marked face reddened with the effort. Then without warning his strong hands made a grab for Kel. He grasped nothing and called out in surrender as a right fist was launched towards his head .It stopped a fraction from his jaw.

"Where'd you learn that?"

Kel shrugged.

The skipper grinned. “Had to know I’m not wasting my time.”

Kel said nothing but he stepped back a pace his eyes still alert.

The skipper saw no anger in him just a determined efficiency. “You’re up against a hard crew.”

Kel shrugged. “What’s it to you?”

“Steady on son, I’m on your side” The skipper spat out into the water again. “I owed him. I gather you want a lift.”

“In, then out a day later.”

“I can’t go down near Biarritz...It’s out of my water.”

“Pick a place. I’ll be there.”

“Holland’s good.”

“Why?”

“I used to smuggle stuff.”

Away across the river the ferry launched itself out from South Shields pursued by a posse of seagulls.

“How much do you want?”

The skipper pulled aside the top of his shirt and scratched the dirty Long Johns that protruded. “We’ll go halvers on the diesel. That’s all. I owed him,” he said.

Two boats down, a crewman emptied a bucket of bilge and the shrieking seagulls swooped.

The crewman cursed. “Flying shitbags.” He turned cheerfully to the trawler and noted the groomed young man in the black sweatshirt and crisp new jeans. From the safety of two boats away he shouted. “Watcheor Arnold! New crew or is he just selling his arse?”

“Fuck off Bennie,” the skipper replied with an absence of venom.

He turned back to Kel. “When will you be ready?”

“Dunno yet. A month ...six weeks. I’ll get in touch.”

“I’ll need a week’s warning right.”

“Sure.” Kel nodded and clambered up the metal steps to the quayside.

The days took over. For the time being he had no purpose, merely a goal. The plotting and planning filled the holes in his life

“What do you believe in?” Jean had asked him. He’d believed in Billy but now Billy was dead. Billy was the man who could shift his life to an exciting plateau and together they were winners. Billy was dead.

The train from the coast hit the buffers at Central Station bumping him out of his thoughts. He joined the passengers getting out. The platform was crowded with people waiting to take the return trip. The billboards were everywhere with the news that Snaith was helping police with inquiries into a contracts scandal.

He grabbed a paper and stood reading it in the concourse. There'd been rumours for weeks. Snaith was pictured leaving his large terraced house; the excellent cut of his Italian suit still discernable after the attentions of the Chronicle's printing process on pulp paper. And above all the same confident smile of a man who believed he was impregnable and that he must prevail.

The smile had been there a week ago when Kel had last called at his home.

Snaith must have known that at the very least he was fatally marked but as he spoke his voice had grown stronger and his body more animated. It was as though a composer had invaded the body of a businessman.

Even the question of guilt didn't dent his inner belief that his was the one statue the pigeons wouldn't find.

"We are all guilty," he said softly and his left hand slid slowly along the large fireplace feeling the cold smoothness of the white marble. On the wall above hung a battered but polished fiddle. He caught Kel's glance. "My Grandma's," he said. "She used to play in the back lanes." And then as he was struck by the contrast between the relic and the beautiful marble he murmured. "Money is the consequence of success. I never sought it for its own sake. It was always to furnish my schemes." He looked at Kel "You're the same."

The memory came through Kel's mind like a cold wind in August as he stood in the station's portico.

He followed the story into Page three and was confronted by the news that Edwards had died. He felt as though he had been struck and the air briefly left him. Edwards had lain for two days before his body was found at his flat in Jesmond. He tried to remember their last meeting, their last words but they were lost in recent events. He walked to the club and rang Dave.

"Why didn't you tell me about Edwards?" He demanded.

"I tried. I've been out all day at the Snaith thing."

"Oh right." He was about to replace the phone when Dave said. "He was buried today. Behind the cricket ground."

Kel felt his eyes fill with tears.

As he replaced the phone he noticed he'd attracted the attention of John Paul who was standing massively at the entrance to the bar.

"A friend's died. I suppose you must think me pathetic," he said wiping his eyes.

John Paul stared at him. "I cry when I get injections," he said. "How much longer have we got to put up with Conway's bastards?"

The question chased him away from his memories. "Not much longer. I've got to go to France and then I'll settle it when I get back. "

In the beginning Conway had looked at him with a wariness that a lazy eye might have mistaken for respect. But as the days had turned into weeks he became more confident and had begun to show the primitive man's contempt for the weak.

He and his crew strolled into the club at weekends loud and brash, pushing to the tables. They wore the same sort of suits and ties favoured by the hard men from London.

Kel looked on as Joey, one of Conway's collectors, started to complain about a bet on vingt et un.

"It's not the money it's the principle see." To prove his point Joey flicked a match and lit a five-pound note, which he then used to light a cigarette.

Kel gestured to Conway who grinned. "What's the matter squire?"

He was standing under one of Billy's chandeliers that hadn't fallen off the back of a lorry. Kel told himself if the chandelier had fallen on Conway at that moment he might have started to believe in an Almighty...albeit an Old Testament version, but it would have been a start.

Kel forced himself into a smile. "Look this is bad for business."

He fought back a desire to nod to the men from Liverpool. Instead he shook his head at John Paul and gestured for the croupier to pay out.

The gamblers who had stopped to watch this little drama returned to their play. The balls click clicked and fell with their death rattle, the cards slapped on to the green baize and the calls from the croupiers filled the room again.

Conway glared and let the thick ash from his cigar drop to the carpet where he crushed it into the pile. "Whaddyamean?"

Kel held the reins of his rearing fury. "I'm giving you 10 per cent to protect the business. Fair enough there's been no trouble but your people...they have reputations and they're frightening the customers away which is no good to either of us."

Conway sucked on his cigar. "Joey meant no harm." The blood had gone to his face again and he dabbed his red neck with a handkerchief.

"The point is he's doing harm."

"He meant no harm," said Conway again. He sucked on his cigar and sent the smoke spiralling up towards the chandelier. "I expect life's a bit tougher now Billy's gone." Somewhere in the depths of the room someone shouted, "YES! YES!"

Kel tried to deflect the tension with a joke. "It's getting worse. The ones who are staying are winning."

Conway ignored the comment. "Never could see what he saw in you," he said and then began to cough. His face reddened as he gasped for breath. Joey came trotting up with a glass of water.

Conway took a drink and coughed himself into silence.

"You OK boss?"

"Yes.Yes."

Kel took note of his slow recovery and his veins opened in hope.

Conway glared at Kel as though he was the author of his misfortune.

Kel took the empty glass from him. "You should have a check-up." He saw Conway's face redden with anger. Like many tough men he was frightened of being ill, frightened of being diagnosed.

Kel handed the glass back to a waitress and then strolled off down to the bar. John Paul was standing at his usual position by the entrance. He'd told Kel in a touching moment of intimacy that Billy had given him the scar above his right eye. "Tough bastard," he said in his laconic fashion. Billy had said John Paul was a "good un" and that was enough for Kel. Joey caught up with Kel as he left the bar. His black oiled hair glistened in tight curls. He was a big man, with deep dark eyes and his smile could change to a scowl in a second. Kel thought he looked like an extra in a pirate film, an extra always trying to push his way to centre stage. Joey took hold of Kel's arm as he came alongside him. "Hey I want a word with you."

Instinctively Kel flicked the hand away.

John Paul approached. "You OK Kel." His eyes were on Joey.

"Sure." Kel smiled. "Just going to get some air. Coming Joey?"

Joey hesitated. Kel turned to John Paul. "See you in a couple of minutes."

Northumberland Street stood wide, silent and empty. Down the road a light burned through the police station doors. A lone car cut across into Market Street.

Kel walked down the alley that ran by the Odeon and turned to Joey. "I'm glad you wanted a word with me Joey because I wanted a word with you."

"Yeah. Where's you're friend?" Joey sneered.

"He's dead. Haven't you heard? I'm on my own."

"Where's the big man?" He motioned with his head towards the club. He looked up the road and saw it was empty. "Whoooopsie," he fluted his voice. "You're on your own pretty boy."

It was then that Kel hit him, driving his right fist into the full stomach with the strange primitive elation of a man gaining release.

He heard the air whoosh out of Joey and watched as he fell holding his stomach, his mouth open, desperate for air. Joey rolled over into the gutter and slowly raised himself to his knees.

A street fighter would have stepped in to finish him off but Kel needed to beat Joey properly just to regain his self respect after weeks of grovelling.

"Take your time." Kel watched as Joey regained his feet and the two eyed each other from across the lane. Then Joey came at him, head lowered and fists flailing. Kel stuck out a straight left twice but Joey came on through hitting him a glancing blow above the eye and following through with his head, which struck Kel in the shoulder. The two of them grappled for seconds and then Kel broke free sufficiently to get the leverage for another right hand to Joey's stomach. He felt Joey's grip on his jacket loosen and stepped back before dancing in again, fists swinging. In the struggle he had been pushed to Joey's right so he moved his body round to southpaw stance and pushed his right fist out twice into Joey's face. Joey staggered backwards and Kel followed him quickly with a flurry of punches until Joey fell back against the wall crying "No More."

He hit him twice more to the face sending him staggering along the wall and then on to the ground. The initial rage had left him and there was a cold economy about his movements as he walked over to the helpless man and spat on him. "Scum," he said, and then walked away to the top of the lane. John Paul was standing at the corner's edge. Kel gave him a wink.

"He'll say I jumped him. Best they believe I've done a runner."

He took a cab to his flat, picked up a small suitcase, and caught the early train to Kings Cross.

The summer had gone and the fog oozed in from the sea to deny him one last look at the Tyne as the locomotive punched through the thick mist on the High Level Bridge.

"I don't like this bit." A large, dark-haired woman took the seat opposite him.

He looked at her, conscious of the swelling to his eye. "Pardon?"

She stretched up to the rack above them and disembowelled a large suitcase scattering papers and sweets on to the table between them.

"Oh I'm so sorry." She started to sweep the sweets towards her with her forearm gathering them in a pile. "The thought of water beneath us," she shuddered, unwrapped a boiled sweet, and started to suck it noisily

She pushed the remainder towards him.

He looked her over slowly...thirties, horn rimmed glasses, no make-up, hair tied in a bun, and a large bust that overwhelmed the constraints of her tweed jacket. She belonged, he decided, on the prow of a ship breasting her way through waves with indomitable if disorganised energy.

She pushed the pile of sweets nearer to him. "In the 1850s Queen Victoria stopped the train on this bridge to look at the aftermath of a fire and an explosion."

"It's OK. She's not on the train today," he said.

"Oh I say." She blinked, laughed, lit a cigarette, and then told him her name was Samantha Lewis and she was going to London because she worked at the Guildhall School of Music. He assumed she was a contralto but she told him she played the piano.

"Piano e forte," he said without thinking.

She smiled and said "Soft and strong. Not a lot of people know that."

At Kings Cross he helped her with her luggage. She watched him hesitantly as he put his case into a locker.

"Are you off to see her?" she said.

"Who?"

But she just smiled and said "The papers have got it wrong. I think you're a lovely man." Then she was gone, striding straight into the crowd until it swallowed her.

He looked back up the long platform, which was now empty save for a single guard, and he remembered the lovers clinging to each other at Pau station. He was still thinking of the couple as the tube rattled into Hampstead. It was warmer in London, the trees were not yet bare, and a faint sun lingered in the Autumnal sky. There were leaves on her lawn though and he wondered whether she had finally sacked the gardener, as she'd threatened so often. He walked slowly down the long path. Why was he here? Why? He knew why. It was their last meeting before his life must change forever. Soon there would be no going back and no going back to her, and he wanted to say goodbye with some feeling of tenderness. Who was he kidding? He wanted her to say she would come back to him when it was all over. Some hope.

A gust of wind lifted the branches of the weeping willow. There were no lights and the house stood in silence. He was about to turn away when he heard her laugh from the back garden.

He moved quickly along the gravel path to the French windows, which looked out over a flagged terrace to the rose garden. The laugh came again and he looked down to the little grove of trees that surround the two tall pines. There filtering through the bushes and branches he saw Jean lying side-on in the hammock. She was dressed in a red bikini and across her flat white stomach lay the dark hairy arm of Zimani who was snuggled up behind her. He had no recollection of how long he had stared but eventually her eyes caught his and she screamed. Zimani fell back off the hammock. The sudden movement threw his dressing gown open. He was naked. Kel made for him and the famous director of many heroic movies squealed in fear and ran into the bushes. In the same moment Jean called Kel's name in an anguished voice that came down the ages. He stopped and turned to her. She was sobbing and calling his name to herself in a strange rhythm and the anger in him was replaced by a sense of doom. "I came to say goodbye properly Jean..." he left the rest of the sentence unspoken. "I guess you do it better."

He looked back at Zimani who had clutched the dressing gown around him. Kel turned and strode to the gate. He heard her calling after him, heard her bare feet on the gravel, heard her crying out in pain, and then he ran down the tree-lined street until her voice faded.

He caught a cab to Kings Cross to pick up his baggage and then took the tube to Euston where he booked onto the night train. He had three hours to kill. London hadn't changed, tramps in doorways, litter in the gutter, traffic charging past to the next set of traffic lights in a city of strangers.

He walked into the nearest pub and ordered a beer. Someone had left a copy of the Evening News on a corner seat. Jean was spread across the centre pages. The columnist had interviewed Zimani who had described Jean as one of the great, natural stars of the cinema. He chucked the paper on to the table and looked around the room. There were no women in the room and thirty men. A number of them were staring at him. He got up and left.

He sat numb on the train until it got to Dover, presented his passport at the ferry stage and then drank at the bar until they reached Dunkirk. The darkness hid the beaches on which his father had fought.

The sight of Zimani's gleaming squat body haunted him. The vision was still spinning in his head when he woke at the Gare du Nord on a damp cold dawn. The broad streets seemed to breathe in the mist as an ancient bus rattled over the cobbles to the Gare Austerlitz. He booked his ticket and sat drinking black coffee at the front of the station watching the swirl of people. Parisian women were not beautiful he decided, but they had a style and self-possession like no others.

He found an empty carriage and fell asleep among gloomy thoughts.

Autumn in Pau was akin to an English summer. He gripped his case in his left hand and made his way across the Grand Prix straight and up the slope towards the town.

His first call was at the Bar des Sports in Rue Montpensier where Madame alarmed the customers by shrieking in delight and flinging her arms around him.

She held him at arms length laughing like a little girl before startling an old man by plucking off his beret and plonking it on Kel's head. "This man he kiss me goodbye and then goes off to shag a film star," she laughed.

She stood back from him. "You have changed English. You are bigger and stronger. Perhaps we should warn the Parapluis eh?" She laughed again. "Your room is vacant but it will take an hour to have it ready." She leaned in to him and whispered in English "A disgusting man. He never empty his pisspot." She kissed him again. "Leave your baggage here and go for a walk. When you return your room will be ready."

He headed for the square at the southern end of the town and walked across to the hotel where he and Jean had said their first goodbyes. He stood there knowing his gesture was futile. But he had done it.

Alphonse, the tiny waiter at the Henri Quatre nodded to him He was standing in a corner puffing a Galois during his break but he stubbed it out and came across to take Kel's order. Kel took a seat at the bench the paratroopers had occupied and looked out into the square. There were no soldiers and no Eloise. The waiter said he had not seen her for a week. A young couple brought in their son and daughter to dine en famille and two teenage girls chatted about boyfriends at the bar. They glanced across to him but he avoided eye contact.

It was on the third night that she came. She had the same peaked cap as ever, she wore black as ever, she smoked a dark cheroot as ever, and her black eyes danced with mockery and fun at the sight of him.

"English," she called and she opened her arms in welcome. He pulled her small young body to him and they hugged in the middle of the café. She had the same vitality, the same spirit, the same fine madness, and he knew she always would.

He feared for her with sudden foreboding. Everything that touched him seemed to disintegrate. He bought her vodka, which she threw back in one with bravado.

"You weren't trained in Moscow were you?"

She leaned back, stretched her long, beautiful neck, and blew smoke rings to the ceiling where she watched them swished away by the fan.

Her large eyes turned on him; dark eyes, long lashes, and a white face ...her own individual sense of beauty among all the sunburned bodies.

They ordered another drink. The little girl began to scream that she had been given the wrong ice cream. Her mother yanked her from the table and slapped her bottom twice as she marched her to the door. The girl's brother grinned at her misfortune until his father snapped something at him threw some notes on the table and took the boy outside. The waiter advanced on the tip like a moth to light.

"I waited three nights for you," Kel reached out and squeezed her arm gently.

"I've been over the border. My brother needed help."

"Is he OK?"

She nodded. "He was lucky." She chose not to elaborate.

He changed the subject." Your letter said everything was ready."

"I need a picture of you."

"And the rest?"

"Let's walk and talk." She rose from the table and he followed her outside.

As they crossed the square in Place Clemenceau she linked her arm into his and he felt her small breast brush against him. She pulled him tighter to her. "Why?" she said.

"Why what?"

"Why did you ask for two guns?"

"I am going to kill two men."

He heard her laugh and then she pulled him sharply into her, turning him so that her lips found his. Her tongue slipped into his mouth but her eyes remained open. He lifted her easily so that her eyes were level with his and then he hugged her. She felt his tears on her neck and then she knew that he was serious.

"Who?" she said.

"They're in England."

"Why have you come here then?"

"An alibi."

CHAPTER TWENTY

Her new apartment, like the old one, was clad in marble but was larger and in a more prosperous area. A smattering of BMWs mingled with the Renaults, Citroens and Peugeots parked under the palm trees along the cul de sac.

The sitting room had one large, leather couch, a glass-topped table resting on a thick metal base, and two thin-legged padded chairs. A colour TV stood in the corner. Two beanbags were placed on a rug in front of the empty fireplace and subdued lighting from the panelled ceiling reflected off the polished parquet floor.

She opened a swing-hinged window at the back of the apartment and the muted sound of traffic filtered through a row of trees at the bottom of the garden.

"They're Elms," he said.

"The English. A hundred years ago this was the Resort Anglais." She laughed. "Now there is only you until the summer. "

He was about to speak but she raised her hand like a conductor before skipping through to the kitchen from where she returned with a carafe of wine, a bottle of whisky, and two glasses.

She poured the red wine for herself and a whisky for him. Then she dived back into the kitchen to pick up a bowl of ice cubes. She noticed him fingering his glass, feeling the quality of the heavy crystal.

"I qualified in the summer," she said.

"Courts?"

"Company Law."

She sipped her wine and smiled. "Tell me about the men."

He drank deep into his whisky and he told her of Billy, of the club, of the murder, and of Jean and Zimani. He told her everything with a rush of words until she asked him "Do you still love her?"

"She is gone."

"That is no answer." She leaned across the table and held his hand. The light from a small scented candle flickered in her eyes.

He sighed. "It's like you and I. We live in different worlds. And I don't like the people in her world."

"So you do love her still." She watched his body slump in answer.

His voice was low. "Once this is over it would be madness for her to come near me."

Eloise reached out to take his hand, which she held softly.

"Once I took a lover as revenge against my husband. But I still loved him."

Eloise ducked her head so that her large eyes looked up into his. "These men. Sometimes I think that you are playing a part."

He did not answer and she pursued him. "You must ask yourself this question because if this is all bravado these men will kill you or you will destroy yourself by killing them." She lit one of her cheroots and sent the smoke streaming up to the ceiling. "You have one great advantage. Everyone who meets you underestimates you. Everyone but me."

She laughed and walked back into the kitchen her hips swaying deliberately on each stride of her slim legs.

She returned with some cheese biscuits. This time she sat next to him. She took a deep drink of her wine and took hold of his right hand.

"Get drunk with me," she said simply. "There's some more whisky in the kitchen. Are you a good lover?" She saw him start in surprise. "Tell the truth," she said. "I intend to find out soon."

He refilled his glass and drank deeply.

"I can't get you a boat," she said. She saw him stoop in disappointment. "But there is another way...a second passport...you can go by train through France and Belgium to meet your fisherman...also I have contacts in Holland...the guns. When do you meet your trawler?"

"Three weeks."

"I'll take your photo tomorrow for the passport...a UK passport. Not French. Your French is not good enough."

He smiled as he watched her at work, a fierce little pixie suddenly full of energy. She faced danger every day and for him it was a new experience. For him there was an end in sight or at least a conclusion. For her perhaps years of struggle and then possibly death or torture and all around her the middle class citizens of Pau were getting on with their ordinary lives.

But to plant bombs that killed children as they played...there was no cause that could justify that. She had laughed fiercely at him when he had put the argument to her a year ago. "First I have never done that. But if I had I would still laugh at you. Do you think we invented it? The Americans dropped nuclear bombs on Japanese cities. The British and Americans bombed Dresden to the ground and murdered refugees. Do you think your armies were full of decent men as you conquered the world? Read the histories of other nations...you raped, tortured, and pillaged your way across continents." Then she had sunk from her anger.

The memory had leapt at him. A year ago he had despised her arguments. Yet here he was planning to kill two men for the murder of Billy...for Billy or for himself?"

He looked at the girl. "You don't think I will do it?"

She shook her head. "No, you have the courage to do it, but it takes a different courage to deal with life after you have killed someone. There is a difference between you and me. My fight goes on. Yours will end just like that." She snapped her fingers. "There will be no revenge to sustain you any more. It will be like making love. When it ends you will be empty and full of doubts. It's then you will be vulnerable."

He saw the truth in everything she said. "What can I do?" he asked.

"Hunt your film star." She reached out and pulled his passive head to her chest and her long, thin fingers ruffled the curls at the base of his neck, exposing the white unburned skin. She pulled him to her thin, boyish body with a sudden passion.

Of all the women he had made love to she was the most petite. Strong for her size but so light he found he could lift her body to any position where, boiling with desire, she bobbed on him calling out his name.

Later she kissed him softly and fell asleep. He lay on her steel-framed bed, eyes open, mind shut. The subdued lighting from the sitting room intruded shyly through the open door.

The bedroom, like the sitting room, had a high ceiling and the minimum amount of furnishing, which gave it a feeling of space. She lay loose-limbed on her belly, the woollen blanket cast aside, her legs splayed, her breath warm on his arm, and he knew that this was the beginning of the end for them. Across the square a church clock chimed into the night. He remembered Fran's painting of the man and woman in the cold moonlight.

Eloise, Jean, and Fran, had he met them all passing?

In the morning she padded over the marble floor, barefoot, bare everything, carrying a plate of hard-boiled eggs. They ate in silence and then she reached into a bedside table and pulled out a Polaroid camera. He pulled on a shirt and sat straight-backed against the white wall behind the bed. The camera flashed twice and a few seconds later she examined the photographs.

"Handsome bastard." She grinned at him.

"Are you complaining?"

"Oh no. Very pleased to take advantage of handsome English man. That is good. But you will stand out in a crowd and that is bad." It was eight in the morning and already she was the Little General, albeit one without a uniform or indeed, any clothes at all, as she wagged an admonishing finger at him from the bottom of the bed.

He reached for her with sudden tenderness but she misread his intentions and avoided his grasp. She moved quickly to the wardrobe, which filled the far wall and operated on a system of revolving trollies. She pulled at the doors that slid open with expensive smoothness to reveal racks of clothes and shoes. She reached into a drawer and pulled out a pair of black lace panties, which she slipped over her small white bottom. "Time for work," she said brightly.

The days passed quickly in a rhythm of their own. In the evenings they drank at the Henri Quatre or walked the long boulevards at the southern end of the town. Sometimes they sat under the palm trees in the main square where he and Jean had first embraced. .

She found him a place to train in the east end of the town. It was a typical boxer's gym with the smell of sweat trapped by the low ceiling in the gloomy main room. There was one, roped ring and a variety of punch bags and speedballs. About a dozen young men eyed him as he walked in on the first night noting the pressed jeans and the tapered, open-necked shirt. They noted too the slim, well-dressed lady who introduced him to Jean Paul, the owner of the gym. Kel stripped off his jeans and shirt to reveal his new training shorts and vest. He appeared to have difficulty taping his hands.

"Can you?" He spoke with a slight lisp as he held out his fists to Jean Paul.

The owner shrugged, spat some chewing gum on to the floor, and tightened the bandages.

Eloise noted the change in Kel's demeanour. Gone was the confident young man with the spring in his step and in his place was a hesitant foreigner who appeared not to belong in these surroundings. Gone too was the fluent French. The accent was more pronounced and hesitant. For a second she too was taken in and she feared for him. Then he turned so he was facing her only, and gave a slow wink.

He spoke to Jean Paul in a slow, thin voice. "I'm told you have a match coming up... perhaps I could spar with some of your team...if it would help."

Jean Paul looked doubtful. He'd already dismissed Kel as a waste of time but he owed favours to the lawyer lady.

"Do you not want to warm up?"

Kel smiled. "Oh I'll warm up as I spar I expect."

Jean Paul looked closely at Kel and didn't like what he saw. At best the Englishman was an unwelcome distraction ahead of the contest, at worst a bloody nuisance. And he looked more like a model than a fighter. He decided the sooner gone the better and shrugged. "Very well we'll see how you go." He motioned to a tall, well-muscled man whose body was gleaming with sweat from his workout. "Maurice? Do you fancy some sparring?"

Maurice nodded. His black hair glistened in the strip lighting and his dark eyes sought out the Englishman looking for signs of nerves or fear. He raised his fist to his chin and wiped his bandaged hand across a two-day stubble. He thrust the stained tapes into a pair of large sparring gloves.

"Certainly Monsieur...how many seconds do you wish."

Kel laughed as though trying to turn the insult into a joke. "We'll take it as it comes shall we." He held out his hands and Jean Paul plunged two gloves over his taped hands.

Kel appeared to stumble as he climbed into the ring. The other boxers were grinning openly now, anticipating the sudden demise of this foreign impostor.

Jean Paul wiped the sweat from his baldhead on the sleeve of his dark shirt and turned to Eloise." Your friend. He has boxed before hasn't he?"

Eloise gave a flamboyant, and purely French, shrug. "I think so. He seemed very keen. He's English you know."

Jean Paul shook his head. "All the Englishmen I met during the war seemed very concerned with survival. This man Maurice is good."

To back his words he gestured to the other boxers who had gathered round the ring like animals at feeding time.

Eloise looked up to the ring as the two men squared up to each other.

The contrast was startling...the white chunky body of the Frenchman with tufts of dark hair sprouting from the edge of his vest, the eyes narrowed to slits, the chin half shaved and the head gleaming through thinning, sweat-damp hair... and Kel, four inches taller, tanned with a sculptured body, and the whites of his eyes flashing. She looked back to Maurice and Jean Paul seemed to read her thoughts. "Fighters deliberately make themselves look mean to live in the mood," he whispered.

She turned to the ring. "It's like one of those ridiculous films where the handsome hero triumphs over the ugly villain."

Jean Paul shook his head eloquently. "I don't think Maurice has read the script."

As he spoke Maurice moved forward quickly throwing out a left jab for distance and then following up with a right cross. Kel caught the left on his gloves and then swayed slightly to his right so that Maurice's second punch went past his head. Maurice's momentum took him forward and at the last second he ducked his head into Kel's face catching him high on the right cheekbone. Charlotte could see the small lump as Kel stepped back. Maurice grinned as the two squared up again and made to move forward. He threw another left and right as he closed in. This time Kel did not move but caught both punches on his gloves and then dipped his legs so that his head bobbed up into the Frenchman's face.

The fighters separated and the boxers at the ringside shouted encouragement to Maurice who angrily wiped blood from his nose and prepared to move in once more. But before he could do so Kel jabbed out two straight lefts then, as the Frenchman's hands came up, sent a left hook under Maurice's short ribs and into his liver. Maurice froze in agony but before he could fall to the floor Kel moved in. There seemed no rush, no urgency, as the quick short step forward allowed him to dip his body and retain his balance as he threw three punches. They came with such speed that had they been merely arm punches they would have been damaging, but the precision of his movement, and the confidence that allowed him to move in close, meant that they had the full weight of his body behind them. There was a gasp from the boxers round the ring as Maurice spun away into the ropes which then propelled him forward on to the canvas where he lay still.

Kel stooped over him, and pulled the gum shield from the Frenchman's mouth.

He did not look at the other fighters who were standing in awed silence beneath him. His eyes sought out Jean Paul who was standing with Eloise at the back of the gym and this time when he spoke his French was clear and his voice strong.

"He shouldn't have butted me."

Eloise came away from the moment to find herself gripping Jean Paul's arm. "My God," she said, "My God."

She watched as the boxers round the ring parted to let Kel through. He stood in front of them breathing easily, the raised lump under his eye the only indication that he had been involved in a fight.

"His nose is broken," Kel told Marcel. "If you wish I will take his place in the tournament."

Eloise recognised she had just witnessed something special. This Englishman had walked into a hostile place; full of tough men who had obviously derided him, and within twenty minutes had taken control.

Outside as they walked back to the square she clung to his arm and told him "You're one crazy bastard! You know that don't you. "

He smiled "You believe me now."

Eloise busied herself finalising the arrangements for his trip. Each morning he returned to the gym to spar and train. Each afternoon he took her bike up into the mountains and rode along rough trails.

It was a week before Maurice reappeared at the gym. . His nose had a dark bruise and both eyes were swollen. He stood at the back of the hall watching Kel work the heavy bag, noting the balance, the slight move of the feet and hips that unleashed the body weight behind his punches. After ten minutes Kel stepped back to towel his sweating body and Maurice moved to his side.

The other boxers stopped their work as the two men faced each other in the yellow lamplight.

They stood in silence for a second and then Kel smiled and held out his hand. Maurice took the hand and then embraced Kel.

A week passed quickly. Kel abandoned his room at the Bar des Sports and moved in with Eloise. For a few days each helped the other escape from their own reality. They dined in cheap bars, walked the town together, and sat out on the boulevard looking out to the mountains. He sampled the delights of French onion soup, sunbathing with his clothes on, and making love with Eloise each night.

Then his passport arrived, suitably aged. His new name was Bill Bryant. Eloise smiled bravely. "Soon it will be time to go," she said.

That afternoon Madame from the Bar des Sports called at the apartment "Ello Anglais," she smiled. "I have a letter for you." He didn't open it .He walked into the sitting room and laid it gently down on the table. It lay for a second as Eloise looked at the envelope and then at Kel. She noted the expensive paper, the neat looping handwriting, the deep blue ink from a fountain pen, and the stony look on Kel's face.

"Open it then."

But he shook his head.

"She may still love you and you her."

He looked into the deep dark eyes seeking signs of sadness. There were none. Instead her eyes were soft with pity. "If I felt I was falling in love with you Kel I would walk away. You knew that from the start."

She moved into him and kissed him slow and soft, writhing her slim body against his groin. For a while he was held by the confusion of his emotions and then her expert hands weaned him away to more basic needs. They made love in desperation. It was as though as long as their twining bodies could writhe, pump, scratch, and pulsate they could stay in a world of their own making. Then, when they lay gasping and defeated, she slid her body across his and reached for the letter.

He lay, eyes closed, as he heard her tear open the envelope. There was silence and then she announced. "She wants to meet you on your beach. She says there are things that she cannot write but that she can only say. She says...."Eloise pulled a face and smiled. "She says a lot." She tossed the letter across the table out of his reach and then slid off his body, off the bed, on to the floor where she rolled over giggling. She got to her feet quickly, wrapped herself in a towel, and disappeared into the bathroom. Through the hiss of the shower she shouted. "Time is running out. We must get to work."

He was still lying on the bed when she returned. Eloise looked at the letter, which lay where she had flung it, and then she looked at him.

As she dressed she told him. "Today I am needed elsewhere."

He rolled over in the bed to look at her. "I'm off to Ogeu," he said.

He caught the crowded bus to the village and walked to the bistro. Half a dozen labourers were sitting at a long wooden bench sipping red wine. Their conversation stopped as he walked across the stone floor.

"The owner. Is he here?"

A short stocky man with a purple face stood up. "Monsieur?"

"You have a hunting lodge near the mountains?"

The man gestured Kel towards a back room.

The others began to talk in ancient French, to create a distance from the Englishman.

The back room was more fashionably furnished though the stone floor was still bare. The patron ushered Kel to a lumpy sofa and offered him some wine.

Kel shook his head.

"Eloise told me you would call...." He hesitated. "She said you would wish the lodge for three weeks...for a holiday." He did his best to hide his disbelief.

"Yes," Kel smiled. "I wish to do some writing."

"Ah writing."

"And training. I'm going to have a fight."

"Ah a fight. Pardon Monsieur. Such things I do not want to know."

"A boxing match," Kel explained.

"Ah yes a boxing match."

"I will need some supplies."

"Ah yes supplies," the owner smiled.

For a week he stayed in the primitive lodge on his own, training by the stream that ran down from the mountains, shadow sparring at the edge of the woods, doing press-ups on one arm and then the other, drinking bottled water, and eating fresh food from the village. At last it was time to go. He bought a week's supplies from the patron, dumped them in the lodge and that night he slipped round the sleeping village, aided by a bright moon. A mile to the north Eloise was waiting for him on her bike. They glided along curved lanes through lifeless fields, their colour bleached by the white light of the moon. Neither spoke but he shivered. It was as though the scene about him had been painted with a bloodless hand.

They sat in her apartment waiting for time to move them on. Her large eyes held steady under his gaze. She was wearing a trim blue skirt and neat white blouse. A red ribbon tied her short hair in the beginning of a ponytail. She could have passed for a schoolgirl. "I shall pray for you," she said.

A clocked ticked in the corner. He had never heard it before but it had been there. It struck five and he stood up.

"Time to go," he announced, aware the words were unnecessary.

She smiled.

"It's better I walk to the station." Kel managed to keep his voice steady.

They embraced and he walked towards the door.

He turned. "Thank you Eloise. I'll see you in three days." He tried to sound confident.

She smiled at his retreating figure until the door closed and in the empty room fought back tears.

CHAPTER TWENTY ONE

Kel carried a small hold-all for his spare clothes.

Across the tracks in the station's café, where he had waited for Paul, a jukebox played a haunting song called A Mourir Pour Mourir by Barbara. The train came, and left, on time as usual and he slept most of the way to Gare Austerlitz from where he took a bus to the Gare du Nord.

There was a two-hour gap before he could take the train to The Hague via Amsterdam. From there he caught a bus to the resort of Scheveningen. He glanced at his watch. It was six in the evening and he was tired, unwashed, and unshaven. He found a small hotel near the front, near the giant pier on which someone had stuck a building, which seemed to be a model of the London Post Office tower. As he looked from his window along the long promenade the town had that strange atmosphere of emptiness common to all resorts out of season.

He slept in a huge, soft bed under a large eiderdown.

In the morning he made his way into the centre of the town through narrow streets with high-walled houses that were decorated with verandas and baskets of flowers.

He followed the map Eloise had given him and after some twenty minutes moved up a side street and knocked on a blue door.

The woman who answered was pretty, in her twenties, and stoned out of her mind. She held together a housecoat with difficulty, which she seemed to find amusing. Her glazed eyes examined him calmly and her lips pouted in approval.

"Eloise sent me to see Sam," he said.

"Eloise eh. You're early."

"Is Sam in?"

She laughed in such a lazy fashion that he suspected she was laughing at him.

"I'm Sam," she said pulling deeply on her smoke. "Sam as in Samantha."

"Eloise didn't say."

He moved into the doorway forcing her to retreat into the hall. There was no carpet and his feet sounded on the polished wood." Have you got the stuff?" He lowered his voice.

"Have you got the money?"

He pushed her suddenly and with force so that she fell backwards to the floor .Her housecoat fell away. She was naked. He felt the fear in her as she tried to gather her clothing.

Sam tried to get up but he pushed her down again. Her body gleamed white in the half-light. "Listen you crazy bitch. You know there's no money involved. What do you think's going to happen when Eloise hears of this?"

She lay on the floor not bothering to cover her body this time. "I need some money," she pleaded.

He looked down and saw the scars on her inner arm.

"Here," He pressed some notes into her hand and helped her to her feet. She ignored him and began counting the money.

Kel watched her in silence. Her desperation was at once piteous and alarming.

She finished counting the notes and, without another word, walked down the hall and into the kitchen. He followed her and watched as she reached into the fridge and brought out a plastic packet, which she handed to him.

Inside were two guns and a packet of ammunition.

"The Luger's been tested." The man's voice came from the hall doorway. Kel swung round to see a short fat man with slits for eyes. He grinned showing broken teeth. "The revolver's full of empty shells as you asked." He smiled again. "Sorry about Sam. She's the front line. He held up a photograph, a replica of Kel's passport picture. You might have been a plant."

Kel nodded, relieved that Eloise was dealing with people who had a veneer of professionalism.

"There's a bag," said the fat man gesturing towards a small black leather hold-all on the table. "And I have to return your photograph. Eloise said."

Kel put the picture in a pocket and pushed the two guns into the bag.

"You're early," said the fat man. "You took us by surprise. If you want to pass the time..." he left the sentence there. The girl grinned .Her housecoat had slipped open again. He thought of Fran, of Jean, of Eloise, of the dozens of girls before them whose minds and bodies he had touched however briefly. But this girl lived in the cul de sac of her next fix and as she leaned back against the kitchen table, exposing the gleam of her naked belly, smiling her lampoon of a seductive smile, he felt the cutting edge between life and death. She was pretty, shapely, and repulsive.

He forced himself into a smile. "Things to do. Too tense."

The fat man's face lit briefly with knowledge. "You've never used a gun before have you." He didn't wait for a reply. "Get close and fire low. The second one's the killer but the first is the one that counts." He had been staring at the girl as he spoke but now he turned to Kel. "It's the shock you see...that's what freezes them...then you can move close and ..." He put his finger to his mouth and grinned. As the man raised his hand Kel saw the stain of sweat on his cotton shirt from his armpit.

"You've tested the Luger?"

The man took the gun and walked over to the fireplace. There was an explosion that banged into Kel's ears as he fired the gun up the chimney. Soot and chips of broken bricks exploded from the fireplace into the room,

The man stood grinning.

Kel tried to disguise his shock.

Outside the air was fresh as he walked towards the coast. He stood on the grass verge looking out across the beach towards the pier and then turned north .The beach was long and empty save for a couple walking a mongrel dog. He walked for four hundred yards and looked out at the grey, rolling seas. Then he returned to his room, put the smaller hold-all into the larger one he'd brought from Pau. Time was moving him on again. He paid his bill, collected his passport, pulled on his thick jacket and walked slowly towards the beach. A mile to the north of the large pier he stopped to stare out to sea, waiting for his boat to come in.

The beach was deserted and he sat on the grass that held the no man's land between sand and land. He thought of Puccini and the ships at sea; he remembered Jean crying on the phone from London, but his sharpest memory was of Billy jogging the long sands at Tynemouth, the sweat steaming from the track suit that covered his short immense body, that, and how his face had lit up like a child at Christmas when he'd seen the rows of books in his flat.

The trawler came out of the horizon silent and slow and he watched as it shed a small dinghy that splashed its way across the flat sea to the shore.

He stood up, waved, and then walked down across the beach to the water's edge.

The boat came to a bobbing halt some twenty yards from the waterline and he waded out through the numbing cold.

He nodded to the two oarsmen. "Arnold aboard?"

"Aye," The nearer of the two men helped him clamber into the dinghy. The smell of fish hung over them even in the cold fresh air. They did not speak as they deftly turned the boat to sea and rowed with easy rhythm.

Kel glanced back to the shore. A man, a distance along the beach, had stopped walking his dog to stare at them. Kel waved and the man waved back, a small Lowry-like figure.

Arnold helped him up the rope ladder as the crew pulled in the dinghy.

He had prepared a meal, a steaming cup of cocoa, some baked beans, and fish fingers.

"They'll not eat owt else," Arnold apologised.

Kel sipped at the tea.

"What have you told them?"

"Just that we're picking up an illegal cargo. They don't want to know. They'll take a bung though."

"How much do I owe you?"

"Just do a good job." He waved aside Kel's protest. "We've had a good catch on the way down." He sipped on his tea and belched. "The truth is he saved me once. There was a hard team after me and he saved me." He shook his head at the memory. "He was a bit like a poliss you know. Except more effective." Arnold did not elaborate.

The crew were packing ice round the fish and Kel sat in a screwed down bunk trying to fend off the rocking motion of the boat. He vomited twice into a carrier bag before falling into a fitful sleep.

It was dark when he awoke to the touch of Arnold's hand on his shoulder. To the bow of the boat he could make out the shape of Holy Island with the castle gleaming in the moonlight. There were no lights from the village but between the island and the Northumberland coastline he could see the stumps of the causeway refuge posts rising like sentries out of the receding tide.

Kel clung to his holdall as the dinghy was thrown about by the waves.

Arnold's voice came out of the dark behind him." We're taking you in two hundred yards south of the causeway. Will you get your bearings?"

"Aye."

Five minutes later the dinghy hit sand and he jumped over the side up to his knees in the cold North Sea.

Arnold leaned into him. "Don't worry. No one will talk. The rest is up to you." He squeezed Kel's arm and called in a low voice for them to turn.

Kel waded towards the shore and, by the time he had turned, the dinghy was lost against the sea and all he could make out of the trawler was a twinkling light from the deck. A cloud overtook the moon and Kel froze in panic as he lost his bearings in the total darkness. He stood in the numbing cold for up to a minute before the moon glided out again lighting the dunes to his right. He waded quickly to the beach and made his way inland until he found a narrow lane. Halfway down he unlocked the white door to a garage and moved quickly inside, closing the door behind him.

He turned on the light, and took a change of clothes from his bag, before reaching for his leathers and helmet which were hanging from hooks on the far wall. It was five thirty. He had an hour to spare and some checks to do.

The stolen Norton had been resting on blocks for a month now, black, shining, and silent. The tyres were still hard and the engine started at the second attempt and settled into a low purr as he turned down the throttle. He cut the engine, opened the door, and pushed the bike out into the dark, silent streets.

The sweat was running like lice under his leathers by the time he reached the causeway. He waited for five minutes for the moon to come out and in the saintly, white light saw that the receding tide was all but clear of the road.

He pushed the bike another hundred yards into the causeway, mounted it, and rode off on a low throttle.

The purr of the engine could not drown the sound of the receding tide which took him with Pavlovian suddenness back to Paul who in his early days on the Chronicle had walked into the office, fresh from University, assertive and cocky. His first job had been to write out the Holy Island crossing times, a chore he which he regarded as an insult to his talents.

A week later an angry reader was demanding compensation for the loss if his mini car and redress for himself and his wife who'd spent three hours stuck up one of the refuge poles.

Paul had shrugged off the incident to Dave and Kel. "If they're stupid enough to take our times and ignore the official posters..."he'd left the statement unfinished.

Kel reached the end of the causeway unscathed and paused for one last look at the silhouette of the castle standing almost precariously on its steep knoll.

As he turned the bike towards Beal and the A1 he knew there was no turning back. During the past few weeks he had had doubts about himself and about what he was planning to do. Part of the time he had evaded the reality by inventing himself as the hero in a paperback novel which, in the hyperbole of the day, had him gunning his bike away from the island and speeding like an arrow down the A1.

But much more potent than that transparent fantasy had been the reality of his memory of Billy, eye to eye, seeking an answer to his question: "Are you in to the finish?"

That and how Billy had spat on his hand before offering it to Kel.

He'd laughed at the time but he shivered at the memory now because he knew that to Billy the spitting had been a bond stronger than one written on paper, stronger than the law... it was a bond between the spirits of two men... primitive and powerful. There was no going back not without betraying Billy and betraying himself.

He turned on to the A1 and headed south at a steady 50mph feeling the bike out. The road was clear apart from the occasion lorry until he hit the early part of the morning rush hour at Gosforth, three miles north of the city. His bike took him through the lines of traffic and it was only a few minutes before he was turning right up the Grandstand Road and cruising in a loop round the vast Town Moor to the West End of the city.

He parked in a side road near a row of motorcycle shops, crossed Westgate Road, turned up a short lane and was confronted by a row of large terraced houses.

They'd escaped the purge of west end building programme, some said, because they were out of sight and therefore out of mind. But Kel knew the real reason they were still standing. Conway had bought them. The deal was local knowledge, which in itself was enough to secure their defence from vandals. But as an added security Conway had installed Big George at number three.

Kel looked along the short street and saw a scene of slow decay. A hundred years ago these grand places had had servants to tend to them and horses with carriages had trotted along the cobbled streets. Now it looked like a street that had died.

He walked up the stone steps to number three, lifted the letterbox, and sniffed.

There was none of the damp musty smell of an empty house. He knocked heavily on the door.

There was no reply. He knocked again and this time opened the letterbox and shouted "Telegram. Telegram."

He heard the padding of bare feet and a few seconds later the sound of chains being removed. The door opened ajar.

Big George did not speak but held out his hand for the telegram. Kel offered it to him, but at the last moment leaned forward and pushed at the door sending Big George staggering back.

"Bad news George."

Big George regained his balance quickly and came forward but he stopped short at the sight of the gun in Kel's left hand. Kel kicked at the door behind him sending it crashing shut. For the first time Big George showed fear.

"Give me a chance. At least tell me what it's about."

"Sure." Kel slowly lifted the visor of his helmet but the gun was steady and out of reach.

Big George's face opened in astonishment as he recognised Kel. There was hope there too because this was the weak man who'd crumbled before Conway as soon as Billy had been killed. The man who'd squealed with fear and pain when they'd roughed him up in the club.

His mind was racing." We can do a deal."

Kel smiled. "Yeah we can do a deal. The sort of deal you gave Billy." And with that he aimed for Big George's stomach and fired. The bullet took him in the chest and sent him flying back to the far end of the hall where he slid gently down the wall. It was as if the world had gone into slow motion and then Kel stepped forward put the gun in George's open mouth and fired again. He felt the spray of blood and brain as the bullet burst a fist sized hole through the back of George's head. He ran through to the kitchen and vomited into the sink. A damp cloth hung from the tap. He wiped down his face and leathers, ran the sink until it was clean, threw the cloth on to the remnants of a coal fire and watched it flicker and then burn. His hands were shaking violently.

Big George's dead eyes stared at him as he left the house.

His bike started first time. A trolley bus tooted its horn as he came out of the side street and he raised his hand in apology before heading up the west road to wait for the night.

CHAPTER TWENTY TWO

The sign on the large warehouse read "FR D MORLEY Construction" because the letter E had been blown off in recent gales and no one had thought it worth the expense of replacing it. Either way it would not have fooled any of the locals who knew that Fred Morley was just a front for the business which was, in reality, run by Kenny Conway. The battered wooden door was never locked because every thief knew the consequences of stealing from Kenny.

On this particular night the premises were safer than ever because Conway's dark Jaguar was parked in the muddy drive.

The door creaked as Kel pushed it gently ajar and stared into the cavernous building. It was here that he had watched Billy demolish the boxer Casey in front of five hundred screaming fans..."The feeding of the Five Hundred," he'd called it at the time. It was here, it was rumoured, that Gary had been taken before his body had been fed into a furnace, and it was here that Conway met his bagman Big George every Friday.

The stone floor was clear except for a scattering of bricks and two bags of cement piled in the far corner.

Across the warehouse, and to the right, some wooden steps led up round ninety degrees to a small office. From there a pale light made a feeble attempt to illuminate the main body of the warehouse.

The stairs gave slightly beneath his weight .One day they would snap, but not tonight. He pushed open the door. Conway was sitting across a stained wooden desk, feet up, reading the Evening Chronicle. Kel had time to read the back page headline (which told him that Newcastle had signed someone called Sinclair) before Conway spoke from behind the paper.

"Everything alright George." It wasn't a question but Kel chose to treat it as one.

"No it's not, Kenny."

Conway slapped the paper down at the sound of Kel's voice and his feet slipped from the desk. Kel gestured to the Chronicle "I'm first with the news tonight Kenny. Big George is dead."

Conway's red face glared at him. "What the hell are you doing here?" he snapped.

And then his brain caught up with the latest development. "Dead. What the hell do you mean?"

"I killed him this morning."

Conway snorted with disdain. "You...you couldn't kill a mouse without shitting yourself."

Kel smiled. Half of courage was confidence in yourself and disdain of others, and Conway had plenty of both. “Wrong Conway. I’m tougher then you think.”

As the two stared at each other in silence Conway tried to work out any other explanation for Kel confronting him in this manner, other than the one which he had been given. He failed.

“Maybe, maybe you are,” he said. “What’s all this about?”

“It’s about my mate and your two bastards who killed him.”

“Who’s told you this shite? It was a team from Leeds.”

“I saw George drive the car at him.”

“Bollocks. George works for me.”

“I saw him.”

For the first time he saw doubt in Conway’s face...if what Kel said was true he had been dealing with a different animal all along. He remembered the respect Billy had had for him. His fingers drummed on the stained desktop. He looked at his watch. If George was just late...nothing made sense. If George was dead...everything fitted. He looked across the desk at the young man standing opposite. The Pretty Boy, he’d called him to his friends. The sort who got it up the arse in jail, and they’d all laughed. Conway stopped drumming the table and raised his hand to ease his collar.

“So what happens now?” he heard himself say.

Kel drew the two handguns from his holdall. “One of us dies tonight.” He looked across the table at the big man and saw the neck had gone as red as the face.

Outside a car tooted its horn. Kenny’s eyes sought the window at this sound from another world, a world he so desperately wanted to rejoin.

“Can we do a deal?” His voice was strained and quiet.

“We did one and you killed Billy.”

“What’s he to you for Christ sakes. He was a two-bit thug who did things that made me look like a saint.”

“But always from the front. And he was nothing like you.”

“Maybe, maybe. But this can’t be worth dying for.”

“We’re wasting time.” Kel held out the handguns. “This,” he said waving the gun in his right hand is what’s called a revolver and we’re going to play Russian Roulette with it. And this,” he said waving the gun in his left hand is a clip loading German Luger which I’m going to use on you if you attempt to cheat in any way.”

“You’re fucking mad.” Conway lunged across the table but Kel stepped back and pointed the Luger into Conway’s head using the barrel to push him back into his seat.

“There are six chambers and only one loaded. So it’s five to one in your favour if you keep the gun pointed at your head.” He smiled watching the sweat break out on the big man, watching the fear build up, watching the swagger drain away until in it's place there remained an overweight, unfit shell of a middle aged man who, for the first time in his life, knew he was the hunted and not the hunter.

He felt the most delicious sense of revenge as he reached into his pocket and pulled out a half a crown which he spun on the desktop.

"Call," he said. But Conway was incapable of calling. His face had gone purple.

Kel sighed and in a gentle voice said, "Tails!" just before the coin lost its momentum and teetered over. It lay heads up.

Conway began to giggle and spittle bubbled from his lips. Kel smiled.

"Well," he said. "It looks like I get first shot."

Conway stared at him in horror. "You stupid bastard. I'll do a deal."

Kel grinned. Conway's mouth had gone slack and saliva was dribbling down his chin as Kel put the gun to his temple.

"If I lose I'd prefer to be cremated," he said. "I gather you're rather good at that."

Conway looked like a man who has forgotten how to breathe as Kel winked at him and then pulled the trigger.

A loud click seemed to fill the office to its walls. Conway stood up; his lips dry, his face shiny. His neck had burst away the top button of his shirt and sweat was running in rivulets down to his chest. The bully in him had gone and with it any semblance of composure. He stared in horror as Kel winked at him again. "I used to tell the girls I fired blanks."

Conway tried to speak but found his throat was too dry. At last he croaked, "You're fucking mad." For the first time in his life he felt completely powerless, lonely, confused, and the pain in his chest was stabbing into his consciousness.

"You know I think you're right. Here." He handed Conway the revolver. "Your turn."

Conway found the gun in his hand. He was not aware of reaching out to grasp the weapon but evidently he had. But most unsettling of all was the disparity between the other man's cheerful tone of speech and the deadly scene he was orchestrating.

The Luger was pointed at the centre of his chest where the pain raged.

"Your turn," he heard Kel say as though he was asking him to choose from a box of sweets. "I'll give you ten seconds then I'll fire."

Their eyes met and Conway knew his only chance of survival was to pull the trigger. The pain in his chest was intense. His head throbbed until it was painful to open his eyes. He kept them shut and pulled the trigger. There was a loud click and Conway laughed hysterically. "I did it! I did it!"

Kel smiled and took the gun. "Your hand was shaking so much you'd have missed any way." He spun the chambers, pointed the gun to his temple and pulled the trigger. There was another click and he handed the gun back to Conway.

Conway stared at him open mouthed. There was no pretence at dignity now. In a hoarse whisper he looked pleadingly into Kel's eyes. "I...I can't do it."

The Luger pointed at his chest was steady." Come on tough guy. It's your only chance to stay alive."

Conway gave a sigh that sounded like the last breath of a dying man. He was now so hypnotised by the situation that he forgot to plea. The arm holding the gun that curved in a slow arc to his head seemed to belong to someone else. He closed his eyes once more and slowly, almost tenderly he pulled the trigger.

The explosion burst into his ears. He screamed, as the pounding pain in his chest seemed to burst out of his breast. He could no longer see Kel through the red mist. To breathe was agony. He slipped to the floor and through all the pain he was dimly aware of one thing, in the far corner of the room a moonbeam pierced through a fist-sized hole in the corrugated iron roof. A hole made by the bullet from Kel's Luger. He saw Kel's lips move but by now blood was coursing through his thin veins crashing in through the aortic valves with a pressure that would not be denied. He stared hard as Kel's mouth moved but did not hear as the young man leaned into him and took the revolver. "Look no bullets Kenny." And then at last there was some comprehension as he saw the smoking Luger.

He started to cough and the pain was such that he slipped away.

Kel stood over him until the struggle for life ended. He waited a further thirty seconds and then removed his thin leather gloves to feel for a pulse. He pressed into the sweaty, fat neck. There was nothing.

He wiped the Luger free of prints and placed into the desk drawer, and then dropped the revolver into his holdall.

Kel pulled on his helmet, zipped up his leathers, and strode out into the night where the cold air hit him like a wave of water. He walked past the Jaguar and up the lane to where his bike rested on a hard surface in the shadows. He looked at his watch. He had three hours before he met Arnold.

The in-tide was lapping gently over the causeway as he sat looking out into the moonlight that lay like glass upon the water. The shape of the boat shivered in the silver light. He stood up, flashed his torch and walked to the water's edge. A dinghy tipped out into the calm and nosed its way through the flat sea. To his left the castle stood on a dark fist of land. All was calm and still except for the dingy that moved in slow even strokes like a boat across the Styx. Arnold looked for clues in Kel's face but saw none.

"Done?" he asked at last.

Kel nodded and together they loaded the bike onto the boat.

We'll dump it further out." Arnold gestured with his head towards the open sea.

"This too." Kel pointed to the revolver in his holdall.

The two of them sat side by side at the oars. They began to row towards the trawler.

Arnold put his back into the oar. "Time of a cup of tea," he grinned. "Then we'll dump the stuff."

CHAPTER TWENTY THREE

Eloise met Kel at the station. A group of Service Militaire soldiers were still straggling along the platform as the train ground its way towards the mountains on its journey to Madrid. It was 6.30 in the morning and the soldiers filled the cavernous platform with false laughter and bravado as they made their way through the grainy light, reluctant to accept that their leave was over.

Eloise had left her short black hair uncovered, a cheroot was smouldering between her lips, and her head was angled high as she stared at him.

"You look OK. Are you OK?"

He smiled, tired from the journey. "I think so. It's odd; I keep waiting for an overwhelming emotion of grief, remorse, or even triumph. But so far there has been nothing." He shrugged. "I want it to be over. But I don't think it is."

She linked her arm in his. "It will be over when you move on." She stepped out with her proud, high step, humming softly a tune he did not know.

They were through the triple arches of the station portico now and crossing the Grand Prix finishing straight. A milk cart tooted a warning as it crossed the finishing line at 10 mph. They hurried across the road.

"I thought you would rather walk," she said.

He stared up towards the shape of the town. "You would have loved Billy," he said in a flat voice that did not require her presence. She saw the tears as they slipped down his face. " I can feel his loss. Perhaps that's moving on."

She pulled on his arm for attention. "You have done everything he would have done for you. This is about you now. About how to survive."

"I'm a killer now!" He was transfixed by the thought.

"No! The men you killed; they were killers. You..." she searched quickly for the appropriate words. "You were an instrument of justice." She pulled at his arm.

"Do you believe that?" He knew in his heart that it was at best a simplification but her voice filled with certainty. "Of course. We are of a kind you and I. We both have duties...you to your friends, I to my people."

They spent the day in town and then she gave him a lift to the mountains, through the village, until the road became a dirt track, and finally across the open land to his lodge. He lit the metal stove and they drank black coffee.

Outside a thin rain was falling. She built up the stove and snuggled against him under a blanket. She fell into a light sleep as he lay still beside her. She woke fully clothed aware of the warmth from his body and in the glow from the stove she saw him staring up into the log roof. She was torn by a terrible sadness as in the gloom of the room she realised with sudden and terrible clarity that this was the end for them. "I must go. Some business." She fought to keep her voice steady.

He smiled "I'll miss you Eloise."

She put a finger to his lips. "A long life and a quick death English."

He moved her hand away from his mouth. "How long are you away?"

She had her back to the stove so her face was in shadow but he felt the catch in her voice. "Until you are gone Kel. You will write though. "

"You are not coming to the fight?"

She lit one of her little cheroots and blew defiantly to the ceiling. "My God you are not going on with that."

"I need my name in the papers." He grasped her arm. "Stay a while."

She smiled. "Best I go before we ...like each other too much." She handed him her black cap. "Here. It will bring you luck."

He was filled with a sudden panic that the dead men would invade his mind in the silence after she left. He watched as she turned to face him at the door. She must have seen the fear in his face because she ran back to him and crushed his lips with hers. Then he felt her leave his body and she whispered. "You are strong like me. You will survive this. You got justice for your friend. Follow your star. Your film star," she smiled away her tears. "Write to me."

This time she did not turn as she reached the door and she left him in the emptiness of the room.

He fell asleep on the thin mattress and woke to the sound of birds singing in the early light. His holdall was packed. He left two tins of baked beans on the wooden shelf above the stone sink. The large key moved smoothly in the oiled lock. The clear mountain air invaded his lungs causing him to cough. He followed the worn track into the mountains and sat by the stream into which a year ago he had thrown his writing. He had wanted Eloise to spend this last day with him but understood her reluctance. He was leaving, always leaving.

There was still one last task before he left the mountain. He took out a clasp knife and cut into the soft turf on the bank. When he'd dug a hole six inches deep he took out his false passport from the holdall, tore out his picture and buried the book. It was the final piece of evidence. He looked back down the valley to the small farms with red tile roofs and smoke curling from the chimneys.

He sighed, rose slowly to his feet, and began the long walk down to the village. After half an hour he picked up the cow trail into Ogeu where he paid off the lodge owner who gave him a huge bowl of white coffee with the skin of milk floating on the surface. He was on his third croissant when the rickety bus arrived. Its departure was delayed for a minute or so to allow a herd of cows to move up the main street towards their pasture.

Jean Paul was waiting for him in the square at Pau. "You're late," he said tetchy with nerves. He got like this before every fight, watching his boys.... "Even English ones," he said attempting humour. "You... you look very relaxed." This too appeared to worry him.

Jean Paul was still on edge two hours later as he sat in the squash court at the sports centre. He finished taping Kel's hands and tugged at his arm as though he was waking someone from sleep. "This boy is a tough one. They say he'll be heavyweight champion for the army this year."

Kel nodded. He was thinking of Mrs Conway. He hoped that the rumours were true and she did indeed hate her brutish husband. Big George, he knew, was a man who had no dependants, a man who came from nowhere.

Jean Paul was tugging at his arm again. "Wake up for Christ's sake."

Kel smiled. "I'm listening." But he wasn't. He started to laugh. All this was just a joke compared with what he had just done. He was still laughing to himself as they ushered him along a white-walled corridor into the dark hall where the ring stood out as clear as an executioner's block under the yellow arc lights.

Some of the soldiers had won their way to the front row to support their comrade. One of them shouted at Kel in an accent that he couldn't place. "Hey Pretty Boy! You're going to get your bottom spanked." The soldiers started to laugh. Kel climbed through the ropes and danced a few steps before handing his dressing gown to Jean Paul. The crowd fell silent at the sight of his strong, long shape. Then another soldier called out. "Hey Pretty Boy! You can spank my bottom if you like." They laughed three rows back at this.

Across the ring his opponent stood with his back to Kel punching into the air with short hooks and uppercuts. Then he turned at the referee's call and advanced glowering into the centre of the ring. Kel had a sense of déjà vu as he stared into the pale, mean face. The Frenchman's eyes widened for a second in recognition. "The Englishman who ran away," he muttered.

Kel smiled. There was an extra purpose to this now. "Tell me did you manage to beat twenty armed policemen? You cretin."

The paratrooper spat on the canvas. He had the stocky body of a street fighter. Tattoos grew out of his short-sleeved singlet. His ginger hair was shaved up to a couple of inches above his ears. Kel guessed he would be fit and that he would not fight like most amateurs behind a jabbing left lead.

He was correct. The paratrooper came at him like an American pro, hands up, head bobbing, before he moved in swiftly behind left and right hooks. The

Frenchman was strong, brave, and prepared to take the left jabs to score to the body to bring down the hands so he could work to the head. Kel moved onto his back foot jabbing and moving as the paratrooper chased him round the ring. It meant Kel's punches lacked power but he stayed out of trouble while he worked out his opponent's style. The crowd began to whistle. It seemed to them that only one man wanted to fight. But the more experienced among them began to notice the clever movement, the way the Englishman was beginning to dictate the distance. The question now was: Did he have the power? If he didn't it was inevitable that the Frenchman would scorn his punches and eventually corner him.

When the bell went for the start of the second round the Paratrooper took the centre of the ring and gestured for the Englishman to come to him. Instead Kel continued his dance, jabbing his left into the Frenchman's face.

"Nail the flash git," A soldier called from the ringside. The paratrooper surged forward and a wild right looped against the top of Kel's head sending him staggering back against the ropes. The crowd rose to a man as their favourite stormed in throwing hooks and round arm rights. Kel leaned into the ropes bouncing in and out using them to change the angle and distance of his body so that many of the Frenchman's punches either missed or landed on the arms. Two rows back a man with a broken nose turned to his neighbour and said "He's going to do him."

"Of course! Allez Ducroix!" The young man leapt from his seat in excitement.

The older man shook his head. "I mean the Englishman." He'd noticed the spring in Kel's legs as he bobbed off the ropes, how his hands were still held high, how his body weaved easily from side to side and, most pertinent of all, that his eyes were cool and clear behind the gloves. "It's a trap," he said. Nobody heard him; they were roaring for Ducroix to finish the Englishman off.

Then it happened. It was just as Billy had told him. The secret was to have the confidence to make the moment, to wait until you got the distance from your opponent that you wanted before throwing your punches. It was all about having the confidence to step in close enough to hit with power.

For the fourth or fifth time Kel bobbed off the ropes and closed with the Frenchman but this time he pushed him away with his forearms. Ducroix was caught slightly off balance and he took a half step backwards.

There was a debate in the hall afterwards, and in the local press the following day, as to the number of punches that Kel threw. There were at least six and they came with blurring speed from alternate fists so that the end of one blow left him balanced to throw the next and from such close range that there was no need to bother about foot movement, the sway of the upper body gave sufficient leverage. It was probable that the paratrooper was unconscious after the second right landed on the point of his jaw but he was caught by at least three more blows before he hit the canvas.

The referee counted to two and then stopped to pull out the fallen man's gum shield. The crowd fell silent as a doctor climbed into the ring but before he could reach Ducroix the boxer rolled on to his side and tried to rise. Kel waited until the doctor helped the boxer to his feet and then walked across to the bank of photographers raising his arms as the flashlights popped. Then he walked over to Ducroix. The Frenchman embraced him and held his hand up accepting defeat. But as they embraced a second time he asked. "You will give me a return match Monsieur Adams?"

Kel grinned and said. "Sure." It was the easiest thing to say.

The following morning he walked to the east end of the town to Eloise's flat but there was no reply to his ring. He stood under a Palm Tree sheltering from the light rain. The windows stood black against the white facade. He waited for a few minutes and then wrote a note. "Good Luck Eloise. I'll miss you. Will write. If you ever want a holiday in England....

PS Won second round...unhurt!!

Love Kel xxxx"

He slipped the note into her post docket and walked back down the gravel path. The air was warm and he could smell the wet grass. He picked up his small sports bag from Madame at the Bar des Sports, kissed her warmly on the lips. She had seen the report of his fight, and the picture of him standing arms aloft. "They say the English lose every battle but the last." She smiled.

Kel said gently "I don't know what you mean."

She broke into a girlish laughter. "Neither do I. Except I don't think you will return."

"Why?"

"I just don't." She traced her fingers along the graze on his cheekbone, careless of the looks she was attracting from customers. "If I had had a son..." she smiled leaving the rest of the sentence unsaid.

He reached and pulled her to him. "Goodbye Maman."

And then he was gone... across the square where he had seen the Olympic flame, down the steps where the Spaniard had attacked Eloise, across the Grand Prix straight, on to the station platform where he had seen the lovers cling to each other with a rare tenderness and on to the train where the Service Militaire soldiers were leaving on short-term passes. A young private thrust a copy of the local paper in front of him and asked him to sign the photograph. "Ducroix, he is a pig," he said in broken English.

The soldier fell asleep at Dax and did not wake until they reached Gare Austerlitz. Kel took a taxi to Gare du Nord.

At Dunkirk the customs officer checked the date in his passport. "A long holiday Monsieur?"

Kel nodded.

The officer examined his face closely. "An accident?" He pointed to the graze and swelling on Kel's cheekbone. Kel took out his newspaper clipping. The officer raised his eyebrows obviously impressed. He gave a little bow before passing Kel through to the ferry with a click of his heels, and that was that. His passport stamped, he stepped on to the boat and sat in the bar until they reached Dover. From there it was a train to London. He pulled out the battered letter from Jean that had arrived at the Bar des Sports.

He read it twice. Its message was simple enough. Zimani had been a terrible mistake. She'd felt abandoned. Could he ever forgive her?

He remembered Eloise's face softening as she read the note. He caught the tube to Belsize and walked up the hill to the grand houses on the Heath.

A fine rain began to fall and the grounds of her house stood damp, sullen, still, and silent. Before he rang the bell he knew she wasn't at home but he rang it anyway. He walked the gravel path to the back of the building. The hammock swung empty. He stood for a second, breathing in the cool breeze that whispered through the hedge where they had made love. As he looked down the long lawn it reminded him of the park scene in Blow Up... the breeze seemed to brush up so many menacing memories.

He took out his biro and wrote a brief note. "You asked me to call and here I am. Must return to Newcastle." Then he muttered "What the hell," tore up the note and walked back up the path.

CHAPTER TWENTY FOUR

Johnson had a trick of edging nearer to you, taking your space as his pale, blue eyes stared with calculated menace. "You're back," he said at last.

A cold wind was coming in from the sea and Kel, who'd been summoned from his bed by the doorbell, shivered slightly.

"You'd better come in," he said.

Johnson was upset. His main meal ticket had gone. "Clever bastard aren't you." His face reddened with anger. "I know you did it."

"What are you talking about?"

"Conway"

"Your friend Mr. Conway I'm told."

Johnson's pale face lit with fury and Kel heard his teeth grind. "Careful sonny."

Kel failed to hide his contempt. "You'd like to get in a kick or two wouldn't you...but you're a little uneasy about what would happen...is that it?"

Johnson said nothing but continued to stare.

Kel continued. "The bad news is I could beat the shit out of you and the really bad news is that I was a thousand miles away when Conway died.

I'm told he died of a heart attack after he shot one of his gangster pals. I gather lots of coppers are saying good riddance to both of them. But not you Inspector. I wonder why?"

Kel chucked his passport on to the table between them and then took out his press cutting. He watched as Johnson examined first the passport and then the Press cutting. He couldn't read French but he could read dates.

Kel waited for him to digest this new information. "So what's your new theory...I hired someone to shoot Big George and then persuaded Conway to have a heart attack?"

Johnson appeared engrossed in the cutting. His long, slim, almost girlish hand tugged at his collar. The hand strayed to his chin, which he stroked gently. "It appears I have underestimated you," he said quietly. He stared into Kel's face noting the bruise under the eye. He had a gift of increasing his menace as he lowered his voice. Even his pale smile appeared threatening. "One day I'll work it out and then..." He searched Kel's face for alarm but found none "And by then the world will have moved on I suppose...new people, new deals, new business." He attempted to laugh but his throat was dry.

It was as clear an offer as Kel could get.

The two men stood weighing each other up and then Kel said. "Do you want a cup of tea?"

That afternoon Kel placed flowers at the grave of Edwards. They'd buried him in the cemetery behind the cricket ground in Jesmond. Gold letters on clean black slate. He was fifty-one...killed by the Japs twenty five years previously when they'd left him with a damaged valve that leaked acid into his gullet. The world had moved on past Edwards.

Business was the new war by other means now. There were deals to be done, treaties to be signed, so who gave a toss about the past except the victims of it.

Kel stood back and looked at the neat stone bordering the grave and the red gravel that kept the weeds at bay.

He would have liked to think that Edwards's spirit would be over the wall with his beloved cricket, but all he knew for certain was that his body was putrefying in a box.

He gave a long low sigh and walked towards his bike. It took him twenty minutes to ride through the town and up the west road to the Crematorium. There in the far corner of the Garden of Remembrance they'd erected a plaque to Billy. The inscription simply gave his name and his dates. There was a second line...Beloved son of...

As he lay down a wreath Kel added a third line in a whisper..."Murdered and Avenged." He moved a fresh bunch of roses to make space for his wreath. The tag flickered in the wind inviting his attention. He smelled the sweetness of the flowers as he moved in closer and then he froze in shock as he recognised the writing before he read the words. "I never did say thanks so I'll say it now. Little Z."

His mind reeled trying to make sense of it. Perhaps there was an Interflora for graves. Perhaps she had travelled up on impulse. She had a generous spirit. He looked at the tag on his wreath. It too had a simple sentiment. "To Billy my best mate." He stood back straight and stiff inviting the ghost to invade him. Across the central lawn a woman tightened her headscarf and then closed her hands in prayer. As he left he could hear Billy singing in his nonsense Italian.

He arrived early at the club. Justin was dealing with the caterers upstairs but he and John Paul came as soon as they were told of his arrival. Justin gave him a hug and John Paul shook his hand with a rare vigor. "Good holiday?" He gave a broad wink.

Kel ignored the wink. "Yeah I've brought you a present. " He reached into his jacket and pulled out the newspaper cutting."

John Paul looked at it blank faced. "I can't speak French," he said.

"You can read pictures can't you."

John Paul's face opened in childish wonder. "You sly bastard."

He thrust the page at Justin. "What does it say?"

Justin read a few lines. "It says he's the best amateur heavyweight in the south of France."

John Paul nodded his head. "Ah," he said." But they're just Froggies."

Kel went behind the mahogany bar and poured himself a drink of orange. The other two shook their heads as he offered them a couple of glasses from the rack.

"How's business?" He sipped at his orange.

It was Justin who answered. "We're doing great Kel. I'm thinking of upping the maximum stakes. There are some seriously thick, rich people up here." He grinned. "What do you think?"

Kel sipped on his orange juice. "Provided we keep the ratio of stakes to cash assets at the same risk level." He smiled to himself. He sounded quite the businessman.

On a whim he wandered upstairs to the casino where the lights were dimmed and the four big tables stood waiting in the front room. A couple of croupiers sat at the bar sipping coffee. He waved in reply to their welcome. They were dressed in tight fitting low-cut black dresses. There were no rules about dress beyond common sense but the girls preferred the revealing tops because they found it earned them more tips.

Perhaps it was the chandelier but the ghost of Billy seemed everywhere. Not the summoned ghost at the crematorium but a ghost that had a life of its own, a ghost that leapt out at you with sudden memories. Tonight the ghost was reminding him of the night they had stood in this room full of hope for their new venture. He sighed and turned away.

Justin joined him at the door. "Come in to the office Kel I want to show you something."

The "something" was the accounts books, which showed they were averaging £2,000 profit each week.

Justin smiled as he saw Kel's reaction. "It's partly down to the film crew but our membership is also up by 20 per cent in the last month."

"Film crew?"

"Yes. They're back here re-shooting the last scene apparently. They've decided they must have a happy ending." Justin laughed. "It's not been a very happy ending for that little shit Zimani...he's dropped a grand this week." Justin's thin, lugubrious face swelled with amusement.

Kel finished off his orange. "Take him for everything you can."

Justin shook his head. "We don't have to try. He's demented. Wild. I can't understand it."

Kel could...the huge fee for his work hadn't been out of generosity but out of a need to own because Kel had had something he wanted...Jean. And now he wanted to come into Kel's lair and defeat him utterly. Jean must have been really savage with him when she ended the affair. Oh he did hope so.

He came back from his thoughts. Justin was telling him he looked pale. The truth was he didn't want to meet Zimani and see the smirk of cuckoldry. Worse still, he might have Jean on his arm.

But no sooner the thought than he dismissed it. The little director might strut his stuff in the club, no doubt with a couple of bodyguards, but Jean had no such desires. Indeed she would see that she was walking into a situation over which she had no control, and that was an anathema to her.

He'd seen her anger when he'd rejected her in favour of revenge. It was more than just frustration at his obduracy. And in her panic and despair Zimani was the willing, yet unwitting, tool of her revenge.

Yet she, according to her letter, now showed remorse.

The first of the gamblers had come up from the club to the casino. Kel sighed at the sight of them. He was already bored. Most of them were brash, rich, and surprisingly stupid. Occasionally there was the tough, quiet punter who stood weighing up the odds, but in the main they were loud men who hadn't come to play but to perform.

The balls began to bob around the roulette wheels. The calls of the croupiers mingled with the chatter of the gamblers who moved from wheel to wheel, their feet silent on the thick carpet. Soon all this would be paid for and then... he knew he was not a manager. He would not stand here night after night, he must move on to new projects...the trick was to get the initial capital. He already had an idea that he should move into property. Big houses in Gosforth or the estate near the airport. The city had a shortage of executive housing. He was lost in his thoughts when Zimani entered with his entourage, a couple of actors, a couple of starlets, a couple of minders, and Little Zimm.

For a second his eyes caught Zimani's. He noted the apprehension in the director's face with some pleasure. Zimani looked again and nodded his head slightly as though seeking a sign, if not of approval, at least of acceptance. Kel looked through him and turned his attention to the bar where a customer was arguing with one of the barmaids. The girl was near tears when Kel arrived to ask if he could help.

The man turned his red fleshy face to Kel and demanded "And who might you be?"

"I might be the owner."

The red-faced man raised an arm in his too tight suit to point to the bar..."I wanted Canadian dry ginger with my whisky not American dry."

The barmaid shook her head. Her long, blond hair shivered in the light of Billy's chandeliers. "We've run out of Canadian Dry Mr Adams. I told him but..."

Kel turned to the red-faced man. "So what is your point?"

"My point." The red-faced man's face got redder. "My point is that I assumed this was a proper club and that I would be served with such a simple request."

"And how do you advance that by shouting at a barmaid who has no responsibility for the stock? "

The red-faced man was already retreating. "Well I..."

"I will make sure there is Canadian Dry at this bar from tomorrow night." Kel slipped a five-pound chip into the red-faced man's hand. "For your inconvenience." He smiled and raised his left arm to usher him to the tables.

As he watched the red-faced man retreat to the roulette wheels he felt a tug at his arm. Little Zimm smiled at him. "Why did you give the arrogant bastard a chip?"

Kel shrugged. "He'll lose that and more."

She'd tied her hair into a tight bun, a la Jean, though she didn't have the classical features to carry it off and her ears stuck out a little too much. However she filled the tight black cocktail dress and her ample bust attracted sly glances from around the room.

She looked up at him hovering on her three-inch heels. "You look tired."

He gave a short laugh. "Tired of being at crossroads I guess."

"You should have crossed the road to Jean's side. Anybody else would have."

He looked past her as though he was surveying the room, but he was merely wondering where the conversation was leading. "I guess so," he said.

"Stubborn bastard aren't you. But Jean likes that about you. She told me. She also told me of the time you met in France. It was as though she was living it again."

He looked down on her. "Why are you telling me this?"

"Dunno. I went to Billy's grave this afternoon." She had a mind like a butterfly.

"I saw the wreath."

"What would you do if you went back to your flat and found her in your bed?"

"I'd do my best I suppose."

She looked around the room, which was filling.

"No seriously what would you do?"

She watched his face soften, but before he could answer, she moved on.

"It's like he's still here isn't it."

"Who?"

"Billy of course."

He looked at her in surprise. "But you only met him twice."

She shrugged. "I liked him. He was a great big friendly bear." She glanced at him taken by a new thought. "He was a nicer man than you wasn't he. I mean he had a more generous nature." Again she moved on before he could reply. "This isn't you is it." She gestured to the now crowded room with its quiet, urgent sounds. She was teasing him again. It was her way of getting back at him for turning her down all those months ago.

He didn't reply. It was as though she was playing tennis against herself. She'd serve and then run round the net to return. "But then I don't know you." She glanced up at him "I don't think anyone does...witty, urbane, stubborn, naïve...hesitant at times but capable of giving a woman a slap..."

"I'm sorry about that." She'd smoked him out, as they both knew she would. She ignored his apology. Her eyes glinted with the excitement of the chase.

"And what else? Billy said you were the best natural boxer he'd ever seen."

"When did Billy tell you that? You only met him twice." The truth came to him as he spoke the words.

"We were lovers," she said simply. She leaned into him squeezing his arm and whispered. "If you ever find out who did Conway? Give him my thanks."

She knew of course...the who and the why. It was only the how she didn't know and she didn't like not knowing.

"I think the only people who know exactly what happened are both dead," he said.

"Come on Kel." She grinned at him and stuck out her chest. "Do you think there's room for a wire in here?"

He looked down at her thrusting chest. "I doubt it."

"You'll not stay here doing this."

He didn't reply so she returned her own serve again.

"You'll get bored."

He showed her the palm of his hand. "So what's next?"

She shrugged. "You are not without choices. Perhaps you've always had too many choices."

He was filled with a sudden melancholy at her words, which he knew had some truth in them. His face must have betrayed his feelings because he saw her eyes soften. She leaned into him again "She still thinks about you all the time."

The words sent a shockwave through him. He heard himself say. "She wasn't thinking about me the last time I saw her."

Little Zimm shook her head. "It was only a pressing of flesh. It's part of the world she lives in. You rejected her. She can't deal with that. She was, is, devastated and confused."

The desire to believe her came at him in a rush. But he knew there were other, larger obstacles.

"She told me everything." She saw the shock in his face... "It's not how you think...Billy told me all about Big George and Conway. I was with Jean when I read of their deaths and she just broke down sobbing. She was sobbing because she'd lost you. Has she lost you Kel?"

Her stare held his eyes and she saw the hesitation but for once she didn't go for the knockout. "You won't know until you see her will you."

"Why are you doing this?"

"I've always loved your sort. Pretty... but kind of dangerous."

In the long, wide, high room sounds did not bounce off walls; instead they floated out as far as they could before dying in the warm smoky air. Even so, he glanced across to the gamblers to see whether anyone had picked up her observation. No one was listening but she had seen his look and grinned at his insecurity.

He tried to recover. "I never realised I hurt you that much when I turned you down."

He waited for her denial and rebuke, but none came. Instead she grinned. "Yeah I was shattered."

The smile fled her face and for the first time he saw her after the curtain came down, tired and anxious. He reached for her hand. "I'm sorry." His voice was low and gentle.

"Patronising git." She squeezed his hand briefly. "Here," she reached into a small leather purse. "It's from Jean." She smiled. "I've read it. She wants to meet you on Billy's beach tomorrow morning."

"Not Bamburgh?"

"That's too far to go for one of you to tell the other to fuck off."

She kept her face straight until he looked at her, and then she winked.

As he walked along the Long Sands he took a line near to the incoming tide. He was coming from the north on the same trail that Billy used to run. The cliffs that jutted into the sea rose out of the morning mist.

He was alone, no Billy, no Jean. Ahead of him the white-topped waves reared and broke against the walls of the open-air swimming pool and above him the seagulls called.

Then he saw her walking slowly down the slope above the swimming pool. No sunglasses, no scarf. Her long hair shivered in the sea breeze and she clutched her cream raincoat at the throat. She cut straight down to the sea and then walked towards him along the waterline. They moved a little inland as they approached each other warily, almost like gunfighters.

For almost every waking minute since he'd left Little Zim he had considered what he should say to her...considered but never concluded, and when he did speak it was with an extempore flippancy that surprised him.

"Lost your glasses then?" In the instant before her reply he remembered their first meeting in Pau and his silly joke about sunglasses in the dark.

He felt a flicker of alarm just before she smiled. "No. It was time to change."

He considered the potential of these words.

"How much how far?" he asked.

"I don't know. But it's like the dead man walking. The first step is the miracle."

He laughed at her little joke. They'd stopped a yard apart and he could smell her perfume. His eyes softened and he wanted to reach out to hold her, but he didn't. Instead he asked her. "It's now or never eh?"

Her eyes did not leave his. "Yes."

"You know what I've done."

"Yes."

"I feel no remorse Jean."

She said nothing

"And I feel no guilt. They were evil."

They began to walk up the beach back the way she had come.

He felt her hand at his arm. "Have you been thinking what to say?"

He smiled. "I failed utterly."

"Me too. "

They walked on not speaking. The gulls circled them screaming.

"The no-remorse thing. I think that's good."

He tried to make sense of this but gave up. "Really?"

"Really." They were approaching the slope by the pool. Someone had left an old Cortina parked overnight. "It means that you won't be destroyed by it."

He turned to face her and for a second was frozen by her beauty, the blond hair that whispered across her white face, and the ice blue eyes. She seemed to be a vision that had been borne from the mist that curled in from the cold grey sea.

"I think," he said suddenly. "You could destroy me Jean."

They stared into a long silence and then she said. "I came back here for a happy ending Kel."

He saw her face soften and his eyes filled with tears. She moved into him and gently laid her head against his chest. Behind her the tide was licking up the beach, washing away their footprints, and out at sea there was the faint shape of a cargo ship with its smoke stack trailing in the sky.